The Secret Van Tams

CARLY BISHOP

Copyright © 2025 Carly Bishop

All rights reserved.

ISBN: 978-1-0682422-0-5

The Secret Van Tams

CARLY BISHOP

The gripping and emotionally-charged family mystery with a shocking twist

PUBLISHED BY VALENTE PRESS

This book is a work of fiction. Names, characters, places and incidents are either a product of the author's imagination or are used fictitiously. Any resemblance to actual people living or dead, events or locales is entirely coincidental.

For Big Bird

For my wonderful nan, Gwen

'If nothing is going well, call your grandmother.'

- Italian Proverb

Prologue

'belofte maakt schuld'
Promise, is debt

I was fifteen years old when Mum told me the story of how my Dutch grandmother Johanna died: squashed flat under the wheels of an Amsterdam tram whilst drunk on French chardonnay. It was a grisly and unfortunate death, she'd said, one she would never wish on her worst enemy.

She'd come into my bedroom in the early hours of Sunday morning, after the last round of 'shithead' had ended, a card game, pretty thrilling actually, where the object of the round is to lose all your playing cards and avoid being the shithead of the group. I'd been declared shithead three times that night, something which neither dismayed me nor pleased me, but which meant I had no choice but to wear the obligatory pink mohawk wig that had been passed around so many times that it made your hair stink of cheese. It was a forfeit that had grown old and no one found it that funny anymore, but no one had the heart to tell Mum, or in fact the balls, because Mum liked tradition and she liked everything just so, and she didn't like anyone to tell her otherwise.

It was two o'clock in the morning and our neighbours had finally upped and left, including old Eddie and Elaine, who were the only neighbours I could suffer for more than an hour or two. I adored them, to tell you the truth. They were the closest thing I had to grandparents of my own, and even though I only saw them on the occasional weekend, I'd grown to love them dearly. I'd watched as plump little Eddie with his gentle stoop and bandy knees had wobbled off down the garden path, followed by purple-haired Elaine, with her wide smile and shaky lip liner that was so far off her own lips it joined her cupid's bow to her nose. Eddie gave me a fiver every week for pocket money and the way his old speckled hand trembled as he reached into his wallet made my heart burst every time. Sometimes, Elaine would do the same, but her rummaging around in her purse didn't quite give me the same feeling as with Eddie. Perhaps it was the lack of a father figure in my life, or a grandad figure even, but old men just seemed more vulnerable with money somehow. Perhaps I'd just got used to women having lots of it. Lots of money, that is. And when I say women, I mean Mum. My mother is extremely rich. Which I guess makes me rich, too. In the money sense, anyway.

It was summer time and we'd put on a *kleine bijeenkomst* for our neighbours, which Mum once translated to me as meaning a small gathering, or a get together I suppose, except I never truly knew what her Dutch terms really meant. She'd only ever use Dutch if she was trying to be ambiguous, or worse, when she was trying to make a point. She'd say peculiar things like *de kogel is door de kerk*, which I'd later Googled as meaning *the bullet is through the church*, and I'd usually just nod enthusiastically to appease her. Language had always fascinated me, but for one reason or another, Mum had never passed the Dutch language on to me. On purpose, I suspect. Anyhow, this particular *kleine bijeenkomst* ended up being a pretty large gathering, with twenty neighbours at least, all nattering on in our Tudor-style living room about very highbrow things, like the sorry state of inheritance tax, how preposterously overrated the Maldives is, and how much dog muck they seem to be finding on the pavements these days. Conversations that a wide-eyed, fifteen-year-old girl like me couldn't contribute much to, thankfully. Well, except for the dog muck, which I'd have had to agree was becoming a bit of a problem, but it did make me chuckle, thinking of these little smelly bombs lying in wait for my neighbours, who thought treading in dog muck was such a lowbrow thing to do. God forbid it ruined their fancy suede loafers.

That particular evening, as the neighbours were busy debating the rugger, or comparing their diamond-encrusted watches, or discussing their next destination for their holibobs, I'd had my first puff of a cigar with Eliza 'big tits' Thompson, who lived with her parents three doors down. It was an obvious nickname that was bestowed to her by our Year Ten geography class at Langswood House, but she didn't mind it, in fact, she'd said that she was rather pleased with it. It got her a lot of boyfriends, she'd said. That, and her ability to steal cigars from her grandfather's place, made her one of the most popular girls in school.

We'd sat together at the back of the neatly mowed garden lawn on Mum's wicker swing seat, taking the occasional swig from a carefully hidden bottle of WKD Blue, and Eliza had whispered to me that she'd stolen two cigars from the travel-sized box of Hamlet her grandfather kept by his bedside, just for us. I'd felt a rush of nervous adrenalin when she'd handed me mine, placing it between my teeth, sucking in my lips prematurely as she'd brought the lighter towards me, igniting it with a crackle. She'd giggled as I'd coughed and spluttered, a puff of grey filling the air. If I close my eyes, I can still taste the smoky bitterness and warmth of the tobacco now. I can still feel the uneasiness in my stomach, the quiver in my fingertips. That hot, prickly feeling of doing something I shouldn't be doing. The panic of my overbearing mum finding out. Her perfect only daughter doing imperfect things. The swing seat sat behind a large oak tree, which was large enough to shield us completely from view of the kitchen of our palatial red brick home, where our mums were picking at the candied nuts and dipping rosemary focaccia into hummus. Vintage champagne coupes that had never seen a single drop of champagne sat on the kitchen table, filled with sparkling elderflower water.

Mum, unlike all of our visitors, had forever been a devout teetotaller and the guests had got used to the severe lack of alcohol at our house. The prohibition house, the men would call it. Mum argued that it was a fair price to pay for a free supper and entertainment. Besides, it was *'particularly ghastly to get so blotto that you behaved like an indigent circus clown,'* or so she'd say in front of the neighbours. She pretended to ignore the fact that the men would bring hipflasks filled with whisky, which they'd take glugs from during regular bathroom visits, and the women would meet sixty minutes earlier at Catherine's, who offered an all-you-can-drink happy hour of gin and tonics to get their fill. Mum was a good cook, an extravagant cook, and they only came to us for the food. And to gawp enviously at the latest designer purchase that Mum had made for the house.

I was brave, thinking about it now. Trying my first cigar, when Mum was already fuming about my getting drunk the night before. It was the very first time I'd done that, too. And I don't mean the kind of drunk where you slur a lot and you can't walk or see straight, and your mum has to help you up to bed. I mean the kind of drunk where your mum grabs you by the face and holds a mirror up to it.

'Look at you,' she'd said. 'Look at the state of you, you stupid, stupid girl.'

Shakily, I had looked back into her mirror, witnessing a swirl of black, red and orange. Black mascara running down my cheeks, red-raw watery eyes and orange chunks of sick around my mouth. It was a scary sight, for the both of us. In the morning from my bed, I had erratically explained to her that it was tequila from my friend Amber's house, and that it had tasted exactly like what I thought bleach would taste like. And for goodness' sake, that *of course* I would never touch it again. Then, I threw up all over my vintage oak dressing table, over all my most precious things: my gold-plated jewellery, my antique perfume bottles, and a framed photo of me as a baby with Dad. That last one upset me the most. They were all sopping wet with bile.

I expected her to be mad. I expected her to make me clean it up. What I didn't expect Mum to do was scoop everything up, including my treasured framed photo, and dump it into a bin bag, then march it out to the wheelie bin outside, never to be seen again. As I slowly mopped up the remainder of my puke on my empty dressing table, with heavy teenage tears rolling down my eyes, I knew then that I'd done something serious.

When she'd appeared in my room at two that next morning, she'd crept over to my dressing room stool and sat tensely in the dark in silence. She was facing towards me, the moonlight peeking through my bedroom window and reflecting into her disappointed eyes, which looked wild, like we were buried in a Gaston Leroux novel and I'd somehow transformed into the Phantom of the Opera, repulsive and vile. I lay there, still, waiting for the story to come.

There was always a story with Mum. A moral. A commandment. A thou shall not. A worry. I knew it would be a story about why I should never get drunk like that again, but I also knew that this story would differ from all the others that had come before it. I knew by her excruciating silence and her crazy eyes that this story was the biggest story of all. The one I'd been waiting to hear my whole life. The one that Mum had not wanted to have to tell. I knew it would be a story about why she never allowed alcohol in our house. I knew it would be about someone close to us. And I knew it wouldn't be about my dead father. I'd heard that miserable story before.

Eventually, she'd begun.

'*De zeug trekt de stop uit het vat*,' she'd said firmly, cutting through the darkness. 'The sow pulls the bung from the barrel. Do you know what I am referring to, Remi?'

I'd stayed deathly silent, frozen with apprehension. Obviously, I'd no idea what she was referring to. These obscure Dutch phrases were becoming the bane of my life.

'For crying out loud. Why did I not teach you Dutch, eh? Negligence, girl. It means negligence will always be rewarded with disaster. Do you know what negligence means?'

I didn't, really, even with a private education and some posh-twat neighbours, but in that moment I'd very much wished that I did. I'd gone to hazard a guess, except that she'd spoken right over me.

'Carelessness. That is what it means, Remi. You want to be careless, you silly girl?'

There it was. I'd been waiting for the putdown, ever since she'd wiped my wet belongings off my dressing table and dumped them in the rubbish.

'Because carelessness is not a joke, Remi. Getting tipsy, or having a few too many, however these... these friends of yours would like to refer to it. For heaven's sake, it is not a joke.' She'd paused then and cleared her throat, letting out a frustrated groan. I wasn't quite sure why she was using the word joke. I'd never suggested it was anything of the sort.

'I see it all the time at work. Do you think it is my responsibility to mop up the drunks of Langswood? And now here in my home, huh?' She'd come closer to my face then, her warm, stale breath reaching the insides of my nose. I had become the punching bag, and she was wearing her boxing gloves.

'You will see it for yourself one day, girl. Because you need to see it. I want you to see it. Then maybe you will know just how hard it is.' She'd snatched my empty water bottle from the floor and slammed it down hard on the table.

But I don't want to see it, is what I'd wanted to say. *I didn't mean it, I swear.*

'You want to know why else it is not a joke, Remi? Aside from the piss it takes out of us paramedics?'

'Why?' I'd replied with warm, shaky breath. The sound of my own voice had startled me, and I'd wished she wouldn't keep saying my name like that.

'Me and you,' she'd said, jabbing her finger at me in the moonlight. 'Carelessness is exactly why we are alone.'

Alone. I knew that feeling. It was something that touched me on the shoulder every time my friends were discussing their family reunions, their weddings, birthdays, or christenings. Their funerals. It felt like a crystal tumbler that dropped on me every so often, catching me inside, the thick glass wall blocking my screams from anyone who could hear them. I knew my grandparents were gone, I just didn't know where. Dead, I'd assumed. Like Dad. I was used to invisible people and navigating this ocean without them. I'd learned how to replace them and how to form make-shift connections with people, mostly with people I didn't like.

Besides, Mum had never mentioned my grandparents. And I'd never felt that I could ask. Until now.

'Why *are* we alone, Mum?' I'd said. 'What happened to the rest of our family?'

'Dead,' she'd replied plainly, as if it were the most matter-of-fact thing in the world. 'Your dad's side. Both of them, as fat as a horse's arse. It was a horrifying sight in the end. I mean, how could you not be embarrassed? It was disgusting, really. They ate themselves into an early grave.'

She'd paused, catching her breath as if to stop herself from saying the unspeakable. 'They were not keen on me, anyway.'

'And what about your parents?'

'Your grandfather, he had no chance. Poor sod was plagued with illness. Diabetes, arthritis… nothing anyone could do about it. It is unfair when it is not your fault. Not like my mother.'

'My grandmother?' I'd said. 'Why? What happened to her?'

I'd been fascinated with grandmothers growing up. Grandfathers seemed good, solid fun. But grandmothers appeared just like superheroes to me. They were strong, full of life experience and womanly wisdom. The head of the family. Or was that just in the mob movies?

One of my favourite grandmothers was the hilarious and scandalous Grandma Swag from Janet and Allen Ahlberg's Cops and Robbers. Or Grandma Annie from the film The Proposal. A mother figure, someone to guide you, but someone who is not your mum. An outlet, a fact checker. At fifteen, I'd have given anything to have one.

'We called her Johanna,' said Mum. 'She insisted on it, said it made her feel less like the dreaded authoritarian. She wanted us to be friends as well as family. Which was part of the problem, really.'

'Why?' I'd asked. Asking Mum about anything was such a rare opportunity that I was trying my luck.

'It just was. And stop asking questions, for goodness' sake. I am talking, you are listening, remember?'

'Sorry,' I'd mumbled.

The air in the room had grown hot and congealed, and Mum had stood up to leave. Her feet had seemed heavy on the floor as she'd stomped towards the door. I'd lay back in bed trying not to breathe, and then she'd turned her head to me once more.

'Drunk,' she'd said in a malicious tone. 'Your grandmother, Johanna. If you really want to know. She was hit by a tram in Amsterdam. Pa had flown her there for her birthday. He was always doing nice things to surprise her. Not that she deserved it much.'

I'd clutched the edge of my blanket, my knuckles white with

tension.

'It was getting dark when it happened. Not dark enough that people did not see her, collapsed on the tram line like a demented puppet after too much French Chardonnay. Those are not my words, by the way. I am only going by what I was told.' The floor had creaked as she shifted her weight from one leg to the other. Then, she'd stood eerily still, and I could have sworn I'd stopped breathing.

'It was almost inevitable, really,' she'd said. 'That the very worst thing that could happen to Johanna would happen during the Silly Season, the season when nothing much was supposed to be happening. During *komkommertijd*, as she called it. The slow season. I always wondered why she bothered to define the seasons, as to me, her life was a constant state of *komkommertijd*.' Mum had paused, as if waiting to see if I'd understood. I hadn't.

'When I was seven, Remi, I'd asked Johanna what this Dutch term meant. *Cucumber time* had been her reply, which I later thought was quite ironic, because to me, Johanna was very much like a cucumber: full of liquid and not much else. Nowadays, I can't even bear to look at one.'

She'd inhaled a long, deep breath, and I'd lay there wondering how a lowly vegetable could bring back such painful memories for someone.

'That day, it changed my life forever, and I did not deserve it, Remi. So, don't you ever remind me of that day again. You promise me. Ever, OK?'

'I promise,' I'd whispered in reply. And with that, she'd slammed the door shut.

The moonlight was dim enough that I hadn't seen Mum's face, but I could tell that, although there was plenty of anger, there was very little emotion there. For reasons I didn't know, her lack of feeling terrified me, and I'd gone to sleep that night distressed and confused. My Mum left so brutally without a mother. Was she so scarred by it all that she'd forgotten how to cry? Was this why she had an eternal hatred of alcohol? Of risks of any kind?

In the morning, I'd woken with a familiar stabbing pain in my chest. My hair was wet and stuck to my forehead like sad, soaked ivy clinging desperately to a wall. I'd tried to shout out to Mum, who was back in her bedroom across the hall, but my voice was trapped inside clenched teeth. I'd felt like I was choking, but my mouth wouldn't open for air. I'd known that I was probably going to die, so I just lay there, trembling underneath my feather and down duvet, waiting for the inevitable.

Mum was right. My grandmother was irresponsible. I was irresponsible. What if something had happened to me? What if something happens to Mum? How would we survive alone?

As I lay now, six whole years later, replaying that memory on the ceiling for the hundredth time, it's Johanna's story which haunts me the most. Even more so than my father's. My grandmother, killed so brutally, through no fault but her own. Is that what Mum expects of me? Is that what she's always seen in me? My selfish, negligent grandmother?

I turn my body to Luke, whose chest is gently rising, then falling. I'm not denying that it's a big responsibility, being the only daughter of an orphaned, sibling-less mother. But I will not let my mum down again.

Not like Johanna did.

PART ONE - ENGLAND

Chapter One

*'om het dak te laten bedekken
met taartjes'*

To have the roof tiled with tarts

It's morning, and I was supposed to have left ten minutes ago. And I can't even lie to her. Because Mum can see me on the *Find My iPhone* app. I could kill the person who invented that sometimes.

At least my car is fast. One benefit of having rich, dead grandparents and of being an only child is that I get to drive a Porsche Cayenne; a silver automatic one with a light leather interior, a panoramic sunroof, and top of the range sound system. Usually, I don't like driving over seventy, but I might have to push that to seventy-five today. Needs must, and all that.

The Porsche is parked outside my university house, and I'm standing on the pavement next to it, flicking the start of a tiny spider's web off my wing mirror. It sticks to my finger, and I rub the soft grey thread onto my dark indigo-blue jeans. That's one thing this city isn't short of, spiders. Lately, the intrusive little things have invaded every dark corner of my large but damp double room, encroaching on my privacy whilst collecting more dust and debris, something the old house could really do without. I'm a bit OCD like that, I like everything just so – an exasperating trait that's both a blessing and a curse and something that I've inherited from Mum – which isn't easy when your student house is like a billion years old and smells of a mix of soggy cardboard and *eau de mold*.

It was slim pickings in terms of finding a decent student let in this place, even with the backing of a rich ghost family. The Dutch in Mum would tell me that these spider visits are a good thing, anyhow, that they are weaving my fortunes in their intricate webs and bringing me good luck. Good job, really, because I may as well be running a six-legged bed and breakfast for arachnids. I don't kill them now she's told me that, just like I don't walk under ladders or stroke black cats. And I will always look people in the eye when clinking glasses. Because in Germany, that's seven years of bad sex if you don't. Or that's what Ingrid told me, anyway. And she's a quarter German.

'Are you coming?' I call out to Luke, who is eyeing up the overpriced houses on sale in the window of the estate agent next door. Houses that I could afford, but that he couldn't. His football socks are gathered around his solid ankles, his blonde hair dark with wax.

'You know I can't be late. I never like to be late. Not today, especially.'

It's true. I really can't be late. Today is the start of the Easter holidays, which is also Mum's birthday, and I'm supposed to be home in time to treat her to an afternoon tea consisting of some Marks and Spencer extra strong tea bags, the finest prawn mayonnaise sandwiches and her favourite red velvet cupcakes from Lila's. The really expensive ones with the silver sprinkles on top. Then, it's straight to getting ready for our annual Easter *kleine bijeenkomst*, the same type of neighbourly get together that we have had almost every Easter for the past ten years, despite the fact that Mum detests our neighbours almost as much as I do.

I used to wonder why she does it, but over the years I've worked out that – aside from using it to showcase our vast array of designer furniture and antiques – it's her way of keeping a hold on the cul-de-sac, of hovering over it, over all of us, like a vigilant griffin. She believes vehemently in the whole *keep your friends close, and your enemies closer* type thing, and has always used our parties as a way of gathering valuable intel into the goings on of Copthall Lane. Mum likes to have eyes on every house in the street. And for someone who craves social approval and validation in our neighbourhood as much as she does, although she'll hate to admit it, she doesn't half complain a lot about every person who we know. *What a bighead he is! How tight-fisted can you be? What dreadful bad breath she always has! Why wouldn't you get your teeth done?*

Last Easter, it was all about food preferences. 'Margaret opposite is such a fussy cow,' she had grumbled to me, whilst carefully seasoning the leek cream cheese dip that she makes for each *bijeenkomst*. 'She is forever asking what is in everything, like I am supposed to list out a full set of ingredients just to cater for her dislike of butter? I have a good mind to put double in everything just to spite her! See if she can taste it then!'

'Perhaps she's allergic?' I'd dared to suggest. 'Perhaps she's not just being fussy, and some things might make her really sick?' Suggesting things to Mum only happened on days when I knew our house would soon be full of guests, when I could guarantee that I could soon skulk off into the background and our pretense of a delightfully happy mother-daughter relationship would begin. She might try to ignore me, but she'd never want to speak poorly of me in front of the neighbours. That wouldn't quite fit with the image now, would it?

'Oh, please, Remi. Allergic? To everything, is she? It probably just gives her the *shits* now and again. And she does not want the *shits* before she sees that god-awful-ugly, man-baby new boyfriend of hers. Do you think she would cater for us like that, do you? No, she would not. We would have what we were given, like normal people do.'

'*Als de kat van huis is, dansen de muizen op tafel,*' is what I'd hear her mumble angrily. When the cat's away, the mice will dance on the table. Basically, she has an unhealthy obsession with people crapping on us left, right, and centre. So, we know everything there is to know about our neighbours, who wear yellow bouffant hair and designer cashmere scarves. The men smell of Dominique Ropion's Portrait of a Lady, of Turkish rose and blackcurrant. The women's choice of fragrance is so floral that it burns my nose. What's strange is that they all kind of look the same. They have narrow eyes and upturned mouths, which speak loudly of *my darling* this and *my darling* that. They tut and mock and coo and cluck. The women tell the men to shut up a lot. '*Bet your mother is so frightfully glad that she does not have to put up with a ghastly old husband,*' they tell me. Which I think is downright rude, considering my dad died of a heart attack when I was barely a toddler. *Actually, Suzanne, with the revolting black hair growing out of her chin. I'm confident my dad was a pretty great guy. Perhaps he'd have had a hard time putting up with her.*

I always knew our neighbours were posh because they all have double-barrelled surnames like Walter-Jones and Calthorpe-Stewart. Every man is an *old boy*. They finish their sentences with phrases like *jolly good* and *golly gosh*. Growing up, they'd scold me often about the way I talked. Once, during an afternoon tea at our house, I'd pronounced the British tea cake scone like *scoan* and it was as if I'd held a Union Jack flag over a fire. The adults were shaking their heads in frightful amusement, and I think it was Betty from number forty-six who'd scoffed something along the lines of *oh sweetie, how awfully precious of you not to know that it's skon, not scoan,* while my apologetic teenage face flushed red with embarrassment. Not that I cared much about what they thought, not particularly, anyway. But I'd learned to respect my elders, and I cared about embarrassing Mum. Mum very much cares about what they think. So gradually, I got to learn all the posh English pronunciations – off like *orf*, glass like *glahss* with a short vowel sound, bath like *bahth*.

We've become very much one of them, in the end. Part of the elite, the clique, in a metropolitan cul-de-sac in the most expensive suburb of London, the one nicknamed the Beverly Hills of England, where magazines suggest you can live the suburban dream, and everyone lives in a spacious period property with a wine cellar and a home theatre and a cocker spaniel named Winston. Which, to be fair to those magazines, isn't far from the truth. We'd originally been outsiders, though, having moved from the countryside of Cambridge when I was three, which I know is part of the reason why Mum tries so hard all the time. I was sent off to a private school. We learnt the rules of cricket. We bought wellies, even though we never walked. Not in mud, anyway.

The thing is, we probably have more money than all of them combined, so I've never really understood Mum's fascination with approval, as there's never really been anything much to prove. Our neighbours must have known that Mum's job as a part-time paramedic for the National Health Service wasn't enough to maintain a small mansion and a private education for her daughter. They must have known there was a long line of filthy-rich – and apparently, preposterously tall – Dutch relatives in our past, who all started with a man called Johan, a politician and diplomat, and his wife Gerde, whose family ran a large chain of breweries. Except I can't ever remember Mum talking about her wealthy family, neither to me nor to her neighbours. I only know because my friend Hannah once looked up the Van Tams, our family surname, and put two and two together.

I look down at my watch, which shows the time as just before eleven in the morning. 'We need to go,' I say to Luke. 'Sorry. Otherwise I can't take you. Sorry.'

Luke turns away from the glass and steps towards me self-assuredly. 'Just picking out the mansion that's going to be my next house. *Our* next house, should I say, once I've got my fancy new marketing job and you're a superstar paramedic.' He wraps his long arms around my waist and draws me closer to him, leaning down to give me a peck on the forehead. 'We need a big garden, somewhere I can put a barbecue, like. Not one of those shite little ones like my dad had, where the coals fell out of the bottom and set fire to the grass. I'm talking about a proper chef's type one. I fancy myself as a bit of a pit master, you know.'

His lips touch just above the scar on the left of my forehead, above my annoyingly overplucked eyebrow, one of two scars that I have on my heart-shaped face. I only know I have a heart-shaped face because of my widow's peak hairline and my narrow, pointy chin, and since my Teen magazine told me so in one of those trivial *is your face round, heart, or square* quizzes. It was the same magazine that told me I'd marry a *brainy babe* and not a *dreamy dude* because I'd ticked yes to *I'm not crazy about boys with curly hair; I think they look kind of like Ronald McDonald.*

'How did I get these funny marks?' I'd asked Mum when I was old enough to let them bother me. The other scar is on my jawline: a slender, silvery mark. She'd looked at me with raised eyebrows.

'Don't you dare blame me,' she'd quipped through tight lips, doing that typical mum thing of pre-emptively defending herself against any potential criticism that she thought unfair. 'And they're not funny marks, Remi. There's nothing funny about them. You were a curious child, and all curious children end up with scars on their faces. *Zodra het hek van de dam is, lopen de varkens in het koren.* When the gate is open, the pigs will run into the corn.'

I'd rolled my eyes jadedly. If it wasn't a pig, it was a sheep in these Netherlandish proverbs she seemed to love so much. And I didn't especially love being compared to a bunch of unsightly animals.

'And stop saying sorry, will you?' says Luke. 'I just need one more minute like this before we go, like.'

I lose myself for a minute in his embrace. 'Does the house have high ceilings and parquet floors?' I say. He smells musky-sweet, of sandalwood and vanilla. 'Real wood floors are a non-negotiable. And some exposed beams would be nice. The more rustic, the better.' I quickly remember that the bored estate agent had described our university house as rustic before he'd shown us around this rough place. 'Well. Rustic in a charming way, anyway,' I correct myself.

'Whey aye,' replies Luke in his soft Geordie accent, the accent that makes him sound like a friendly Viking. 'As long as I can have my seventy-inch TV and a sports channel subscription, it can have whatever you want it to have, like.'

I stand looking up at him with a happy smile and sad eyes. We've been doing this quite often lately, Luke and I, throwing out ideas for our imaginary life after university. It seems to have become the way we flirt nowadays, as if our make-believe suggestions might somehow demonstrate our true feelings for each other. Like agreeing on paint colours and tile options might mean that we're destined to be together. *Oh, you love green in the bathroom, too?*

Being destined to be together doesn't mean we will be together, though. Luke grew up in Old Malden, near Newcastle, which is four hundred miles away from mine and Mum's house in Langswood. Verborough University is somewhere in the middle of both of our family homes, which sounds like the perfect imaginary compromise, except Verborough is an absolute dump. Neglected storefronts with fading paint and graffiti line the high street, and the few green spaces that there are look overgrown and sombre. Cheaply built housing estates sit like bags of cement randomly plonked around the city. The sky seems lower here, the air squeezed together like the inside of an aeroplane. I'm so looking forward to leaving this place, but I'm not looking forward to facing up to the reality of our relationship, if you can call it that. With only a few months to go until we graduate, and the prospect of beginning the long slog towards finding a proper job, we're both trying to ignore the fact that the most likely scenario is that we'll both move home to our parents, and we won't see much of each other again.

It's a sad thought. Except I'm trying hard not to think about it. I'd never thought I'd meet someone like Luke here, just maybe some red-hot acquaintances, like the ones that Samantha meets in Sex and the City, like that fit *Smith* guy, or whatever his name was. Or that was the hope, anyway. Surely, everyone is due one of those types of acquaintances in a lifetime? Or else, why would they bother projecting these things on the TV?

'You know, there's something about a man in sports clothes,' I say, whilst clumsily wriggling free from Luke's grasp. 'But if we don't leave now, my mum is going to kill me. Sorry.'

Luke relaxes his grip. He pushes my tortoiseshell frames from the tip of my nose back onto my lightly bronzed face. 'I know, I know,' he says. 'But I'm sure she won't kill you, Remi. You definitely don't want to stay one more night here with me instead? Pretty please, like?'

God, he's persuasive, I think. *If only his toned quad muscles weren't so on show right now.*

I look down at my things, two designer duffel bags' worth of things, stuffed with hordes of make-up, unwashed clothes, and the afternoon tea bits for Mum. They're slumped on the floor next to the Porsche.

'I'm sorry,' I say, immediately regretting the use of the S-word for the fourth time in two minutes. 'You know I want to. But the term's over, and I promised Mum I'd head home for her birthday.

She needs help to get the house ready for tonight, and she says she's cooking her special apple pie for me. Plus, I'm desperate to see Copperfield. And to wash my clothes in a machine that isn't full of fungus.'

It's been three months since I last saw Copperfield the cat, our majestic Siberian male with huge, pleading golden eyes. He's a house cat, which Mum likes as it gives him less chance of getting run over, or eaten by wolves, or vampires, or cat-hungry aliens from Mars. Except, we have the least housey cat ever. True to his name, he loves to find any escape route possible to leave our home. Mum gets so cross with him. I love him like the sibling I never had.

Luke smiles softly and starts walking towards the passenger door. 'That's a good enough excuse, like. Tell you what, though. When you get back, hows about we go on a date? A proper one, like. My treat. There's a new cinema that's opened up a few miles away. There are sofas we can snog on and everything.'

I let out a schoolgirl-sounding giggle. A nervy but secretly thrilled giggle. I'd hoped, wished even, that he felt this way about us, but I wasn't sure at all, because Mum once pointed out that I'm never quite sure about anything, even something that's a fact, like one plus one equals two. A kind teacher once told me to work on probabilities, but I've found that only works if you focus on the positive. *Is it probable that Luke likes me because he's asked me on a date?* Yes. *Is it probable that he's using me for sex? Or for frequent lifts to football?* Probably.

Besides, the most date-like experience we've ever had was a late-night dine-in Subway meal deal on the way home from Elysium nightclub. But I can't deny that I'm excited. I make sure Luke isn't looking, then reach to touch the small piece of wood around my neck. I rub it between my fingers. *Touch wood touch wood touch wood touch wood.*

'Sounds perfect to me,' I say, trying to sound casual whilst bouncing into the driver's seat. Except for one thing.

He won't want to date me once he's met my mum. Nobody ever does.

Chapter Two

'het leven gaat niet altijd over rozen'

Life is not always beautiful

Although I have a catalogue of beautiful things, like this car for one, I've resigned myself to having low expectations in many areas of my life. *Het leven gaat niet altijd over rozen.* Life is not always beautiful. It was Pieter Bruegel who taught me that.

    Mum will stare at her favourite painting by her favourite artist, hung high above the hallway table, as if it's a work of moral art. Like it contains the rules of the universe, demonstrated by the hundreds of ugly figures enacting proverbs in a tapestry of how the world works. The 16th century *topsy-turvy* world. They've always bothered me, these merchants and villagers, each of them focused on some peculiar task. The man who is passing an enormous bell around his cat's neck. The woman who is tying a devil to a pillow. The man who is hanging backwards out of a window, holding a deck of cards. I've spent hours staring at the characters, trying to work out their literal meanings, wondering why the man on the foreground is hitting his head against a wall. I'd stare closely at the painting, until my eyes were crossed.

'Those two weird men, those ones, *there*. Are they trying to pull each other by their *nose*?' I'd asked Mum in confusion. With furrowed brows and determined expressions on their faces, their noses were locked in a comical tug of war.

'They are tricking each other,' she'd replied. 'Pulling someone's nose. It is a saying, Remi. It looks like they are playing, huh?'

'Kind of. They look kind of scary to me.'

'Scary?' she'd said. 'They are important, Remi. This painting is very, very important. Have you seen this one?'

She'd pointed to a man playing the violin to a disinterested cow. 'The cow is incapable of appreciating the music. No matter how skilled the musician is, their efforts are wasted on that cow. And this one?' She'd gestured to a person attempting to carry a burning stick in a horn. 'They cannot control the fire, no matter how hard they try. But of course, the fire represents something. A person, you know. You cannot control people, Remi. They are unpredictable. Volatile, even, like fire. The trick is to realise this early on. Do not waste your efforts on an incompetent cow. Do not try to change the unchangeable. It saves a lot of the disappointment later on.'

I'd nodded my head, not really understanding anything that the pictures were saying to me, but instead finding myself chanting her words over and over. People are volatile. Efforts are wasted. I assumed that applied to love, too.

I put the Porsche into drive as Luke jumps into the passenger seat, sliding his hand over onto my knee and squeezing it gently. A bolt of lightning runs through my body.

'Now don't get freaked out, OK,' he says. 'But it would be cool to meet your mam one day, Remi. Meet the person who knows you best.'

I feel myself stiffen, my fingers folding around the steering wheel tightly. *For goodness' sake.* That is the last thing I thought he was going to say.

'I'm sure she'd love to meet you, too. One day,' I reply. There's a pause, and I can tell I've dented Luke's ego a bit. He moves his hand off my knee and nods slowly.

'The thing is, Luke, is that my mum isn't that... well, she's not that easy-going,' I say. 'Sorry.'

I focus my gaze on the grey sky ahead, on the tops of the sad trees trying desperately to reach the light of the sun. The car radio is humming a sad song quietly as I imagine Luke and Mum meeting for the first time. Him, with his confident cheek bones, well-mannered and gracious and forthcoming. Her, with her nostrils flared wide, standoffish and sombre and snide. Her, irritated by his casualness and threatened by his mere presence. I imagine her asking him pointed questions, interrogating him even, and then growing impatient when he stumbles over the answers. And then afterwards. *Remi, don't waste your efforts on the incompetent cow.* I imagine myself trying to justify it to Luke later, feeling upset that he can't see what I see. Trying to explain that she's not always that good, but neither is she that evil, and that parents aren't meant to be Wonder Woman or Maleficent because, as a matter of fact, they're just human. And she happens to be a particularly lonely human because, other than me, she's had every person she loves die on her. In tragic circumstances. So, perhaps she deserves to be bitter. And perhaps a little twisted.

I can almost feel the discomfort of their awkward first encounter in my belly.

'Oh, aye,' says Luke. 'I'm sure she's just worried about her only daughter and that. Seeing as you've not had a boyfriend before.'

Boyfriend. The way he says it brings my breakfast to the inside of my throat. 'Uh-huh,' I say.

Luke rubs his shoulder inelegantly. 'Well, how does your mam like mouthy, unemployed northern lads?' He reaches out his hand and fondly brushes my scar with his fingers, the silvery one on my jawline. 'Come on. She'll love me.'

My fingers are still gripping the wheel tightly. 'Well, she should love you,' I say, glancing in my rear-view mirror and indicating to pull out. *Like I do*, I want to say. But my stomach isn't ready for the L word yet, and if I'm working on probables, for me to say the word love to Luke, I'd need to be as sure as the sky will be blue tomorrow that he would say it back. Because who can think of anything more mortifying than telling someone you love them and not having it reciprocated?

That will never happen to me. I won't allow it.

'My mum's just a person who's... sceptical,' I say. 'And she has a thing about drinking. She has a thing about a lot of things, really. She's a paramedic, Luke. She's seen death a hundred times. She's seen the worst that can happen to people. Seen the worst that people can do to themselves.' I check my mirrors again. You can never be too careful, to be fair. It's Sunday morning, and Sunday drivers are the worst.

'I mean... and sorry, I don't mean to sound rude or anything. But she definitely wouldn't like the fact that you go out drinking with your footy mates.'

Luke raises his eyebrows in surprise. 'She'd hold it against me, like?'

'Probably,' I say, debating now whether I should have sugar-coated it, or perhaps not mentioned it all at. Except, I know Luke prefers honesty. I fiddle with the small diamond stud in my ear. 'She'll say you're a bad influence, which, of course, you most definitely are not. But she's shit-scared I'm going to end up like my grandmother, dead under the wheels of a tram.'

'Haddaway, man!' hollers Luke, turning his whole body to face me. 'Your gran died under a tram?'

His brow furrows as if he's meticulously trying to process this morbid information in the space behind his eyes. 'Your poor bloody grandma. And your mam, of course.'

'I know,' I say. 'It's bad, isn't it?'

Luke wipes his forehead, looking genuinely distraught. His

ability to show compassion, even when I've just told him that my mother will probably hate him, is one of the beautiful things about him. 'Terrible. But hang on. How would *I* be a bad influence?'

My fingers grip the wheel again as I signal to turn left into the battered old Verborough high street. A pub proprietor is busy washing last night's sick off his pavement with a snake-like hose, in the watchful view of the customers of the café next door. The wind flicks a ketchup-stained napkin, fresh from an overflowing bin nearby, onto my car windscreen, and I switch the wipers on hurriedly. *Please don't let me have to pick it off, for goodness' sake.*

'Drinking,' I say to Luke quietly. 'The tram accident, well, it wasn't technically an accident. Mum said my grandmother was to blame. Although I prefer to think alcohol was to blame. She stumbled blind drunk into the path of a tram. And well, trams can't stop quickly, can they?' I brake abruptly as a light turns red. 'I mean, that's mad, isn't it? Losing someone like that. Although I was too young to remember her. Mum's the only family I have.'

'Bloody hell, Remi,' says Luke. 'That is rough *as*, like.'

He places his hand back on my knee, and I stare at him until the light has turned green and someone beeps their horn at me to move. My palms are sweating. I've never told anyone about how my grandmother died, and I feel eerily guilty about it, guilty about laying the blame on her out loud, like I'm speaking ill of the dead and it might come back to haunt me. I can feel my heart beating through my chest. It's not that Mum told me not to tell anyone. But she never made it clear that she was OK for me to tell someone, either.

'Was it in the news? In Holland, like?'

'I looked for it,' I say. 'But I couldn't find anything. It's difficult to sift through websites when I don't speak Dutch. I did find one site, though. The Institute for Road Safety something or other. They say there are at least twenty-something deaths each year from accidents involving public transport in Holland, so she's not the only one, I guess.' I'd felt like I'd gotten somewhere when I'd found that statistic, even though it had told me absolutely nothing about my grandmother's death whatsoever.

'And what about your grandad? Was he there when it happened?' Luke stares back ahead. 'Christ, Remi. How horrendous to witness something like that, let alone if it's your *wife*.'

I'd thought about my grandad, when I was tracing the whole scene out on my teenage ceiling. Had he seen it? The love of his life splattered like a cracked egg on the tram tracks? Or had the poor soul been spared the gory details?

'I don't know if he saw it,' I say. 'My mum made me promise to never speak about it again. Too horrific for her, I guess.'

I take a hand off the steering wheel and tuck the left side of my biscuit-coloured hair behind my ear. 'I knew nothing about my grandmother until this one weekend when I was fifteen, the very first weekend that I got drunk. Mum was furious with me. She only told me the story to scare me, I think. She loves a scaremongering tactic, does Mum.'

'Yeah, like the Little Red Riding Hood story, you mean? *Never trust a stranger, always listen to your mother* type thing?'

'Exactly. And from then on, I stayed away from it. The drinking, I mean. Not completely, but to show her solidarity, you know? I'm all she has, Luke.' I lay my head back on the headrest, feeling tired. It really has been a long term.

Luke swallows loudly. 'Yeah, I get it.'

'She's got this real hatred of it, though. Says the devil comes out when you drink. It's extreme, Luke,' I say. I wipe at my eyes, under my glasses, which are starting to give me a headache.

Luke chews on his cheek and sighs. 'Remi, I can see how your mam blames alcohol for her mother's death. That is traumatic, no doubt about it. But you can't live on edge your whole life. Bad things happen to good people, right?'

He gives my knee a sympathetic squeeze. 'Or maybe your

gran wasn't a good person, maybe she was just a selfish alcoholic. My dad's a borderline alcoholic, and he's a goddamn selfish prick. Sorry. But your mam needs to realise that you are not your grandmother. And that I'm not a bad person because I choose to get mortal with my mates once in a while.' He sucks in his chest and moves his hand back onto his own thigh.

'Get mortal,' I say, pulling myself towards the steering wheel. 'I love how you say that,' I smile.

And it's then that I realise it. This will be the last time Luke sits next to me in my car. I will need to end our relationship. Before it's even begun.

Chapter Three

*'wie boter op zijn hoofd heeft,
moet niet in de zon lopen'*

He who has butter on his head, should stay out of the sun

Once Luke is gone and I'm out of the football ground, I turn the radio up and start accelerating towards the motorway home. *Turn up the feel-good in your area* a voice sings out, as I cough loudly to clear my throat. I bring my wooden pendant up towards my mouth and hold it between my lips. There will be no traffic today. I'll make it back for one o'clock, just as Mum wanted. *Touch wood touch wood touch wood touch wood.*

Travelling out of Verborough, even without Luke, is always a pleasant experience. Throughout the depressing city the mildew suffocates your lungs with its stagnant aroma of decay, burning under your nose like an invisible moustache. Arriving in Verborough three years ago was like the disappointment you feel when you slice open an avocado and it's all hard on the inside. It's not clear if the vast number of undergraduate students here have made it like that, or if it was made like that especially for the students – as a dank hole for them to burrow their way out of, like a post-graduation challenge. *Congratulations on lasting the years in this cold and unyielding concrete jungle! Your next task is to escape it!* Even the motorway gives a heavy sigh of relief as it sends cars north towards fresh air or south towards freedom.

An hour and a half and what feels like a hundred dual carriageways later, I start to see the houses look happier, with their windows washed and their curtains flung open as if to say welcome home. An hour and a half and what feels like a hundred dual carriageways later is when I feel the trepidation coming on.

It starts when I'm near our cul-de-sac.

I've spent whole afternoons driving around Langswood, timing my arrival home perfectly to what I'd guess would be the best time for Mum's mood. I've spent a lifetime contemplating how to navigate the delicate balance of daughterly appreciation and assertiveness. If I catch Mum at the right time, I can often avoid being on the wrong side of our strange power dynamic. Which means my Easter break at home will start off on the right foot, at least.

My stomach aches for warm toast and jam, washed down with a milky cup of hot coffee. As I turn onto our driveway, my tires roll wearily on the paving stones near Mum's meticulously manicured front lawn, where blades of grass stand like bristles on a hairbrush to create this lush, velvety-green carpet. It's incredible how well she looks after this lawn. How well she looks after everything, really. Her belief that appearances count for everything explains why I can't count a single weed around the flower beds, which are filled with heathers and tulips, and a large Californian lemon and lime. Bees hum around the perimeter near to a wooden bug hotel, which we won together at a summer fête. A rainbow-coloured pebble painted with *mummy* is placed in a pot next to some beautiful red primroses, my favourite colour. The pebble was a gift, a primary school art project, something that made Mum's face light up as if it were a stone made of gold.

I smile as I remember the pink rollerblades she bought me in return.

The clock says twelve forty in the afternoon. I breathe out as I realise I've made it, and in plenty of time, too. The car door feels heavy as I push it open, in a hurry to stretch out my cramped-up thighs. A scrunched-up crisp packet of Luke's falls onto the paving, and I tut as I pick it up, crumpling it in my palm. I reach into my door compartment for any more rubbish to remove from my car, finding a parking ticket and a tarot card I'd collected from last weekend. *The Whispering Grove card* it reads. *The Whispering Grove symbolises introspection and the subconscious mind. The whispers of the forest invite you to delve deep within yourself, to uncover truths and find clarity amid uncertainty. This card reminds you to trust your inner voice and embrace the mysteries that lie within.*

I shudder, remembering how I'd acquired it. The problem that day had been a thin man in a dirty suit who looked like he smelt of sour baked beans and cabbage. He was following us like a rat following cheddar, shouting *get your tits out for the lads* at the top of his gravelly voice while staggering in and out of the road. My housemate Aoife, a quiet but quick-witted Irish girl from Galway, had spotted the door of the arcade at just the right time and dragged me into it.

'Jesus the lord save us,' she'd panted heavily. 'Doesn't the scoundrel see that we have tits as flat as pancakes, like?'

I place the rubbish – including the card – neatly into my new car bin, a purchase that my OCD me had been very happy about. I'm looking forward to showing it to Mum this week. Not the card – she thinks arcades are a gambler's paradise – but the bin. Perhaps I'll order one for her car after our afternoon tea.

Glad to be free of the confines of the Porsche, I tread around to the boot and start to unpack its contents. Patrick from number ninety is out on his front driveway, tinkering with his prized vintage Mercedes like a giddy little lad playing with a toy car. His sweet dog Pickle, who's regularly moaned about by the cul-de-sac for his tendency to howl throughout the night, is sat staring at him, grumpy at having to wait for his walk. Patrick gives me a nonchalant nod as I grip the handle of one of the duffel bags and pull it up onto my shoulder.

'Hi, Rosie,' he shouts. 'Whoa, that's one hell of a bag you've got there. Where are you hiding the dead body?' His laugh is one that regurgitates around the cul-de-sac.

It's Remi, I want to correct him, but I don't.

'Bodies,' I say instead, flashing him my least genuine smile. 'Only in here, it's just the heads.' I let out a pained snort and then a strange cough that seems to escape from nowhere. 'Apologies. That was a joke, of course. Sorry.'

His face turns sour, and I move quickly towards the house. He watches me as I lug the heavy thing – carrying enough dirty cotton to clothe an army – past the red tulip border and towards the side door of the house. As I drop it there in a heap, he treats me to an arrogant rev of the car engine. *Oh, sod off, Patrick,* I think. *Your engine impresses me about as much as your non-existent chivalry.*

The lock on the side door turns easily, and I step inside, carefully placing my shoes where Mum likes them. The house smells divine, of lime and patchouli, like one of those expensive home interior showrooms with rustic stone pots and fake white hydrangeas everywhere. It feels like a sanctuary compared to damp and dreary Verborough, and I am suddenly very grateful for Mum's insistence that the house be kept spotless. Sunlight streams through the entryway like a spotlight onto more tulips, freshly cut ones this time, which are sitting neatly in a vase on the glass hallway table. Without even looking around, I can tell that every inside surface has been freshly dusted and hoovered and mopped and wiped over with not a clinical cleanliness, but a considered one. My six-legged bed and breakfast residents would be mortified.

Sunday is the only day that Mum doesn't clean. We're not

religious, even if Mum did sign me up for Sunday school so my Church of England Prep looked favourably on me, but Mum likes to leave Sundays for rest. She won't work Saturday night shifts as they leak into her Sunday, and I'm glad of it, because I worry about her being on any night shift, let alone the night before the Sabbath, when all the devils come out to play. The devils that come out when you drink.

She doesn't clean on Sundays, but she likes to tidy. She always likes to tidy. But the house is peaceful, and I know she'll have already finished her tidying, and she'll be upstairs in her dressing room, the one she's lovingly decorated with pearlescent wallpaper and expensive branded reed diffusers, sorting through one of her many cupboards, with her *getting the most out of midlife with Liz Clark* podcast on, lost in the world of menopause and financial planning and empty nest syndrome. Either that, or a podcast on true crime stories, an intense political debate, or some graphic medical discussion that includes a personal trauma experience or two. All taxing and triggering topics to me that I try my very best to avoid – in order to maintain a life of ignorant bliss – but that I know I'll hear about over afternoon tea later. And rightly so, Mum would say. You can't avoid the *world*, Remi. You just have to learn from it.

I carry the lumpy bag from the doorstep to the washing machine, pop my shoes back on, and step back outside to fetch the rest of my things. The clouds have parted, and our cherry blossom tree is standing magnificently in the spring sunlight. I'm grateful to have caught the stunning sakura in full bloom, and it suddenly makes me feel sad for the residents of Verborough. It makes me feel sad for Luke. Then it makes me feel sad full stop. That's what beautiful things do. You can't help but fall in love with them, and then they break your heart.

As I reach the Porsche again, I see an unfamiliar red Ford Fiesta pulling up to the pavement – a bit of a banger, and a rare sight for a Sunday down our sleepy end of the cul-de-sac. Patrick must be thinking the same thing as he revs his engine again. Standing in the shadow of my four-by-four, I watch as a frail, balding man of around seventy steps out. He's older, but not elderly, a similar picture to most of our neighbours, but he seems out of place, confused by his surroundings. Or perhaps just confused full stop. He's a stranger who doesn't belong in our neighbourhood, that's for sure.

I can picture the posh women of Langswood watching from their windows, tutting at the creases in his shirt and the frayed edges of his jeans. I smile as I think of them, criticising his parking, cursing him for daring to pull up on the street that's very much open to anyone but that, in their opinion, is so obviously not open to anyone except them. Especially on Sundays. At any moment, I expect one of them to run out into the cul-de-sac and try to defend their right to his parking spot, even though their cars are all parked neatly in their massive driveways, which are all extremely accessible, due to their excessively wide dropped curbs. *It's not the point, though, darling, is it?* I can hear them grumble. *What if I have a delivery? Or need space to turn? Or just don't want an old banger near my Ferrari?*

I feel the need to keep eyes on him, to defend him from their watchful gaze. Clutching onto his car door for what looks like dear life, he surveys the semicircle before settling his gaze on our house. His eyes look glassy, a bit like Copperfield's after he's ripped open Mum's best cushion for the tenth time, the strawberry-coloured one with tassels that sits on her linen armchair near the glass conservatory.

Copperfield. It hits me that, in my haste to get the bags inside, I've left the side door wide open, meaning Copperfield the cat could be executing a Houdini-style escape at this very moment. Panicked, I abandon the man and dash back to the side door, feeling relieved to see him sitting regally in the long hallway when I return. I kneel and stroke his soft fur. His squidgy feet that look just like little snowshoes pitter-patter around me as he nudges his head against my jeans. His purr is so comforting, and I find my shoulders instantly dropping.

I'm about to shut him safely in the utility and go back out for my second duffle bag when I hear a loud *ding-dong* of the doorbell.

Ding-dong ding-dong, ding-dong ding-dong. Then again. *Ding-dong ding-dong, ding-dong ding-dong.* Someone is either very heavy handed with their index finger or seriously eager for us to answer.

I grab at Copperfield, trying to scoop him up into my arms, but he starts walking inquisitively down the hallway towards the front door. It can't be a coincidence that I just witnessed someone near our driveway looking over at our house. Then, a few minutes later, there's a ring on the doorbell. But what does an old, confused-looking man in a battered Ford Fiesta want with us on a Sunday? I stand still for a while, willing him to go on his way. He's frail, but the *don't open the door to strangers* rule has never got old for me. Mum still hides a can of extra strong hairspray in the shoe basket in the hall. Could he be lost? Spreading the word about his church, perhaps? Wanting a donation to charity? There's always plenty of those who come around here. It's like they think that most rich people aren't rich because they're tight.

Ding-dong ding-dong, ding-dong ding-dong. The doorbell chimes vociferously again.

Bugger. Copperfield looks back at me with an excitable expression, then carries on towards the noise. Worried that he might make a dash for it, I grab at him and pull him back towards the utility by his collar. I can't see the front door, but I can hear Mum's slippers coming down the stairs.

'Yes?' she says as I hear the door creak open. 'There really is no need to keep pressing the doorbell like that. It is a long way from upstairs, you know.'

'Oh, yes, well, 'ello dear,' says the man, with a whistle in his nose. I can tell by his elderly voice that it's him from the red car. 'I'm very... extremely sorry to bother you on a... err, on a Sunday afternoon,' he says. He speaks painfully slowly and with a slight stutter in his voice.

'Well. Yes. OK,' replies Mum. I imagine him as that one pesky ant, the one that's somehow got into the house from a secret entryway near the kitchen countertop. I imagine her leaning on the door, pulling her shirt collar higher into her chin, determined to eliminate him from her porch as fast as possible and get on with her afternoon. It's obvious from her voice that, like me, she has no idea who this man is, and that she has absolutely no intention of finding out.

'I just... ah. I just 'ope I've got the right place,' says the man.

Copperfield's fishy breath fills the air around me, and I shake my head at him fondly, like a mother to a baby. I pull him into my chest. *The poor old man's got the wrong address,* I mouth to him.

'What place are you looking for?' replies Mum. There's a strange pause, and Copperfield's purring sounds loud against the silence.

'Well,' says the man. 'I, umm. I was 'opin to, err. To talk about Johanna, as a matter of fact.'

'Johanna?' blurts out Mum in a high-pitched, peculiar voice.

I stand puzzled in the hallway, still hidden away from view. Johanna? My grandmother, Johanna? Why would this old man be wanting to talk about Johanna? I can hear Mum's slippers shuffling busily on the porcelain tile.

'I travelled to Cambridge to find 'er, you see. Tried turnin' up at the 'ouse a couple of times, even shouted over the gate. But no one was there.' He sounds livelier now, his sentences more coherent, like someone's turned his battery up to high. 'So, my son did a bit of diggin' for me, you know. On the internet and that. He can crack into all sorts of things, that lad can. And I've got reason to believe that this is the residence of the Van Tams, if I'm not mistaken?'

I wait, wondering how long it will take for Mum to admit that his son is a possible IT genius, because he's absolutely right.

'And who are you?' challenges Mum instead.

'I'm grateful that you've answered your door, Ms. Van Tam,' he says, completely ignoring her question.

'Elise,' says Mum. 'My name is Elise.'

The man pauses. 'Well, Elise. I don't mean to startle you, dear. I don't know 'ow to say it, really. But I've thought about this moment for a very long time.'

'Look,' says Mum. 'I really do not understand what you mean. And I am actually right in the middle of something.' I hear the door creak as if she's starting to close it.

'The thin' is, you see, dear.' He speaks louder and more quickly now. 'I'm comin' to the end of my life. I've been livin' with cancer for a while now. Bowel cancer. It's terminal.' He pauses, as if to catch his breath.

Mum doesn't say a word.

'I don't want any *pity* or anythin'. That's not why I'm tellin' you.'

'Right,' says Mum, with an edge to her voice. If he hadn't had just said he'd got cancer, I'm sure she'd have slammed the door in his face by now.

'Yes. Well. You want to know why I'm 'ere, I'm sure. Why I'm 'ere askin' after your mother. It's just,' he does what can only be described as a really ugly, phlegmy cough. 'It's just I've never been able to forgive myself for what 'appened to Johanna.'

There's a long silence now. Mum's slipper shuffling has stopped.

'What the…'

'Just 'ear me out, dear, please. I'm just desperate to know that she's OK. That she went on to live a good life, you know? I know it's a surprise, me turnin' up unannounced at your door. But please. It will mean I can go in peace.'

I stand with bated breath, frozen on the spot. Copperfield

wriggles, and I hug him tighter until he stills. *Never been able to forgive myself?* What is this old man on about?

Then Mum speaks, differently this time, as if it's finally sinking in to her who this man might be. 'Wait a minute, you can't be…'

'Yes, dear,' he speaks over her. 'Gerald. That's right. The driver of the motorbike.'

Motorbike?

'You have got to be kidding me,' replies Mum. 'You mean the motorbike that ran over my mother?' She's loud now, with short, shaky breath. 'You mean the man who left her there to die? You turn up on my doorstep all these years later, asking how she is? So that you… so *you* can go in peace?'

It's Gerald's turn to shuffle now. I can hear his shiny coat ruffling on the doorstep.

'You should be ashamed of yourself.'

My mouth drops open as Copperfield is now trying to fully maneuver out of my grip, like he wants a front row seat to view the action.

'I understand your anger, dear,' the man says calmly now. 'And I regret that. Oh, do I regret that. I regret that every day, believe me.' There's a sombre pause, and I have a vague vision of him trying to battle with Mum to hold the door open. 'But we all make mistakes, don't we, Ms. Van Tam? And I don't mean that to sound disrespectful, of course. But surely you, of all people, would understand that?'

I can hear Mum's heavy gasp, the door creaking in her grip. The man's coat crackles as if she's pushing him off his standing spot. 'Get. The. Fuck. Off. My. Doorstep,' she hisses. 'And don't you ever come near me or my mother again.'

Then she slams the door, and I hear her, for the first time ever, start to sob uncontrollably.

Chapter Four

'wat kan rook met ijzer doen?'

What can smoke do to iron?

Don't come near me or my mother again. *Me or my mother.* Not dead mother. Just mother. It doesn't make any sense.

I grab the handle of a door just off the hallway to steady myself, my glasses sticking uncomfortably to my nose. I'm breathing mostly through my mouth, but I can still smell the strong, fishy aroma from Copperfield. His golden eyes are frozen on mine, like he knows something's off.

It's weird, the way my heart is pumping, and I'm not expecting those funny black dots to move across my eyeballs like this. Mum has never sobbed before. Not sad sobbed, anyway. I drop Copperfield gently to the ground, a perturbed expression creeping across my face.

Why do I feel a bit faint?

Perhaps it's the surprise, the surprise of knowing that this man's story, and my mum's story about how my grandmother died, don't quite tally up. I mean, they don't tally up *at all*.

So, who is lying?

I pull my body closer to her so I can see her. Her legs are shaking, rather violently it looks like, and she collapses down, the palm of her hand touching the wall, her head dropping towards the floor. I can almost taste the saltiness of her tears. Part of me wants to run to Mum, to comfort her, like she would comfort me when I was a child and my best friend wasn't my best friend anymore. To tell her that everything's going to be alright. But my legs don't move. They stay rooted to the spot. Their intention, I realise, is to go quickly in the opposite direction.

Before I can give it a second thought, I shake the black dots away from my eyes and tiptoe down the hallway back towards the side door, grabbing a startled Copperfield and throwing him into the utility room with a bit more force than I'd intended. He meows an angry meow at me as I whisper *sorry* apologetically to him. Usually, I'd be far too intimidated to confront a man I don't know, especially a potential murderer. I know Mum would *hate* that I'm doing this. But what if she needs protecting? How can I protect her if I don't know the truth?

I click the utility door closed and run out the side door after him. Trying to be as quiet as I can, I move my soft Bambi legs past the tulip border and the perfectly green grass and up onto the driveway. Sooner or later, Mum will see my car outside the house, and all my bags in the utility, and I need to get to this man before she has the chance to come out and stop me.

I run faster, so I'm on the pavement, then on the road, until I'm in touching distance of the man's car. He's rummaging around in his shiny jacket pocket for his car key.

'Excuse me,' I hiss, urgently. 'Gerald, isn't it? Please. I need to ask you something.'

The man turns around and looks at me, his old eyes surprised. I stop still, wheezing slightly, and I realise that *I'm* surprised, too. This man is a stranger, a potential threat, a cold, hard killer for all I know. What if he gets mad and attacks me? What if I get mad and attack *him?* Why can't I have gone to Mum on the floor and demanded that she tell me the truth?

'I'm Elise's daughter, Remi,' I say. I square my shoulders and clear my throat like a seasoned actress might do, determined to get something out of this old man's mouth that makes sense. Because none of this makes any sense right now. Not least, me begging a random man to tell me stories about my past.

'Remi Van Tam,' I confirm. 'I'm Johanna's granddaughter.'

I immediately wonder whether I should have given him all of that information, and curse myself for not being more composed.

'I'm part of the family, you see. And I just need a few things clarifying,' I say. 'And quickly, if that's OK.' The man stares at me for a while, and I sense that nothing he does is going to be done quickly. I tug at my sleeves until they are covering my hands entirely.

'Right,' he says. 'Right.'

He is a poorly sight up close. His face is putrid and grey with random dark spots that resemble small countries dotted around a well-polluted globe. His hands are rough and solid, and his nose looks broken at the bridge. Despite all the warning signs, I can't seem to feel scared of him, though. He looks like a man suffering from terminal cancer. He looks thoroughly exhausted with life. He does not look like a person who would want to attack me.

'First off. I'm truly sorry for upsettin' your mum,' he says. The skin around his mouth is all dry and cracked, and as he talks, a white piece of spit lands on his bottom lip. 'It's not what I wanted to do today, dear. I can promise you that.'

He tries to lean on his car but loses his balance, and he sways slightly towards me. I take a cautious step back, not knowing what to make of it. He's poorly, that's for sure, but I have no allegiance to this man. And according to what Mum just said, he rode off on his motorbike and left my grandmother for dead, or whatever the hell that means.

'I just need you to tell me exactly what happened to Johanna, as quickly as possible,' I say, more sternly this time. I glance around the cul-de-sac, feeling eyes on me already. My face stings in the Spring sunshine.

The man looks perplexed. 'Why dear, you don't already know?' he says.

My fingers twist the fabric of my sleeves. *Well, I thought I did*, I want to say. But I don't say that. 'I'd just like to know your side of the story,' I say instead.

He sways again, looking hesitant. Expecting him to blurt out how he killed – or didn't kill – my grandmother in the middle of the street, to someone he doesn't know, might be a long shot after all. I start to beg. 'Please, Gerald,' I say. 'It's important.'

Painfully slowly, he pulls his skinny arm up and looks down at his watch. The brown leather strap is all cracked and fraying.

'Meet me at the coffee place,' he says. 'The one in that 'ome store. The one that I would 'ave passed on my way 'ere. I'll 'ead there now. If we're goin' to do this, dear, I'm goin' to need a cup of tea.'

~

Ten minutes later, and I'm pulling into the home store car park, into the empty spot next to Gerald's red banger. I jumped into the Porsche and followed him all the way here, eager to make sure that he kept his word about meeting me. I mean, I can't imagine I'd have chased him down the motorway if he didn't, but given the mood I'm in right now, maybe I would have.

I'd left home without telling Mum, of course. No way would I have risked her disdain for me even considering speaking to someone like Gerald myself. She might have locked the door and blocked me from leaving. I feel sick imagining what the conversation will be when I get home, but I can deal with that later. This could be important, I remind myself. Whoever Gerald is, his sudden appearance has upset Mum more than I've ever seen before. She might not want it, but I could be protecting her. And I'm not the child that she thinks I am. Perhaps this is one way that I can prove it.

The home store is a vast, multi-level emporium filled with mid-priced home goods, with a small coffee shop on the second floor. Large glass windows look in on wide aisles, which are flanked with vibrant displays of faux flowers, kitchenware, and various types of home décor. I touch my phone, checking for signs of a missed call from Mum. Thankfully, there's nothing but a WhatsApp message from Aoife reminding me to cancel our food delivery service for the three weeks that we'll be gone from our student house. I glance over my shoulder at the cars parked behind me. She doesn't know yet.

I have time.

I turn my phone onto silent and put it back into my pocket, watching as Gerald moves from his car, slothfully pulling himself out of his front seat. It's a struggle for him to stand upright, and a mystery why no one has given him a stick to help him in situations like these. If he were my dad or my grandad, I wouldn't allow him to leave the house without some sort of walking aid. But that's not my concern. I'm not here to help this guy, for goodness' sake. I'm here for information.

I step out of the car and stand awkwardly near him, waiting for him to be upright. As he finds his feet, I wonder if we'll make it all the way up to the café at the top of the store. Before I can convince him that he really doesn't need that cup of tea in order to tell me exactly what he knows, he starts to shuffle over to the glass double doors, and I follow him until we're there, surrounded by people coming and going with big plastic bags stuffed with bedspreads and curtains and other random bits and bobs to decorate their beautiful, massive houses with.

Gerald takes a tentative look inside the store and then glances at me, holding his arm out in what can only be described as a gentlemanly way, as if to say, *after you*. I take an eager step forward, unsure whether to say thank you, which would of course be the polite thing to do. But I say nothing. I just walk quickly into the home store in silence.

Thankfully, the escalator is right in front of us, next to a collection of white Scandi furniture, set up like a cute mini living room. I decide to let him go first this time, and I almost have to push him onto it, standing behind him so that he doesn't topple backwards. As we get to the top, I feel the need to hold out *my* arm, to help him off the escalator. He takes the arm, and I'm treated to a strong whiff of old wood and menthol. My body is stiff as I lead him onto terra firma, dropping his arm as soon as it feels reasonably possible. It is so surreal to be helping him like this. To a passerby, we probably look like we're family.

We reach the café and I gesture at Gerald to take a seat while I order a cup of English breakfast tea and an espresso. *If only Eliza were here with one of her grandad's cigars*, I think. He picks a seat near the window, close enough for him to stagger to, but far enough away from the families with small children watching noisy episodes of some tiny tot programme on their parent's phone. I'm grateful because, whatever he has to say, I want to hear him loud and clear.

While I wait not so patiently for the barista to finish making our drinks – *why are they always so slow?* – I decide that I want to be the one to speak first. I start to try to work out ways of approaching this. I need him to tell me everything, but I don't want to push him into a corner. Now, Remi, is not the time to blurt out a jumbled mess. I need to stay composed, for my words to be succinct and to the point. I need him to trust me in order to tell me everything. Isn't that what they say in all those detective books?

My confidence wanes as I remind myself that I don't know this Gerald from Adam, that he still might be an absolute monster, a heartless assassin who knocks people down for fun and leaves them for dead. I look around, now feeling grateful that the coffee shop is full of bodies, bodies that I could call on for help at any moment. I know he looks decrepit and feeble. But looks can be deceiving, can't they? Isn't it always the quiet ones that you need to watch out for?

Finally, the barista pushes my drinks at me, and I carry them over to our table, leaving Gerald's on the round black tray and placing it in front of him. He picks up his teacup and blows gently on it, pushing a ten-pound note across the table in my direction.

'For the drinks, dear. Call me old-fashioned, but I wouldn't expect you to 'ave to pay for them.'

I nod appreciatively, surprised by the gesture. No one said that serial killers can't be generous, though.

'Would you prefer I start?' he says.

I take a seat opposite him and down my hot espresso in one, burning my tongue in the process. I don't feel quite as brave now that I'm sitting here facing the man.

'Yes, that would be best,' I say. So much for wanting to speak first.

'You really know nothin' about this at all?' he says.

I'd thought hard about this on the drive over here. Do I tell him the story that Mum told me? Or do I leave him to tell me his own version of events?

'I know nothing,' I reply firmly.

Gerald takes a sip of the tea and rests the cup down, spilling hot liquid into the saucer and onto the tray. He lowers his head towards me.

'First off. I'm not a murderer, if that's what you think.'

'I don't necessarily think that,' I say. My hand goes to my necklace.

Touch wood touch wood touch wood touch wood.

'Good. I can sense you're more open-minded than your... than erm, than other people might be, dear.'

I notice that Gerald's left eye is looking straight at me, while the right eye keeps drifting off to the right, and I'm completely unsure as to which one to focus on.

'It was an accident, I can assure you. The whole thing was a terrible accident.' He takes another shaky sip of his tea while I wait silently for him to continue.

'Cambridge, it was. The summer of two thousand and five. Down Petworth Close, do you know it? Past the primary school on the right, and over the mini-roundabout. Just up from the fish and chip shop, and it's there on the left 'and side.' I watch as he marks it all out with his bony finger, and I nod, wondering why old men have such a tendency to focus on meaningless directions. 'Petworth Close is where your grandmother lived.'

'Right,' I say. 'So, this accident, it happened outside her house?'

'That's right, dear.'

'And you were driving a motorbike?' I say. His face looks surprised. 'It's just I overheard you, talking to Mum.'

'A Kawasaki Vulcan eight 'undred,' he says. 'A cruiser, beautiful it was. I was drivin' 'ome from a mate's 'ouse. I'd been 'elping 'im build a shed in the garden, you see. We worked into the night as long as we could, right until dusk fell and it grew too dark. It was about ten-ish when I came down Petworth Close, maybe just before ten. I wasn't goin' fast, around thirty or forty miles an 'our, perhaps. I wasn't one of those reckless motorbike riders like you see nowadays.'

He takes another sip of his tea and winces when he swallows. I should hate this man, but part of me feels like I want to offer him paracetamol and a blanket.

'OK. So, you were driving your motorbike, in the almost-dark, down my grandmother's road,' I say, trying to piece it all together in my head. 'And then what happened?'

Gerald leans further into the table. 'The thing you 'ave to understand, dear, is it's a country lane, Petworth Close. The 'ouses are big, they're set far back from the roadside, covered by shrubs and bushes and the like. There are a couple of street lights, of course. But when it starts gettin' dark, it's quite difficult to see down there at night. And their 'ouse, it was on a bend.' I can hear his raspy breathing getting hoarser, and I feel the urgency to speed things up before he keels over right in front of me.

'I understand that,' I say, using my most polite voice. 'But let's get to it, shall we?' My knees knock together under the table. 'What was my grandmother doing outside her house at that time in the evening?'

Gerald takes his time to fold his hands, one over the other. 'That, I don't know, dear. All I know is that she was already in the road when I went over 'er.'

He blinks a hard blink as I imagine the poor woman, savagely battered by flying metal.

'So, she'd walked out in front of you and you'd hit her, is that it?'

'Oh no,' he croaks. 'That wasn't what 'appened at all. Well, not quite.'

'So, *what* happened?' I say, less sympathetically this time. I say it loud enough that the woman on the table next to us looks over, and I'm forced into flashing her a reassuring smile. I turn back to Gerald. 'I just need to know the main part of the story, please.'

'Right, well. I didn't knock 'er over, if that's what you mean. She was already layin' there.'

'What do you mean, she was lying there?' I say.

'Before I even knew what was 'appening, my motorbike bumped right over 'er. It seemed to go on forever. I mean, my motorbike was a big, old chunk of metal. I lost control and almost came off the bike.'

'So, you ran *over* her?' I don't know why, but imagining someone being run over, as opposed to knocked over, feels worse somehow.

'She was right in the middle of the road. I wasn't sure if she was face down or face up or whatnot. Like I said, it was gettin' dark. At first, I thought she was an injured deer or somethin'. A large, dead fox, maybe. I stopped for a second, and the figure just lay there.'

I crumple up my face. Why was Johanna lying in the middle of the road? Was she blind drunk, like Mum had said?

'But then, she started movin'. She made it onto all fours. Then she stood up. I could just make out a person, a woman. She was stumblin' around, and I panicked.'

My face starts to redden again. Suddenly, I don't give a monkey's how ill or how old this man is. 'You didn't just *leave* her there, did you, Gerald?'

'I promise you, I didn't,' he says, his eyes widening seriously. I wonder if he's intimidated by me, then, and I shrink quickly back into my seat.

'I called the ambulance. Anonymously, I admit. I didn't tell them what 'ad 'appened. I just said that I'd seen a person movin' around on the road who looked like they might be injured.'

He scratches his forehead, and I watch as bits of skin flake from it.

'I waited nearby until the ambulance arrived. 'id the bike and pretended I was a passerby. Your grandmother was delirious. She 'ad no idea. I thought that if she'd got up, she would be OK. I had a family at 'ome to think about. I was scared. I'd been in trouble with the police before, been in a fight when I was a teenager. GBH conviction, dear. I didn't need another reason for them to come knockin' on my door.'

'Right,' I say, staring hard at him. My heart feels like it's filling with hot, gooey fluid.

'I know I should 'ave told the police what really 'appened. It would 'ave saved all this mess that 'appened afterwards. But I didn't leave 'er to die. I can promise you that.'

'You sure make a lot of promises,' I mutter, without meaning to say it out loud. 'So, you never got caught?' I ask. 'And what do you mean by *all this mess*?'

'Caught?' he says. 'Well, there wasn't really anythin' to get caught for, dear. It was an accident, like I said. Two people in the wrong place at the wrong time. But I couldn't live with myself. I 'ad to know what 'appened to her. So, I rang the 'ospital a week later and managed to convince them I was a family friend.'

'And they told you she'd died?' I say.

'Oh no,' he says. 'They told me that she was very much alive.'

I'm stunned into stillness, then.

Johanna was alive?

'The doctors said she was doin' well, all considerin'. But I never knew if she made a proper recovery. Which is why I turned up at your 'ouse today.'

My mind goes to Mum, distraught at Johanna's bedside. And just now, sobbing on the floor. 'Didn't you get charged with anything, though? Surely you can't just run over someone and pretend like it never happened?'

'Actually, don't tell me,' I say. 'The police never investigate anything unless the person dies, do they?'

I'd seen it on TV. Countless true-life documentaries where people have gone through terrible ordeals, been raped, been attacked, and the police don't take it seriously. Until someone else winds up dead.

'All I can say is that I'm sorry.' Gerald sits back now and slowly pushes his empty teacup to one side. 'But now I've told you what 'appened, dear. Well, I expect you can now 'elp me with what I need to know.'

'What do you mean?' I say, trying to pretend that I didn't know that the only reason Gerald was here was to find out how Johanna was doing. *It would mean he could go in peace*, I'd heard him say.

'Just now,' he says. 'You asked if the 'ospital 'ad told me she'd died.'

'Yes,' I nod, spinning my empty espresso cup on the table. It crashes loudly to the floor, and I reach down for it, my fingers fumbling around the handle.

'Does that mean what I think it means, dear?'

'That Johanna's dead?' I whisper.

'Yes,' he nods. 'If so, I'm ever so sad to 'ear it.'

His sorry gaze makes me look to the ceiling, and I realise that I don't know what to say. I most definitely do not want to reveal to him that, in fact, after hearing his version of events this afternoon, I now have absolutely no idea whatsoever if Johanna is dead, alive, or has relocated to Timbuktu.

'I'm surprised your mother never recognised me, you know,' he says. 'I mean, I know it's been eighteen years, and I've lost a bit of weight. But I recognised 'er alright.'

I look down and find his gaze again.

'Sorry. But, how would you recognise her, Gerald?'

'I saw 'er on the night it 'appened,' he says. 'She was there.'

The old man senses the surprise in my eyes.

'Your mother, Elise. She didn't tell you what she did?'

'What she *did*?' I stutter.

'Your mum. She doesn't tell you much, dear, does she?'

I adjust my glasses, wiping my damp fringe away from my forehead. 'Sorry, but... what did my mother do, Gerald? Is it something I should know?'

'Well, yes,' he says, much more slowly than I would like him to. 'If it were me, then I'd want to know. I mean, I think you should know. Yes.'

My teeth clench. 'Then can you tell me, Gerald?'

It's the old man's turn to show me some sympathy now.

'I'm afraid, dear. That's goin' to 'ave to come from your mother.'

Chapter Five

'om tussen twee stoelen in de as te zitten'

To sit between two chairs in the ashes

You should know. I sit hunched over in my car, playing Gerald's words back to myself in my head.

Your mum didn't tell you what she did?

I stamp my heel down in the footwell, an action that seems a bit toddler-like, I'll admit, but I feel better for doing it. And quite frankly, I may as well act like a toddler, seeing as I'm being treated like one. I'm the deflated child that's being kept out of the adults chat, I decide.

Except I am not a child.

It's not particularly warm outside, but I turn the air conditioning up to full blast. What the hell is this all about? Should I trust what this old man, Gerald, says? I can't see a reason not to. There doesn't seem to be anything in it for him to tell me lies about my grandmother's death. Unless it wasn't an accident. But then, why would he come back here? An attempted murderer wouldn't go out of their way to contact the person he attempted to kill.

Not if everyone knew that he'd done it, anyway.

Before I can think to do anything else, I pull my phone out of my pocket and tap the screen. I exhale sharply as I see a missed call and a message from Mum.

Remi. You are late. What on earth are you doing at the home store? Call me.

Shit. I scratch at the eczema on my wrist, the skin flaking away in a similar way to how Gerald's did on his forehead. Before I can curse Find My iPhone again, I search for Luke's name, click call, and hold the phone up to my red-hot ear, surprised by how much I want him to answer. After a few anxious rings, he picks up.

'You alreet, babe?' he says, in his deep, comforting tone.

'Luke, have you got a minute?' I say.

'Yeah, course,' he replies. 'Is everything OK?'

I want to say no, that actually everything is really not OK, but I know that's not what anyone wants to hear. No one wants to be burdened with the *I'm not OK* chat, especially not someone who you've been having casual sex with.

'Sorry for calling, but… something really weird has happened,' I say instead.

'Weird? What do you mean, weird? You're OK, aren't you?'

'Please don't worry,' I say with shaky breath. 'But I got home, and, this man. Well, he just turned up at our house. Mum answered the door. She didn't think I could hear them, but I could. And he started talking about my grandmother, Johanna. And then I followed him…'

'Woah, hang on a second,' cuts in Luke. 'You'll have to slow down a bit, Remi. Say it again slowly. You followed a man somewhere. Is that what you said? Wait a minute, are you in danger?'

'No, no. Not in danger! He just suggested we come to a café. I bought him a cup of tea. Which I know sounds a bit odd. It's…

it's hard to explain but…'

I study my own face in the rear-view mirror. I still can't quite believe I pretty much forced this man to tell me everything. Well, everything except what my mum apparently did.

'Basically, this man knows what happened to my grandmother. And it's not what I thought it was.'

'The drunk grandmother who got killed by a tram?' confirms Luke. 'Sorry, I didn't mean for that to sound the way it did.'

'Yep! That's the one!' My voice is sounding bizarrely high-pitched, like the more I talk, the less it believes what it's saying. 'Well, according to this man, it wasn't a tram that hit Johanna. It was a motorbike. *His* motorbike. And she didn't get killed,' I say. 'Well, not instantly, anyway. Unless she was involved in two life-threatening accidents involving a vehicle in her life, which I think is highly unlikely.'

'OK,' says Luke. 'So, what do you mean? That your grandmother is alive?'

'I don't know,' I say. 'But she didn't die at the scene, like Mum told me. Not according to this man, anyway. And she was most definitely not hit by a tram in Amsterdam. Whatever it was happened in Cambridge, right outside her house.'

I tug on my ear, just as a tired child would do. I'm reeling from the possibility that the whole Amsterdam thing is a lie. If only I'd have known that it happened in England, I might have got somewhere with my internet searches.

'So, your mam has lied to you?' asks Luke. 'I mean, it's a whopping great lie to tell, don't you think? You really believe this man is telling the truth?'

'He has to be,' I say. 'He's on death's door, Luke. That's the reason he wanted to see Johanna, to know how she ended up. Before he goes, you know? So that he can go in peace, he said so in his own words. I can't see any reason for him to lie. Not now, anyway.'

'But why on earth would your mam lie to you about your

nanna being dead?' asks Luke. 'I mean, have you confronted her about it?'

'No, not yet. I'm still in the car park at the home store. It's where we met for the tea.'

'Well, you'll have to talk to your mam about it when you get home.'

'I know. And I definitely should. She's messaged me asking where I am. So, I need to get home… but…'

'But what?' says Luke.

'I just… I can't talk to her about it, Luke. I know I've got to face her, but…'

There's a long pause, and for a second, I wonder if I should have just said *yes, will do! I love talking to my mum about things of the heart.*

'Remi. Are you scared of your mam?' asks Luke.

His frankness surprises me.

'I'm just… angry,' I insist. 'She told me my grandmother was killed instantly by a tram, and now this man shows up saying he ran over her with his motorbike. And then she gets all upset, I mean *really* upset, like sobbing and stuff, and I've never seen her like that before, and, well, it just doesn't make any sense. And I can't work out why she'd lie to me about it. And it's pissing me off, to be honest.'

I take my glasses off and wipe my eyes, feeling an overwhelming urge to cry. The dread of going back to the cul-de-sac washes over me.

'Bugger.'

Rarely do I swear, but it feels so good that I mouth *fuck, shit, fuck* into the steering wheel. All the time that I've been coming to terms with losing a grandparent I never met in the most terrible of circumstances, all those years suddenly feel like they're stacked on top of me, like hot, itchy woolly blankets I can't shake off. And now, the story I was told might not be true.

But why? Why would you lie about how your mother was

killed? And if she's alive, why is she keeping me from her? Or, keeping her from *me*? Does my grandmother not want to see me? Is she a *danger* to me, for goodness' sake?

'Remi,' says Luke firmly, as my head jolts back into real time. 'I think you need to go and have a chat with your mam. Just hear her out. It might not be what you think.'

'It's just…' I start.

'Ring me back if you need me, OK?' he says.

And then I hear it. There's a loud clattering in the background, and I hear it again. A woman's voice calling for Luke.

'Look, I can't really hear you, Remi. Just let me know how it goes, OK?'

I hear the woman's voice again. She's definitely close to him. She definitely said his name. Or did she? Is he really with someone else? I know I can be paranoid sometimes. Or is he just pretending he can't hear me, because he doesn't want to hear anymore?

I press my glasses back onto my face. Now I'm questioning if I should have opened up to him. Should I have told him about this horrendous story?

Am I being that needy fling?

Am I going crazy?

All I know is that he's already hung up.

Chapter Six

'de zeug trekt de stop uit het vat'

The sow pulls the bung

It was an easy decision to take the long route back, through the town and past Langswood train station, a gleaming white art deco building designed by lighthearted folk, people who imagined it more as a glamorous museum than a dimly lit passage for the much less flamboyant trains that run in and out of the smog of London. I turn the Porsche towards the south bank of the river, contemplating the thought of being back here for good once my final term at university ends in just a few short months.

Even on a Sunday, it's bustling around here. Pavements are full of the hum of animated conversations between families and friends, all spoken in various languages, including *posh twat*, that familiar English dialect. There's a packed car park at the wine merchants on the corner and a long queue of cars waiting to leave the croquet club after their usual Sunday event. A middle-aged running club, all dressed in parakeet yellow, jogs cheerily past a row of early Victorian villas. Three teenagers sit chatting on a bench, scooping out whipped cream from their pistachio Frappuccinos.

There's no doubt that Langswood is a lovely place. A safe, affluent, multilingual place. But is it *my* place? I'm very aware that I have wandering feet, feet that can be contained, for a while at least, by regularly re-wallpapering my bedroom walls, and occasionally moving my bed from one side of the room to another. And, by knowing the realities of the grimy alternative of Verborough. But my fate is to be here in Langswood forever. Mum's already prepared me for that. The house will be mine, she's said. And I shall keep it. She's only had to hint that she'd be rolling in her grave if she ever saw me list it on Rightmove.

'What will you spend your money on, Remi?' Mum would ask me more often than I liked. 'Because one day, our house, the money. It will all be yours, you know.'

I'd glance at her uneasily. 'Don't say that,' I'd reply, miserable that we were talking about money, *again*, and haunted by the thought of my mother dying one day, leaving me well and truly alone. It's one thing to feel suffocated by an overbearing mother. It's another to feel choked by grief when they're gone.

Once, I'd dared to suggest that I'd move to America, or at least buy some sort of holiday home there.

'Ha!' she'd replied. 'America? You won't find a house like this there, you know. You young people would not know gratitude if it smacked you in the face.'

Gratitude. I'd imagined Mum then, forever like the devil on my shoulder. *You cannot change that carpet! You need to brush the stairs, not hoover them! This great house has become a cesspit!*

'I suggest you think about it very carefully,' she'd said. 'Money is both a glorious and a gluttonous thing.' She'd picked at a curl in her hair, like she was the Governor of the Bank of England announcing her quarterly review.

'You know, once upon a time, money did not exist. Whatever people needed, they traded or negotiated. They would swap what they had for something they wanted. There were no coins or notes to squirrel away. Coins do not bring joy to people; things do. It was a much simpler way of life, I think.'

'Well, I'd fail miserably then,' I'd replied. 'I'm not very good at bartering with people for stuff.'

She'd ignored what I'd said and carried on picking at the curl, turning the ends in her fingers like a wise old woman with a point to vent. 'Most people try to spend their money and keep it, too. But that is impossible, Remi.' She'd tilted her head. 'No. The Dutch believe that there are three types of people when it comes to money.'

'Three types?' I'd ask, trying to hide the fact that I really didn't care all that much about this sort of thing, and anyway, I'd heard this story a hundred times before.

'Three types,' she'd confirmed. 'There are those that are honourable and strong-minded enough to keep just enough coins in their piggy bank long enough for them to become *schimmelpennigs*.'

'Schimmel-how-do-you-say-it?' I'd said.

'*Schimmelpennigs*. Mouldy pennies, remember? These people, they are smart to save just enough for a rainy day. These are the ones who share their wealth with their friends, family, and the needy.'

'Is that us?' I'd asked on cue.

'I like to think so,' Mum had nodded. 'The next group, well. Those are the ones who hide their coins away. Many, many coins, too many coins to count. Except they *will* try to count them, every night, looking at their shiny coins thinking how great they are to have this many coins when others go without.'

'Right.'

'And then there are those who spend their pennies, but not on their family, friends, or the needy. Instead, they spend it on themselves, in the pub, buying drinks for other insignificant souls, while their children are at home with nothing good to eat and not a pair of shoes that fit them.'

'Well, that's just selfish,' I'd said, knowing that this would satisfy her. 'Why have kids if you don't intend on looking after them?'

'Oh, I am sure they did intend on it,' she'd said. 'It is amazing the hold things can have on you if you do not learn to control them, Remi. Drink. Drugs. Money. Life is all about self-control.'

I'd nodded, thinking about the fiver that was sitting in my purse, the one that she'd given me earlier, the one that I knew wasn't really mine to spend.

'But what if you can't control *everything*? What happens then?'

'You can control most things, Remi. Unless you allow someone else to influence your decision-making. Or, you get greedy.'

She'd raised her eyebrow at me, and I'd crossed my arms defiantly.

'I'm not greedy. And I definitely wouldn't let someone else tell me what to do,' I'd said, proudly delivering the punchline.

'That is my girl,' she'd smiled, giving me a hard tap on the shoulder.

We rehearsed this speech often. We talked about money a lot. We talked about what we should and shouldn't spend our money on. Mum talked, and I listened. Most of the time I listened, anyway.

Except I realise now, as I pass the recreation ground full of screaming children, that Mum was wrong. There aren't three types of people; there are four. The fourth type is much like the first, in that they distribute their wealth among their friends, family, and the needy.

Except they don't *share* their wealth. Sharing would suggest financial support, backed by trust and benevolence. Instead, these types of people use their money to assert power and control. It's their way or the highway, a *strings-attached* kind of deal. There's enough showering of extravagant gifts to maintain a façade of generosity, while subtly exerting control over their loved ones' financial independence. Mum would withhold my dinner money when I didn't pick the friendship groups that she wanted me to. She wouldn't allow me to get a part-time job due to *safety* travelling home alone. She gladly provided me with cash for my tuition fees, but on the prerequisite that I *choose* a course to be a paramedic. I'm sure it's so I can witness the results of someone else's poor choices on my day job.

Langswood is a strings-attached kind of deal. And, I decide, I'm not staying here unless the terms and conditions are fully disclosed, including knowing exactly how we ended up here and, more importantly, what the hell happened to my grandmother.

Chapter Seven

'te kijk te worden gezet en vernederd'

To play on the pillory

I'm home. My car rolls to a stop on the driveway, and as I'm gathering up my belongings – keys, phone, handbag – our next-door neighbour Joyce appears at my window. *Bugger.* Joyce is probably the last person I want to see right now.

'Remi, my darling! You're back *already*?' she says, with that wide, intrusive smile of hers. 'My goodness, these universities have the longest holidays. Students nowadays, you're never there, are you!'

I muffle a sigh and force a smile back. 'Joyce! Lovely to see you, as always. And yes, I'm happy to be back! Can I… erm… help you?' She's no doubt here to offer unsolicited advice. Or to moan about the window cleaner.

'Well, I couldn't help but notice you had a visitor earlier,' she says, doing her usual thing of probing for details. 'One I'd not seen around before.'

I hesitate, wondering how to deal with my extremely nosy neighbour. 'Yes… oh, he's just someone from Mum's work. An old friend, you know!'

'On a Sunday?' she asks, raising her eyebrows suspiciously. She's clearly not satisfied with the vague response.

'Yes, on a Sunday,' I say.

Our eyes lock in some sort of strange tug of war, a bit like the noses in Mum's painting. Then, Joyce leans in, lowering her voice as though she's conspiring to carry out some secret plot on the cul-de-sac. 'That's really surprising,' she says. 'Because Elise is not usually here on a Sunday. Not lately, anyway.'

'Oh, really?' I say. I don't know what she's on about. Mum is here every Sunday.

'Oh, yes,' she says, looking pleased with herself. 'Every Sunday, around late morning, she leaves here in the car. She's gone for hours, she is! Gets back around teatime, you know. Oh, she wouldn't mind me saying it, of course. I only know because Sundays are my gardening days, and sometimes I'll water the plants for her when she's gone.' Joyce twists her freckled, bony fingers in her hands, and I have the urge to grab at those fingers and chop her long, yellowing talons off.

I sigh inwardly. I feel like I should be shocked about this. Left out of the loop again? *She goes out for hours every Sunday?* But I don't want to give nosy old Joyce an inch of satisfaction.

'Of course she does,' I say instead. 'But thanks anyway, Joyce. For watering the plants I mean. Got to run, anyway! Sorry!'

I turn and retreat to the doorstep of our house, unable to shake Joyce's watchful gaze that's lingering on my back.

'I'm always here if you need me, darling!' Joyce shouts back. 'It's important to have a strong neighbourly support system, especially in these trying times.'

'I'll keep that in mind,' I mumble. A woman who keeps a list of who does or does not decorate the exterior of their house for Christmas is the very last person I would want as support.

I put the key in the lock of our blue front door, gearing myself up to go in, waiting until I'm sure Joyce's gaze is gone. I know

Mum will be furious that I went after Gerald. And now, that nosy old Joyce saw our visitor, too. Damn living in a cul-de-sac.

I can feel my palms clam up. It's ludicrous to be this nervous about speaking to my own mother, but, I realise, Luke is right. Maybe I am a bit scared of her. Who *isn't* a little scared of their mother? Mothers are just generally a bit scary, aren't they? Even other people's mothers, like Eliza's, who I swear never used to blink. Or Aoife's, who speaks in this low, unnerving voice that never changes. It's almost robotic. It's eerie.

I breathe a deep, uncomfortable breath in and unlock the door. The entryway is quiet, so I move through to the kitchen, where Mum is standing at the kitchen island, vigorously scrubbing the quartz countertop with a thunderous look on her face. She's wearing the same sort of clothes that she's always worn: a plain, white, round neck top with a long, itchy-looking taupe cardigan over it. Her blue denim jeans that she's had since I can remember are tucked into some beige Ugg boot slippers. Her skinny lips are a rusty red. She has black dots under her eyes where her mascara has run from crying.

Sporadic curls, ones that don't blend with her hair's natural pattern, make her ash-blonde hair look frizzier than usual. The crazy hair is something I never inherited. Of the things I did inherit, are Mum's glittery, pale blue eyes. Eyes that can look right through you.

She doesn't acknowledge me when I walk in. She turns to the dishwasher and starts emptying it, grabbing at cups and slamming them noisily into the cupboards. The cupboards rattle in fright.

'Mum,' I start. 'Are you OK?' She turns towards me, and I see it in her eyes. She knows.

'What did you go out there for?' she shouts, signaling towards the front door. 'Were you listening in? Did you go after him?'

Her thunderous firing of questions at me gets my back up instantly. I want to say *do you know what Mum? I did it. I followed him. I went against every single little rule in your overbearing notebook of life and I followed him. And in ten seconds I had more clarity from him about Johanna than you've given me in ten years.* But I know better than that.

'Mum,' I say instead. 'I wasn't listening in. I was bringing my things in through the side door, and… I was trying to stop Copperfield from running out and… I wasn't trying to pry, I promise. But yes. I heard him talking to you about Nan. And I just wanted to hear what he had to say.'

I have never said the word Nan before, and it makes Mum wince.

'*Talk* to him about it?' she cries. 'Where the hell did you go with him? To the home store? What, so you had a coffee with him? I cannot believe you went after that man! You do not know what he is capable of!'

I stay silent, crossing my arms defensively. She does have a point. But still. This is exactly how I knew she'd react.

'So, what did he tell you, then?'

'Not loads,' I lie. I could sit here and tell her *exactly* what the poor, dying man told me. But based on this reaction, there'd be no use in that.

She goes back to scrubbing the quartz like a woman scorned. 'Well there is nothing to talk about then,' she says through gritted teeth, the bangles on her wrist clanging loudly against each other as she makes one harsh swipe after another. 'I have told you the story. And that is the end of it.'

'I…' I stammer, not wanting her to have the last word. It's too soon to just shut the conversation down. 'I was just confused when he started talking about a motorbike, that's all.'

As soon as I've said it, though, I can tell I've gone too far. Mum stops flinging things into cupboards and comes at me. 'So, you are going to believe some man you have never met over your own mother, are you?'

'Are you?'

'No, I...'

'I do not *need* this right now, ok, Remi? It is bad enough that I just had to face the man who... well... to have this all dragged back up again! And you have gone and run out there in front of the neighbours! They will all be fucking talking about us now!'

I decide it's not the time to tell her about my conversation with Joyce.

'You're being paranoid Mum,' I say. Except now I'm worried that perhaps paranoid wasn't the right word. I start picking at my bleeding nails, just like I used to when my teacher asked me for an answer in science class. One about the periodic table that I didn't know.

'Paranoid?'

I wince as Mum comes right up to my face now, wet cloth in hand.

'It is *my* mother, not yours! I have told you what happened, and I do not appreciate you running around behind my back trying to meddle, OK?'

'Meddle?' I say, biting down on the inside of my cheek.

As if it's not my family too.

'It's just... I know what I heard, Mum, and I think it's my right to know the truth.' Usually, I'd have retreated by now. Taken my petulant self off to my room, in the guise of a naughty teenager. But this time, I'm not backing down. I widen my stance and stand tensely.

'The truth! The truth! Are you calling me a *liar*, Remi? After all the things I have done for you! You are choosing his side over mine?' She jabs viciously at her chest.

'I'm not choosing sides, Mum! This is ridiculous!'

She's right in my space now, spitting the words at me. 'I will tell you what is *ridiculous*, Remi. You, standing here in my house, questioning me about my own mother. How dare you?'

Her arm comes up, the one with the cloth clenched between her fingers, and she holds it there above our heads, a threatening look in her eyes. I imagine the whack across my face, like the whip of a belt, the burning sensation across my cheek, and I brace for it.

But she doesn't hit me with it. Instead, she brings the wet cloth down hard until it's on her thigh, the fabric slapping against it with a *thwack*, her face bearing a steely look of morbid shock and satisfaction. *Thwack*. She does it again.

Thwack. And then again.

She doesn't flinch as she looks at me and says, 'Happy, now?'

My eyes sting with shocked tears. I was fully expecting her to whack me one. I was not expecting her to start whacking herself.

'Mum, stop!' I cry, trying to grab at her arm. She pushes me off, and I fall hard against the sink. 'I don't understand why we can't just talk about it!'

Mum drops the cloth and picks up a fork from the dishwasher, then, slamming it into the drawer, just as she was doing before. 'Oh, do shut up, you ungrateful bitch,' she says, wiping a hot tear from her eye.

Chapter Eight

'harnas aandoen'

To put your armour on

It's not the first time she's called me a bitch. Or a cow, or a fucker, or even a see-yoo-enn-tee. But this time, it felt uncomfortable. I decide that I will not allow her to call me a bitch like that again. Especially an ungrateful one. That was a bit unfair.

I do think I've pushed it too far, though. In fact, I know I've pushed it too far. *Don't you ever remind me of that day again*, she'd warned me. And what did I do? I did exactly that. I made her cry again. There's really no one to blame but myself. Except for Gerald, the man who turned up unannounced on our doorstep. Yes. She should also blame Gerald, the man who has interrupted our lives, for some sort of selfish atonement project.

I catch myself in my bedroom mirror and can see the familiar rash spreading across my neck. It looks like the one that my old school friend Genevieve would get when she was standing at the front of the class presenting something, like the full lifecycle of a plant or the origin and importance of the Magna Carta. It was the one that you couldn't stop staring at, the one that would spread like wildfire all over her upper body. The one you felt sorry for. You wouldn't be able to listen to a word that Genevieve was saying. You'd just be focused on the rash, like it was hot, molten lava that might spill dangerously out of her, fresh onto the classroom carpet. I take my weighted blanket out of the cupboard and lie down on top of my bed, pulling the heavy yarn up over my own molten lava rash, and then up over my shoulders. I roll my head towards the wall and follow a tiny crack running all the way from the floor to the ceiling. Even a wall can't resist cracks forever.

I listen out for Mum, who, like me, has retreated to her bedroom, having scrubbed the kitchen to within an inch of its life. I lay thinking about Mum's leg, wondering whether it hurts, whether she regrets slapping a wet cloth hard over her own thigh and not across my face instead. Perhaps I *should* give her a break. She's right when she says that she doesn't need this right now. She's been working a lot lately in one of the most demanding jobs there is. I wiggle my toes free of the blanket, which is swaddling me as though it's a thick layer of warm butter over a hot ear of corn. It feels soothing and stifling all at once. Soon, it will be my job. Soon, I'll be the one who can say I don't need this right now.

I'm well aware of the stress that being on the front line of the health service puts on people. I'm prepared for the long and inflexible hours and the grueling twelve-hour shifts. I'm mindful that paramedics face extremely high stress levels, leading to a higher chance of suffering from depression, anxiety, post-traumatic stress disorder and fatigue. I often wonder what Mum has to suffer with under the surface. She keeps a lot to herself. But sometimes, she'll give me brief snippets of the horrors she sees.

She says the streets are full of drugs, much worse than what the news tells you. Some patients are extremely hard to manage, apparently. She'll say that some days, being a paramedic is the best job in the world, and other days it's the worst. She's warned me it's not like in the movies, and there are, in fact, long stretches of time where you're not doing much at all. Being a paramedic, you quickly learn that life is not always beautiful. But for some people – people not like me – there's a certain excitement about heading to work for your shift and not knowing what the working day is going to bring. Fun fact – Mum's helped to deliver three babies!

I'm aware that I might witness people die, of course. *All medics have that one call, the one that will haunt them for the rest of their lives*, my least favourite lecturer warned me off the record once.

I sat all day picturing what that call would be.

A few months later, I mentioned it to Mum while we were at the table having dinner together. 'Do you have a call… I mean, was there an incident… one that has stayed with you, you know, that you think about a lot?' I'd asked her.

Mum had sat back for a second, chewing noisily on her spaghetti vongole. 'Things happen,' she'd said, gulping her mouthful down hard. She'd put her fork down slowly and looked me straight in the eyes, my eyes that are so identical to hers.

'Unfathomable, incomprehensible things. Things that will make you feel like tearing your heart out and swallowing it whole.' She'd reached over to me and picked a stray hair from the arm of my shirt, flicking it quietly to the floor.

'Things that will make you want to swallow it just enough, so that your heart will sit firm in your throat, and you can never talk about the dreadful thing again. *Met de mond vol tanden staan* is how my mother Johanna would have put it. To stand with your mouth full of teeth. To be speechless, forever.'

I'd sat silently, trying to process the enormity of what she'd said. Not quite believing that this was a world that I'd allowed myself to be thrust into.

'And what if you make a mistake,' I'd asked. 'Like, a really bad mistake?'

She'd gone back to eating her spaghetti then. 'Everyone

makes mistakes,' Mum had said. 'But you see what you see, Remi. Some patients are an absolute nightmare to treat. They do not want the help. Sometimes you get attacked. Verbally abused. You have to be prepared for anything.'

I knew exactly what she'd meant, then. We'd had lessons on how to deal with challenging or uncooperative patients, how to de-escalate situations, and how to utilise sedation if necessary. We'd even been told to involve law enforcement as a last resort. But I hadn't really thought about putting that into practice. I'd hoped it wasn't a common thing.

'But what if you misdiagnose someone?' I'd asked. 'What if you think it's nothing, when actually it's something? Something big.'

Mum had twirled some pasta around her fork and set it down on the side of her bowl. 'Can I give you some advice, Remi?' she'd said, touching the scar on her wrist from where a patient had bitten her. She'd had to go through six months of testing for hepatitis and HIV.

I'd tapped my red-painted nails against my teeth.

'There was this person who we used to pick up a lot. His name was Joe. Joe was a total fucking nightmare. Joe was always taking drugs, hardcore drugs, you know, and he was always getting into fights. He was always punching things. Walls, doors. People. He would end up with bleeding knuckles, and we would be called out to attend to him, and usually to attend to the poor sod who he had punched, too.' She'd taken a long sip of her sparkling water.

'One busy Friday night, I had a new paramedic with me. There were not enough ambulances to go around, which is a thing, by the way. Expect a lot of bullshit excuses from the powers that be on why they never seem to have enough resources around here. Anyway, we were called out to Joe, and we had him in the back of the ambulance, and he was hurt, as usual. Bleeding knuckles. High as a kite. I kept telling this new paramedic that it would be just his right hand, and that he had probably punched something, but the new paramedic would not listen. We spent ages checking body parts that did not need checking.'

'So, what happened?' I'd asked. 'Was Joe alright?'

'Was Joe alright? Oh, of course Joe was alright. Druggie Joe was *fine*.' Mum had rolled her eyes.

'But do you know what happened next, Remi? Our next call was to a man who had passed out inside a restaurant. By the time we turned up for him, he had been waiting for over an hour for an ambulance to arrive. It was his heart. It had packed up while he was waiting for his dessert to arrive.'

'Oh my goodness,' I'd said. 'Was he OK?'

'He wasn't,' she'd said. 'He died, Remi. All because we had spent ages checking on Joe.'

We'd sat in silence while Mum had finished her spaghetti.

'That is beyond awful,' I'd said eventually, wrinkling my nose in astonishment. I'd thought hard for a second. 'But what if Joe *did* have something else wrong with him? Wasn't the new paramedic just following protocol?'

'He was not following common sense, Remi.' She'd tilted her head like she had all the answers. 'And to be quite frank, as far as Joe was concerned, I wished it was him who had been in the restaurant, and him who we had been too late for. He would have bloody deserved it, anyhow. You just cannot help some people.'

Mum had taken another long sip of her water, and I'd nodded, thinking about the poor man who'd been left there, slumped on a restaurant chair, waiting in vain. Sixty minutes is such a long time to wait. What a dreadful situation for Mum to have been in.

I'd pushed my plate away, my food unfinished.

'Oh, and one more thing, Remi,' Mum had said then.

She'd leaned in to me closely.

'If you do make a mistake. And I am sure that you won't. But if you do? Admit *nothing*.'

Chapter Nine

*'als het niet mijn verantwoordelijkheid is,
dan bemoei ik me er niet mee'*

If I am not meant to be their keeper, I will let geese be geese

It's morning, and slowly I sit up from my slumber and tap my phone. It's five minutes past seven. Mum had cancelled yesterday's *kleine bijeenkomst,* and we'd stayed in our bedrooms for the rest of the day, avoiding each other except for occasional trips to the kitchen for food and water. I'd eventually drifted off to sleep but found it so hard to stay asleep that I'd left my bedroom and moved to the sofa in the living room, with the cashmere throw as a cover, my sweaty body sticking to the beige leather seats. The house is quiet, and I realise I've slept through any sound of Mum getting ready for work this morning. Her grumbling into her muesli. Her throwing her uniform on in a huff. She's never been one to forgive and forget easily. Sometimes she can ignore you for days. And even then, she'll only talk to you when you've admitted that it was probably all your fault in the first place.

She would have started her shift at six thirty, so she'd have left home more than an hour ago, which is something that I'm grateful for. After last night, I'm not ready to face her yet.

The living room smells clean, like that very first sip of a glass of sparkling water. Light is spilling through the cream shutters, casting a warm glow across the bare walls. An impeccably polished glass table sits on a recently hoovered silk rug in front of the antique fireplace. Everything in here is cream or beige, except for the green plastic of the leaves in the designer faux bouquets and the dozens of ocean-blue coasters, which have been placed on every flat surface going. Coasters that don't just protect the furniture, but that set very important boundaries. Most of my life has been spent dodging these luxury items, like glass tables and bespoke armchairs, and marble worktops. It's been learning to live alongside them, not with them, in case I scratch them or dirty them or, heaven forbid, devalue them. Often, I find myself tip-toeing across the carpet rather than walking on it. Much like Copperfield the cat does with his little snowshoe boots.

One of the ocean-blue coasters holds my water bottle, and I reach for it, glugging down the last of its contents. My throat feels extremely itchy and dry this morning. I sit staring at the glass table, picking at a strand of matted hair, my jaw sore from clenching. My neck's stiff from lying at a weird angle. According to the sleep tracker on my watch, I woke at midnight and then at two, then again at two thirty. I think of Luke, who'd have gently cuddled me back to sleep, stroking my hair and getting me paracetamol if I needed it. A nice doctor once told me that I should have grown out of the night terrors by now, except that growing out of something means forgetting it, doesn't it? And how can you forget to be terrified about things? It just doesn't many any sense to me.

My leopard print dressing gown – one of a collection of five animal print robes – is laid over the beige armchair and I reach for it, grabbing at the banana soreen bar I'd left tucked into the right pocket. One of the reasons I love my dressing gowns so much is their ability to house food, empty wrappers, TV remotes, tissues, an iPhone, a full, fat belly and anything that should not or cannot be placed on a coaster. I unpick the wrapper and tear a gooey piece off, quietly shoving it into my mouth. And then the doorbell goes.

I should mention that one reason I *don't* love my dressing gown so much is that it is bright pink and orange and is not exactly the kind of attire that looks great on the doorstep in front of neighbours or strangers. I spring to my feet, pulling the fleece across my body and tying the cord around me. I consider ditching it, but all I have on underneath is a cotton nightie that is slightly see-through and no bra. Copperfield appears by the living room door, pitter-pattering down the hallway. It's a very long hallway – *we have the largest square footage of all the cul-de-sac*, Mum would say – so with me pitter-pattering behind him it takes us a good while to get to the front door. And I don't feel particularly comfortable about opening it, considering that I'm the only one home. I quickly locate the hairspray, just in case.

There's a heavy bang on the door. 'Open up,' comes a voice from outside. It's a deep, burly voice, like the voice of a broad-shouldered – and possibly very scary – man. Copperfield scarpers and for a second, I stand in silence, considering how I can convincingly pretend that I'm not home.

'We know you're in there.'

Bugger. I'm stuck.

'How do you know I'm in here?' I whisper.

'You are required to answer the door,' says another voice. This voice is slightly less gruff, but robust all the same. A bit like Phil or Grant from Eastenders, or like one of those faces in Mum's painting, the crazed one who is biting on a pillar, or the miserly one sitting between two stools in the ashes.

'I'm afraid we don't open the door to salespeople,' I call back. 'And we already give to cancer research. So, if you wouldn't mind trying another house. Thank you!' I grab at my necklace, the wood smooth against my fingertips. I squeeze it four times while Copperfield meows loudly from the safety of the stairs.

'Shhhhhhhh,' I murmur to him.

'We are certificated enforcement agents,' says the first voice again, a little more politely this time. 'You will have received a letter informing you of our visit. So I ask that you open up the door.'

'Sorry, what did you say you were?' I tiptoe to the study, which has a little window overlooking the porch. Two men who are, as suspected, very broad-shouldered are standing on the front porch, their faces looking as impatient as they sound. They both carry important-looking identification around their necks.

'Certificated enforcement agents,' I hear them chant again. 'Also known as bailiffs. You will have been informed with plenty of notice that we were coming. And I would suggest that this is much better done inside than out here on the front porch, with all your neighbours watching.'

I shudder in a sudden panic, then tiptoe quickly back to the door.

'You see, this is where you are quite wrong,' I shout through the keyhole. 'Because we most definitely did *not* know you were coming. So, I'm certain you must have got the wrong house,' I say. I'm unsure why I'm suddenly pronouncing my words like the posh women of Langswood. 'I mean, I'm clear on what a bailiff is, of course, and I'm just stating that we're clearly not the people that you're looking for.'

'Van Tam,' one of them says. 'Miss Van Tam. That's you, ain't it?'

Shit. How does he know that's me? *Do I admit to them that's me?*

'Well, you see, that's the thing,' I shout back. 'We haven't had any communication from a *certificated person* of any kind. So, I really think this is all a big mix up. I'm really sorry. Perhaps you could call your office and see?' I suggest.

'We could do that,' says the gruffer man. 'But all charges related to the case in question will need to be covered by you. So, we'd have to come inside to use your phone.'

'Right.'

'And, like I say. The longer we stand here, the more obvious we will be to your neighbours.'

Oh Christ. He has a point.

'OK,' I say. 'But I will need to see some identification, won't I?' I pull back the door gradually. 'Otherwise I can't really let you…'

Before I know it, the men are stomping into the hallway and muddying Mum's beautifully polished porcelain tile floor. They shove their ID cards in front of my face in an extremely rude and condescending fashion. I start to panic that I've let two burglars into our home, except that everything on their ID checks out. I mean, I think their ID checks out, but seeing as I've never seen a bailiff's identification before, then who knows? But it does say that they are *certificated enforcement agents*. Which is what they said they were.

And now I'm worried. And a little bit scared.

'I'm sorry,' I say again. 'But you can't just come barging into our home. This is all just incredulous! And please don't stomp all over those tiles. They're really porous, they absorb anything and everything and they're a real nightmare to clean. So you will need to take those off.' I gesture downwards towards their feet, then watch as they completely ignore my request and continue tramping around the place.

'Did someone from around here send you?' I ask. 'Was it Joyce from over the road? You can tell me, it's fine. It was Joyce, wasn't it? Because I know that once upon a time Mum borrowed her special pans, but that was ages ago, and she's since bought her two completely new sets, which were posh ones from QVC.'

Both men are completely ignoring me and instead, charging

around the ground floor of the house, looking intently at the objects on show. 'There should be plenty,' the tall one mutters to his sidekick.

'Plenty of what?'

He turns his body to face me. 'Like I said, you would have received a letter. Seeing as you know what a bailiff is, you'll understand that we are here to collect a debt on behalf of a creditor. We have written authorisation from the local authority due to unpaid council tax and loan agreements.'

'Loan agreements? Unpaid?'

'Yes. You can choose to make a payment now, or alternatively, we will start seizing your property to sell at auction.'

I sway slightly on the spot. 'What kind of payment?'

The taller man shows me an amount, an extortionate, eye-watering sum.

'I would also advise you that non-payment of council tax can lead to imprisonment if you willfully refuse to pay. And that if you attempt to remove us from the property by force, you must know that you can be charged with assault.'

If the smaller man hadn't started picking up ornaments and walking them out to his van, then I would honestly think that this was all a terribly timed joke. But it's so clearly *not* a joke. Two men – whose identification badges around their necks check out as legitimate, certificated bailiffs – have wormed their way into our house and are now carrying our possessions out of the front door. They had no intention of using our phone to call their office. They just wanted to get inside. And now they're here in the hallway, they're going to seize whatever items they choose. In front of the whole of the cul-de-sac. This is very, very real.

Oh my good God.

'Just... just wait!' I shout. 'Let's just have a talk about all this, shall we? We are very clearly not in debt of any kind! And you can't do this without Mum here, anyway!' I sift through the sweet wrappers and tissues in my dressing gown pocket and grab at my phone, jabbing at the screen to call Mum, except that it goes through to voicemail.

'Mum!' I pant. 'There's an emergency at the house. There are people here, and there's been a big mistake and I need you to call me back. ASAP. OK?'

I turn back to the men, who are now clutching onto the edges of a grey granite side table, ready to lift it from the spot.

'You can't take that.'

'I'm afraid we can.'

'I mean, you can't just come in here, picking whatever you like!'

Except it seems that they can. The side table is swiftly marched out of the room. And then I see it. The painting. Mum's precious proverbs painting, the one that she gazes at every morning and every night. The curious rules that she lives by.

'You can't take the painting,' I say as they make a move for it on their return. 'You can take anything else, just not the painting.'

They curl their gloved fingers around the edges of the solid wood frame, lifting it up and away from the wall.

'It's not ours, honestly! We're just storing it for someone else!'

'Do you have any proof that you are storing it for someone else?' asks the taller man.

'Well, no. I don't. But do *you* have any proof that it's ours?'

The men exchange a strange look. I grab another smaller painting off the wall, one of tulips and windmills and blue sky.

'Here, take this one instead. This one is *extremely* valuable. She got it from this place in Utrecht. The woman said it was an original, I mean it's probably priceless…'

I stop as they carry the proverb painting past me and out through the door.

'You're not taking it!' I shout after them.

Then, 'Miss, we're going to need you to let go now.'

'Let go of what?'

'This painting.'

I glance down to see my hands clenched around the frame, holding onto it for dear life. The three of us stand there for a while, and then they yank it from me, and all I can do is watch as they carry it out onto the driveway and into the back of their van.

I run back into the house, grabbing an antique glass clock that looks vaguely pricey.

'This! Take this!' But it's no use. The painting is locked safely inside the van, and the blood-thirsty bailiffs are back already for more.

'That painting,' I cry. 'It's my mother's painting. And it's very, very dear to her. And unless she is here, then you can't take it. I can't authorise it. So bring it back. *Please.*'

The shorter man takes a slow, deliberate inhale of a bright purple vape. He blows the fruity vapour in my direction.

'We don't need your mum to authorise it,' he says. 'Because it's not your mum who owes the debt.'

'Then why the bloody hell are you taking it?' I cry.

'Because the debt is yours, Miss Van Tam. It's all in the name of Remi.'

Chapter Ten

'om een sjaal om hun nek te binden'

To tie a scarf around their neck

But I have no savings to loan against, is what I'd said to them as they'd left. And then I'd slammed the door and phoned Mum again and left another message.

'They've taken the painting,' is all I'd managed to say.

Now, the excited eyes of Copthall Lane are burning into my organs. Being thrust into this topsy-turvy world, where nothing and no one makes sense, has stripped me of my skin. It's as if suddenly the world has x-ray vision and my entire contents are now exposed. They are all staring directly at the monster in my stomach. And now this nakedness, I've learnt, has dire consequences. One of those consequences being the clock that's now smashed to smithereens on the porcelain tile floor.

The hands are laid all bent and crooked next to jagged shards of glass. I have a sudden urge to walk barefoot on the glass, to feel it pierce through the soles of my feet. I have no idea how much this clock is worth, and I know Mum will be furious with what I've done, but I realise it might be *my* clock, and this might be *my* house, and so I run to the kitchen, pick up a dinner plate and smash it in the space alongside it.

I close my eyes and imagine Mum's face when she walks in. The painting gone. Some of the furniture gone. The clock and the plate smashed to pieces all over the floor. I imagine the faces of the cul-de-sac as they watched the men taking things from our home. Because they would have been watching, of course they would.

When I left Verborough yesterday morning, our lives were so normal. Except I'm not sure how normal we ever were, really, now. I guess I did believe a few strange things growing up. Like for every night that I didn't go straight to sleep, a part of the moon died. And that chocolate turned to weeds in your tummy. And if I said a rude word, then my teeth would crack. Odd things that no one at school seemed to relate to. Should I have challenged Mum on these oddities I was told? Should I have challenged Mum more full stop? And where does one draw the line between an acceptable lie of necessity versus a fear-inducing one?

I wonder what my dead father would do if he was here to witness this. I scrunch my eyes up tightly, trying hard to create a face. A legitimate one, not one based on a photograph. One that I saw. One that I remember.

I've done this hundreds of times, thousands even. When I was a child, I used to sit at the base of our majestic oak tree, my eyes held tightly shut like they are now, with one hand resting on the trunk, willing the tree to whisper its memories to me. Willing it to show me the things it witnessed baby Remi do. But nothing came. I don't remember anyone. Worst of all, I don't remember my dad.

Why did my dad have to die when I was so small, small enough that I don't remember him? If he'd died when I was older, I'd at least be able to feel him, to smell him, to hear him. I've tried so hard to conjure up memories of him pushing me on the swings, feeding me in my high chair, playing hide and seek. But it's like my brain never woke up until I was two and a half. Everything before that is gone. It's a scientific phenomenon called *infantile amnesia*, apparently. The brain isn't mature enough to make stable memories of people or events. And as hard as you might try, you can't access a memory if it's just not there.

Ever since I was told about his passing, I've lived with this void that I can't quite articulate. I can't understand my dad's death, because I never really lived it. I lived with it. But I never felt the pain of losing my father. Or my grandmother. Not the real pain, anyway. Just the pain of living with ghosts, ambiguous ones with no faces, that you've been told are related to you.

Instead, I've helped nurse my mum's grief, like it's her pain alone. She was the one who lost her partner. She was the one who lost her mother. She said it herself last night. *'It is my mother, not yours!'* I don't have the right to grieve, do I?

I open my eyes and clutch my phone tightly in my hand. Part of me wants to smash something else. And the other part is crying for what my mother has just lost.

I can't believe they took the painting. The painting that my beloved father gave to her. The painting that connects her to her Dutch past. A past that I've so desperately wanted to be a part of. A past that is slowly coming back to haunt us.

I bare my teeth at the empty wall, as though it's offended me.

I have to do something. Whatever trouble we are in. Whatever mistake has been made. I need to get it back.

Touch wood touch wood touch wood touch wood.

Chapter Eleven

'hij zit met de gebakken peren'
He sits with the baked pears

I've been staring at the empty foyer from the living room sofa – which was one of the few things downstairs that the bailiffs left – for about two hours now. Copperfield swooshes by, with eight feet, three tails and a blurry oatmeal body, as I feel my phone vibrating in my dressing gown pocket. I'm not entirely sure how many seconds go by before I take it out to look at the screen, but when I do, I see it's not Mum. It's a WhatsApp message from Eliza Thompson, who is still living here in Copthall Lane with her strange, aging parents, except that a few years ago they'd downsized, selling their larger home and moving into a smaller cottage a bit further down the road.

We'd never really stayed in touch after school. She went to an acting academy and I went to college to do science and whatever else Mum had told me to study. I was to be a paramedic. I was to follow in her footsteps and become a healthcare worker, except I never did like science. I liked geography and places and people and cultures. I liked maps and exploration, and natural wonders like the Grand Canyon. I dreamt of visiting my ghost family in the Netherlands, of walking the mudflats of the Wadden Sea.

In my case, I could have left. I could have told Mum I didn't want her financial help to get through university. I could have trained to be a cartographer, or a geologist, if I was clever enough. I could have told my only parent that the last thing I would want for my future is to be a carbon copy of her. I could have done all of those things. But I didn't. For many, many reasons, I didn't. Mainly because I'm all she has. But also, because she's all I have, too. We're stuck in an emotionally-charged partnership, trying not to fail each other, but feeling like a failure every day.

I think Eliza works at a drama school now. And here she is messaging me, no doubt about the theatre that's just occurred between me and two debt collectors in the cul-de-sac for the whole community to see.

Remi, it's Eliza from school. I know it's been a while, and this is a bit out of the blue. But I'd been meaning to get back in touch anyway, and there's something I think you should see. Could you come over? I'm at number fifteen.

I read the message back to myself out loud. *There's something I think you should see.*

I lie back on the sofa, studying my options on the ceiling. What kind of *something* could I need to see? It can't be a coincidence that her out of the blue message is so perfectly timed with one of the worst and most humiliating events to ever take place in the cul-de-sac of Copthall Lane. But Eliza has never been one to gossip. She's a keeper of secrets, some of my secrets, in fact, and so I have no reason not to trust her. And I have no one here to stop me.

'*Don't give her the satisfaction,*' I imagine Mum saying. Which is precisely why I need to go and see Eliza at number fifteen immediately.

I shake myself out of slow-motion mode and move quickly

upstairs, jumping into the shower – I just can't do any more of today without a shower – and then throwing my joggers and a hoody on in a rush. I fold the cashmere throw neatly over the arm of the sofa, trying to make the house look as familiar as I can amongst the bleak, horrible emptiness, and then grab my keys and go, out from my hiding place and out onto the stage that is the unforgiving circle of the cul-de-sac.

Please, please don't see Joyce.

I pull my hood up and walk fast, not too fast that I look like I'm trying to escape, but fast enough not to encourage anyone to approach. I know that number fifteen must be at the opposite end of the street, although I'm not entirely sure which house it is. Copthall Lane is a long suburban road with more than a hundred houses – mostly detached, but some semi-detached – with our cul-de-sac at one end and a school halfway down. The school is an all-boys independent preparatory school; a mix of pre-prep and prep, where the little darlings, mainly Tarquin and Maximus, are forced to wear itchy berets and oversized blazer jackets, drowning their tiny pre-teen bodies so they look like they're playing dress up in their grandad's clothes.

It's a quarter to nine and humongous four-by-fours with blackout windows are filling the street in both directions. Inside them, flustered parents on the Monday morning school run are frantically scouring the area for places to park. I start to weave my way between the people, bikes, scooters and prams, looking out for door numbers in the process. I move past a house numbered fifty-six, where a woman with wet hair in a similar leopard print dressing gown to mine is hurriedly pushing her son and husband out the door. The boy is carrying a giant cardboard aeroplane, and neither parent has spotted that he's got two different coloured shoes on. A floral-smelling lady rushes by, dragging an abandoned scooter with her son lagging behind, who's now kicking up the flowers in the neighbour's front garden.

'Well done Hugo!' she shouts back to him. 'Very good walking darling!'

As I reach the school gates, I have to manoeuvre my way through a sea of harassed parents, nannies and child-minders, book bags dangling precariously on their shoulders, who've by now lost their children in the never-ending sea of red berets and long, woolly socks. It's far too warm for woolly socks. I exchange a few forced smiles and nods with faces I don't know. A brother is arguing with his sibling about who will get dropped off at their classroom first. An anxious tied-up dog barks incessantly at being left outside the gate. Horns beep as a car stops in the middle of the road, and a father gets out, casually letting his kids out like they're royalty. This scene of chaos is enough to make you never want children. Not at all because of the behaviour of the little darlings. But mostly, that of their parents. Or at least, to consider the idea of permanent home schooling, so as not to be forced to associate with them at all.

I sigh loudly. It's the first real breath I've let out since Beavis and Butthead – or Phil and Grant – turned up at the house unannounced, and it goes on for so long that I worry I might not be able to breathe back in again. I stop, focusing on closing my mouth and forcing the air up through my nose. I can smell thermos-stored coffee and dew on the grass. My stomach starts to churn, and I pop an Imodium from my hoody pocket into my mouth. I let it melt on my tongue and then I'm ready to move again.

After some final dodging and diving, I make it out the other side, past the gates and away from the noise. I turn to the houses and start my number search again. Nineteen – seventeen – fifteen. Here we are.

I push open the pocket-sized gate and start to walk down the moss-covered pathway. The cottage is small but perfectly formed, with a pink front door and a beautiful antique brass knocker in the shape of a bee. The house is in the middle of a row of terraced period cottages, set behind a small wall with a quaint wrought-iron fence and an area for flowerpots. Every house has a different coloured front door. Pink, baby blue, sage green. The windows are framed with wooden shutters on the exterior and flowery curtains on the interior. The downstairs curtains are open, and as I reach the front door, I can see through to the cosy living room inside. I imagine the real wood floors and the wood burning stove, and the cellar that is probably haunted.

A cat jumps down from the wall of a nearby cottage and startles me. This out of the blue meet up is more nerve-wracking than I'd imagined. I reach back to touch my neck. My hoody is starting to feel extremely tight around the collar. After a moment of deliberating over whether to backtrack up the garden path, I see a shadow at the door.

I take another deep breath and press the doorbell.

The lock turns, and the door opens to a small, smiley face, just as I remember it. Eliza is petite, with glowing olive-toned skin and large, sparkling hazel eyes, each framed with a precise wing of plum eyeliner. Her hair is tied back in a neat bun, revealing large, gold bee-shaped studs.

'Bees,' I say. I press my glasses against my sweaty face, my hands quivering slightly. 'Sorry, it's just that I've realised you must really like bees. I never knew that about you.' My voice is stupidly shrill.

'Remi,' says Eliza kindly. A smile spreads across her face. 'I'm so glad you came.'

'I almost called you big tits,' I say. 'But that would have been weird, wouldn't it?'

'Very,' she laughs back. 'And they're not that big anymore.' She looks down at her chest. 'I've lost quite a lot of weight since secondary school.'

I clear my throat a couple of times, and I notice she is staring at me in a strange, sympathetic way, like she's remembering my school nickname *twitch* for the first time in a long while.

'This is such a lovely little house you've moved to,' I say, shifting my weight from one foot to the other. I immediately regret using the term *little*, like it's something that one of the neighbours would say at a *kleine bijeenkomst*.

'Thank you,' she says politely. 'Do you want to come inside?'

I straighten my hoody and shove my hands into its pockets. 'Sure,' I say, and then I follow Eliza into her cottage, straight into the living room, which is full of trinkets and colourful cushions and empty bottles of craft gin with fairy lights inside. I wonder if Eliza's mother is a bit of a hoarder, with the sheer number of things there are in here, but perhaps I'm just not used to seeing things so lovingly displayed like this. She must be the total opposite of Mum, who has no material connection to anything apart from two things – her prized Pieter Bruegel proverbs painting, and an ugly ceramic duck that I bought her on a school trip once. I flinch as I think of the painting in the back of the grubby van somewhere.

'My parents are at work,' she says, as though she's pleased to have the place to herself. I wonder, too, if at the age of twenty-one, Eliza begrudges living in Langswood, where the high cost of housing means that grown adults are left with little choice but to continue hanging about in their family homes. Or, live in a shoe box.

Following Eliza into her kitchen, I wait as she clears a stool of papers and magazines for me to sit on. A robin chirps cheerily on the windowsill outside, edging closer to us, as if it knows it's about to hear something juicy and wants to listen in.

'Cup of tea?'

'That would be lovely,' I say, even though I'm probably the only English woman who thinks tea tastes like warm, brown dishwater. It's hard to stomach, even with a few sugars thrown in. She flips the kettle on, and I think I can hear Abel Tesfaye – aka The Weeknd – spilling out of a speaker somewhere.

'Do you want to sit down?'

I perch awkwardly on the stool and rest my leg against the footrest. This had seemed like a good idea. The *only* idea. Except now I'm stuck in Eliza's cottage, feeling my glasses sliding swiftly down the bridge of my nose. Eliza seems to be acting kind enough, but I feel desperate to leave. Did I really believe that she'd hold a key to unlocking something – something that might help me make sense of what's just happened to us? Would I have come here otherwise? What else would I have done?

I glance through the living room towards the front door. I could make my apologies and leave now, couldn't I? Except – although I can feel movement in my stomach, its contents fighting against the Imodium – my leg is now firmly wrapped around the footrest, anchoring me to the spot like it knows the real importance of this meeting and what it might mean to my life.

I walked you here, Remi. Now get on with it, for goodness' sake.

'You said you had something to show me?' I start.

'Yes, that's right,' says Eliza. Her almond-shaped eyes that really are quite beautiful stare sombrely into mine. 'I heard about what happened just now. At your place. It was all over the neighbours' chat.'

'Oh,' I say. 'Was it?'

Of course it was. As if I didn't know it would be all over the neighbours' chat, that obligatory chat that every poor suspecting new resident gets lured into under the false promise of *it's good for security* and *we're looking out for each other*. Instead, it's mostly *do you want my old useless thing that I can't be bothered to take to the dump*, or accusations of *who the heck's having a bonfire at this time of the day?*

Alice from number twenty-one has a habit of offering out mouldy fruit to whoever will take it. Usually Dorothy, who takes anything from anyone. Bernadette is forever losing her cats. Peter is perpetually in need of a tradesperson. Cate complains about everything and everyone. I'm one *do you want an Ikea table with only slight scuff marks on the legs* away from leaving the chat, something that feels so impossible, like shouting *fuck you!* loudly through your neighbours' letter boxes.

Eliza places a cup of hot tea beside me on the kitchen counter. 'Yes,' she says. 'I'm sorry, Remi. They're such assholes around here, the lot of them.'

I take a small slurp of the tea, enough to show my gratitude, and then open the chat up on my phone in front of me. I read the latest message.

Does anyone have a cauliflower I can borrow? In exchange, I can offer you some unopened digestive biscuits and a cabbage (bought in error). I must stop over ordering on my Waitrose delivery.

It's from Colette, who's been to a couple of our *kleine bijeenkomsts* with her husband a few years back. She smelt syrupy, of vanilla and earthy old books, and she had a huge wart on her nose that gave her a certain Wicked Witch of the West look about her. I start scrolling through the rest.

Any recommendations for a tree surgeon please? My beloved oak tree seems to need a bit of attention.

Richard is good. He's done our eucalyptus a few times.

Anyone want a small freezer? It's old and needs a good clean but perfectly useable.

Can anyone help? I'm making ginger biscuits and seem to have forgotten the ginger.

Does anyone recognise this doorstep? Parcel says delivered but not to correct address.

I clear my throat again. 'Sorry, but I can't see anything on here,' I say. I turn my screen to show Eliza. She leans forward against the cluttered stove top.

'That's because you're looking at the wrong chat group. There's another chat, called *Copthall Christmas*. Last year, Debs put on a party for most of the street. Except she didn't invite Elise. I thought it was so mean. My mum didn't go because of it. But they use that chat now, if…'

'If what?' I say.

She hands me her phone, gesturing at me to scroll through it.

'I'm so sorry Remi. I just thought you should know. I know we're not best friends or anything, but we're mates, right? And I know it's always been just you and your mum, and I wondered if…'

She trails off, and I unwrap my leg from the chair, sitting upright intently.

'I just wondered if you knew you had an auntie,' she says.

Chapter Twelve

'iemand aan de schandpaal nagelen'

To nail someone to the pillory

Eliza's phone screen is cracked but the *Copthall Christmas* chat is fully legible. The first message is from Valentina, an Italian-born lady who lives next to Patrick. An attendee of our *kleine bijeenkomsts*, and the kind of lady who complains about Patrick's dog.

Valentina: Does anyone know what is going on in the cul-de-sac? There's a large van parked outside Elise's and two interesting-looking men stood outside the front door. Marco says he heard shouting? Did anyone else?

Linda: Hi Valentina, I thought I heard loud voices too. It looks like they're carrying stuff from inside the house out of the front door now.

Amanda: Is Elise moving?

Kate: They're definitely not removal men. They'd have a much bigger van if so. @Christine, go get those binoculars out, will you!

Christine: They're out already, darling! The men have got large ID tags around their necks. They're tall, too. They look more like bouncers than anything else.

Debs: They can't be bouncers. Burly men carrying belongings out of a house – it all looks a tad suspect to me. I'd put my money on debt collectors or something like that.

Wilma: I always knew there was something dodgy about that woman. *(Three people have added a thumbs-up emoji.)*

Valentina: Debt collectors! OMG!!! *(Followed by three shocked-face emojis.)*

Linda: Well, it makes sense doesn't it? If they're carrying items out of the house. That table is granite, she said so herself. Probably worth a few bob.

Kate: Golly, it just shows you, doesn't it?

Debs: Just proves you never know what goes on behind closed doors. Is Elise there?

Christine: No, just Remi, it looks like. She can't have known they were coming, or else she wouldn't be in her dressing gown in the middle of the street. I wouldn't be seen dead outside my house in my dressing gown, would you?

Debs: Remi? Isn't that the one that's got a few 'issues'?

Kate: She had an 'episode' on a school trip once (my son was in her class). Elise had to go all the way down to Cornwall to pick her up, and then she wasn't allowed on any school trips after that.

Valentina: Well, she's in a tug of war with the two men and a rather large painting at the moment! This is comedy gold!

Linda: The proverbs painting, I bet! Is she winning?

Valentina: From what I can see, I'd say she was giving it a jolly good go.

Debs: Go Remi! *(Followed by two strong-arm emojis.)*

Valentina: Bailiffs 1 – Remi 0. They literally ripped it out of her hands. Oh dear.

Christine: OMG guys! She's crying.

Kate: Oh, that's sad. Should we call the police?

Wilma: Police? I don't think so. We don't want it bringing down the tone of the neighbourhood.

Amanda: Did anyone hear that smash? I think she's just thrown something.

Debs: Oh for goodness' sake. It's like an episode of Jeremy Kyle! Someone needs to put a stop to this madness. We're not a bloody council estate.

Valentina: It looks like they're leaving now.

Frank: I hope so, I've got a parcel that I need to pick up from Marks and Sparks and they're blocking the whole of the cul-de-sac.

Amanda: Do you think someone should call Elise?

Kate: I'd assume Remi would have done that already?

Linda: I've just tried her. It rang out and I wasn't sure about leaving a voicemail.

Kate: She looked pretty upset. Is there anyone else we could call? Does Remi have any other family?

Valentina: There was this one lady, if I recall correctly, from a long time ago, mind you. She came to our house once, when Elise and Remi first moved into the street. I think her name was Claire or something like that?

Amanda: It was Clara. She had that really thick Dutch accent.

Debs: That's right. Clara. Wasn't she her sister?

Amanda: Yes, Elise's sister. They looked ever so alike. Like twins. She drove that baby-blue car and had that beautiful Cartier watch with the diamonds.

Valentina: That's it. I remember now. Clara with all the diamonds. *(Followed by a diamond emoji.)*

Amanda: The money is all from the Dutch grandmother's side. I mean, a part-time paramedic who buys caviar? I don't think her husband's job was anything to shout about.

Kate: My Nigel makes seven figures a year and even we don't eat caviar!

Valentina: Shame, though. That'll be the end of their little gatherings.

Amanda: I agree. What a shame. *(Five people have added a sad-face emoji.)*

~

'Remi,' says Eliza, nudging me gently. I realise she's been peering over my shoulder as I read. She lifts her phone from my hands as I try my hardest not to cry. *This is comedy gold?* Fucking Valentina.

Eliza pauses, as if she's expecting me to say something. But I have absolutely no idea what to say. This must be what going into shock feels like. My gums feel like they've turned to rock.

'I can assure you that we had absolutely no part in that conversation,' she says. 'It's horrible, the way they talk about what has just happened to you. Absolutely horrid.'

I don't even nod. I just sit there, slumped like a potato, staring right into her eyes. I pick out specks of gold around the pupils. The eye specks match the freckles on her nose.

'I do hope I did the right thing by showing these to you,' she says. I realise she lisps when she says the word *these*.

'You did.' I manage to say. 'Thank you.'

She shifts awkwardly on her toes, moving away to the sink and rearranging some dirty cups that don't need rearranging. I realise I do that sometimes. I stare at people and make them uncomfortable. I know she feels uncomfortable because she clinks the cups loudly and then runs the tap, changing the subject to talk about drama school and other things that I'm not really listening to. Instead, I continue to stare at the back of her head, imagining asking her a question.

Is someone trying to sabotage us?
And then another.
Is Mum's estranged family trying to sabotage us?
And then another.
*Is **Mum** trying to sabotage us?*
And then finally.
Does Clara with all the diamonds have the answer?

~

I'd tried calling Mum again while I was treading the pavement back past the school, the children now shut away in their classrooms, the stressed-out parents mostly glad to be rid of them for the day. The children, mostly glad to be rid of their parents for at least a couple of hours. I'd tried her for a fourth time as I'd sloped back past nosey old Joyce's house, holding my fist by my side and discreetly flipping her the finger like a teenager might do to her most-hated teacher. At least Joyce wasn't in on the chat. She's probably just as hated as we are.

I bet *she* doesn't know about the secret sister, surely?

I'd silently considered the fact that I have an auntie out there that I never knew about. I wondered what she might look like, this mysterious family figure of mine, kept hidden from me for so many years. Where she lives. What she does for a living. What her passions are. *Clara.* I'll admit it is a beautiful name. It sounds elegant, sophisticated even. I bet she smells exquisite, of jasmine and mint. On my walk back home, I'd imagined my grandmother Johanna holding her children in her arms, their delicate little fingers wrapped around hers. I'd imagined her carefully picking out their names, Clara and Elise. I'd wondered who was the eldest, who had weighed the most. Whether she and Mum both had the same ash-blonde hair.

I'd wondered why they are estranged. And whether Clara is the problem. Or if it's Mum.

Or, if they are both as bad as each other.

Perhaps she's dead, like Johanna was supposed to be. Or perhaps she's very much alive. And if she's alive, then she likely knows what happened to Johanna. Which means that she might know what is happening to us. If Johanna's accident and Mum's problems are connected, of course.

Have I always believed that they are?

Chapter Thirteen

'hij draagt water naar de zee'

He carries water to the sea

Arriving home, I unlock our front door and decide to head to the kitchen to make myself a strong coffee, possibly the strongest coffee I have ever made. Except I'd forgotten all about the sorry pieces of smashed clock and broken dinner plate that are still scattered miserably across the floor. Copperfield has not. He is sitting staring at them in disgust. The swing in his tail is telling me that I should have addressed this scene before I'd left for Eliza.

'Yes,' I tell him as I kick off my shoes in a hurry. 'I fully understand I am a disappointment to you. I am not quite the clean-freak like our mother. But it's OK,' I say as I stroke his fur. 'I promise I'm doing it now. And we won't get into trouble.' I collect the dustpan and brush from the cupboard and fulfil my promise to the cat while he purrs loudly in satisfaction. Moments like this are when I wished I had a dog to vent to, one of those exuberant ones who makes adorable mistakes, like spreading dribble all over the sofa or chewing on your favourite slipper. The dog wouldn't have judged me for something like this or scarpered when the bailiffs came. He might have even helped scare them away. Yes. I should like a dog one day.

Back in the kitchen, I pour hot water into a mug and swirl the old-school coffee granules around. My stomach is starting to worry that, even though Mum will be on a shift, she hasn't returned my call. In an effort to quieten it, I reach for the biscuit tin, something that I used to do far too often, according to Mum. When I was about ten, she came up with the idea that the biscuits should go inside a tin, which is then placed inside another tin, so that every time you come to want a biscuit, you have to break into two noisy tins in order to get to the crumbly, beautiful thing that you wished for, just to make sure that you'd *really* thought through whether or not you should be having one. To make things even more difficult, the lids never fitted properly, which meant it was a total faff to get them back on, and I'd often get told off for leaving the lid a bit wonky when the biscuits had all gone soft.

I pick out three custard creams from a crumbly mess, then take a fourth, if I can carry it. As I crunch through the first one, I spot a note on the kitchen table in what looks like Mum's handwriting. Or at least, I *think* it's her handwriting. It's hard to tell because it's written in capital letters in red pen on a large yellow post it.

Do not let them in. I will take care of this.

I stare down at the note, crumbs falling from the biscuits in my hands.

She knew they were coming. And worst of all, I let them in.

I let the *'we'd need to come inside to use your phone'* sneaky buggers in.

My skin goes cold as my mobile rings. It's Luke.

'Erm, hi,' I answer.

'You alreet?' says Luke cheerfully. 'You'll be pleased to know

I survived another night in damp and disgusting Verborough,' he laughs. 'How did last night with your mam go?'

'I'm, erm...' I say. 'I'm just a bit distracted at the moment, Luke. Sorry.' I'm still staring in horror at the note.

'Right. No worries, like. Did it not go that well then?'

I had almost forgotten about mine and Mum's argument last night. I wonder if I could tell him that actually, Mum ended up slapping herself across the thigh hard with a wet cloth? But some things are just never meant to leave the closed doors of home.

'We had a bit of row, actually,' I say. 'We went to bed angry, then she left for work early in the morning.' I decide I can't face telling him about the bailiffs. Unlike the whole of Langswood, he will never have to know.

'Ouch. That's not good, Remi. Are you OK?'

I can't say yes. Luke will see through my lie.

'There's been a new development,' I say instead.

'A development? What kind of development?'

'I found out that Mum has a sister.'

'She told you that? Your mam, like?' I can imagine Luke's nose wrinkling, his inquisitive blue eyes widening with concern.

'*She* didn't tell me, no.'

'Right.'

'Her name's Clara.'

'Woah,' says Luke. 'Clara, huh. That's a nice name.'

'Yeah. It is.' My eyes don't move from the note on the table.

'C. L. A. R. A.' I can hear Luke fumbling with something in the background. 'Hang on a sec,' he says. 'I'll pull her up on Facebook. Reckon she'd be a Van Tam too?'

'Probably,' I reply.

'Got her,' says Luke after a few seconds.

'Crikey, that was fast.'

'Her profile is set as private, but I'll send her profile picture to you now.'

I hold my phone away from my ear and click on the picture

that Luke sends through. Slowly, I take in her features – ash-blonde curls, a straight nose, high cheekbones and a hint of freckles. Her lips are curved into a rose-coloured, approachable smile. She's not identical to Mum. But she looks just like her.

'Gosh. She's beautiful,' I can't help myself saying out loud. 'She looks like me, doesn't she? I mean, not saying that I'm beautiful, but…'

'Aye,' he says. 'You are beautiful, Remi.'

My cheeks flush red. Now is not the time to address the voice that I may or may not have heard on our call yesterday.

'Does it feel strange?' he asks. 'Seeing a picture of someone else related to you?'

'It does.'

'Do you think you're gonna contact her, then?'

'I don't have a Facebook account.'

It's true, I don't. I don't have any accounts that put me in danger of identity theft or financial fraud or believing some person in Africa pretending to be Jane from school who's got cancer and needs £10,000 to cure it.

'What about in your mam's phone book, then?' suggests Luke. 'If she's anything like my mam she'll have one of those old notebooks with everyone's details in. There might be a phone number or something.'

Luke's suggestion is enough to pull me out of the note-staring trance. I tug at the kitchen drawer, the one containing purses, old bank cards, cash, coins, keys and a book titled *telephone numbers and addresses*. Its worn brown leather is warm between my fingers. Mum has had this book forever. Each page has its own crease or imprint, with hand-written entries crossed out, and new letters and numbers inked underneath. I slowly turn the pages until I get to C. *Clara*. As if she's been in our lives forever, she's there.

'You're right,' I say. 'There's a Clara in Mum's phone book. With a foreign number, mind you. There's a *plus thirty-one* at the start.'

Luke is punching something into his phone again. 'It's the Netherlands. Plus thirty-one is the Netherlands.'

'Right.' The sound of my heart thuds loudly in my ears.

'Should I… should I come and see you, Remi? Jaz said I could borrow his car.'

I drop the custard creams on the table to scratch at the itchy skin around my wrist. I like to tend to the area like it's a fire, keeping it burning so I can warm my fingers when required. 'Come to Langswood, you mean? Now?'

'Yeah,' he says cheerfully. 'I could leave in half an hour, if you want?'

'No,' I say, more abruptly than I want to. 'I mean, not right now. No.' Or next week. Or ever. I can't have him here, I can't.

'OK. What about the weekend, then?'

'No,' I repeat. 'Definitely not the weekend.' My fingers scratch like they are hungry for the shedding skin.

'Right,' he says, his cheerful demeanor gone. 'I mean, I get the message, like.'

'Oh God. Look, I don't mean to be horrible or anything but…'
'It's fine.'
'I'm really sorry, Luke. But if Mum's around… it's complicated. And I need to go now. It's just, I've got… I've got things I need to do.' I go to press the button to hang up the phone.

Then, 'Fuck,' I hear Luke saying into himself. 'Fuck.'

My finger lingers over the *end call* button as I stare back at the note. And then I press it, and he's gone, and I hold the leather book in my arms, and I start to sob, just like Mum had done on the floor of our house twenty-four-hours earlier.

Chapter Fourteen

'men moet het ijzer smeden als het heet is'

One must strike while the iron is hot

It's dark outside, and Mum is still not home. A half-empty pizza box sits lonely on the kitchen table surrounded by the scent of garlic and fried cheese. Mum hates the smell of garlic. The house is silent without the TVs, and I can just make out the beginnings of some dust settling on the cream radiator covers. They look so odd without their usual ornaments loaded onto them.

I've made ten calls. Left three voice messages. Sent two texts. I typed out *I can't believe you knew they were coming and you've left me with them and now you're not returning my calls and who the hell has been impersonating me and I don't even have any money and I can't sleep here on my own and are they coming back or do you just not care?* But I didn't send that. I just asked Mum politely where she's got to and if she could let me know she's OK. Please.

My slippers take me to the window where I peer through the shutters at the expensive cars parked like trophies in the cul-de-sac's driveways. My Porsche is there, with an ugly heavy-duty clamp wrapped solidly around its front wheel, which they'd promised they'd remove if the debt was paid in the next few days, and I wish now that I'd told them they can have the Porsche in exchange for the painting. I curse myself for not being quick-thinking enough. What will I do when I'm a paramedic if I lack the skill of rapidity? Will I fail the thousands of patients who will come to rely on me? Will I end up making the mistakes and then admitting nothing, like Mum told me to do, just to keep my job?

The moon is almost full tonight. Its chubby face looks like it's eaten all the custard creams. I wonder if the sun will be mad that the moon's imitating her. I suppose I should try to sleep, but sleep is not coming easily to me these days. Instead, I find that I'm lying in that unnerving state of half-awake and half-asleep for long periods of time. That state where your leg jerks you into consciousness, as though you've just fallen off a cliff. Last night I was in the water again. Sometimes I'll be in a river, but most often I'm in the sea. I always have goggles on, or perhaps just some supernatural ability to see underwater, like I'm being forced by the powers that be to see the danger beneath me. Sometimes it's a shark, sometimes a crocodile. Last night it was a body, shackled to the ocean floor. The body was lying on its back, deep down in the water, arms above its head, spread out in the shape of a starfish. I was floating at the surface, looking down, watching as they took their last breaths, helpless to do anything. I've heard deaths at sea can be peaceful ones, but it didn't look very peaceful to me.

There's a cream Mum has that's supposed to help you sleep. It will be in her dressing room, and I start to move towards there, pretending that it's not an excuse to go hunting around in her room for things. That it's not a ridiculous excuse to be in there, to be one step closer to something that I know I want to find.

I float across the landing, following the scent of lemon verbena to her room. Mum's door is open, as it always is, like it's testing me.

Her room is vast. It's what those tall Canadian twin brothers on HGTV would call a *bedroom retreat*. High ceilings and walls are covered in expensive cashmere paint, named something daft like Panda's Breath or Marshmallow Dust. Sheer linen curtains fall delicately over the large windows on all sides. The bed is made like it would be in a high-class hotel, dressed in crisp white cotton covers and covered by a chunky knitted throw, plus half a dozen scatter cushions with the fashionable chop down the middle. Next to the bed are two small nightstands, each holding a single object – on one, there's a small faux trailing eucalyptus and on the other, a lamp with an elegant silver giraffe as its base. Wardrobes line the far side of the room, ones without handles, those ones where you've no idea how to open them unless you have a degree in cabinet-making.

Seeing Mum's room, and the way she has tirelessly perfected it, makes me stop, then. For a moment, I stop thinking of the bailiffs and Eliza and the horrific details of the neighbours' chat, and instead, I think of Mum and her large bed which she sleeps in alone. The bed which she would, had the world not been so cruel, share with my dad. I think of us over the years. Of her tucking me in for a night's sleep after suffering through my piano recital, the recitals that she never once missed. I think of her bringing me hot soup and clementines when I was sick and stroking my back after a twelve-hour paramedic shift, then returning to this bed alone. I think of the princess breakfasts she'd always book for us at Disney World. And the way she always makes sure my bed covers are soft and clean and snuggly. I think of me being oversensitive. I think of her being there for me, always.

I think of my world without her.

It's almost enough to make me turn around and walk out. But I don't. Instead, I tiptoe over to her bed, so as not to make marks in her carpet, reaching underneath the bedframe to pull out a large grey box. A box that holds all her most important documents.

The lid opens smoothly with a gentle tug. Her passport lies on top of a stack full of papers, and I open it, smiling at the photo which makes her look a bit like Goldie Hawn in the film Snatched. Her perky cheeks sit perfectly on top of her well-defined jawline, except that her eyes look small and smudged, like an anime character, like someone who can see with their eyes closed.

The passport is useful, as it tells me that she hasn't truly abandoned me and fled abroad. Yet. But that's not what I'm looking for. I want the Title Register from HM Land Registry. Not something she's told me. But official evidence.

And a few papers down, I find it.

Section A – the property register – lists our house. Number ninety-five, Copthall Lane, Langswood, UK. Section B – the proprietorship register – lists the proprietor.

I'm expecting it to be Mum, of course. The proprietor should be Elise Van Tam.

But it's not.

I gasp as the words pulsate on the document.

It's not in my name, either. The house isn't ours.

The house is in the name of Johanna Van Tam.

Which means Johanna is alive. And Clara could be my only way of finding her.

Chapter Fifteen

'de kat de bel aanbinden'

To bell the cat

It turns out that the day before yesterday – after Gerald showed up – I'd completely forgotten to give Mum her birthday things. I'd discovered this as I was rooting around in my duffel bags in the utility room this morning, unloading my dirty washing and shoving it into the washing machine three t-shirts at a time. I was finding something to do to pass the time, something that Mum would approve of. The stench of two-day-old prawn mayonnaise sandwiches had attracted Copperfield, who, since last night, had been lurking hungrily by the utility room door. It was enough to make me gag. It's a real shame, but like a lot of smells – public transport in a heatwave, my wee having eaten asparagus – this stink will be forever ingrained in the back of my nostrils as a memory, and as such, I don't think I can touch prawns ever again.

The red velvet cupcakes are still edible, though. I tuck them under my arm and carry them to the kitchen, where I arrange them on the kitchen table with Mum's birthday card neatly on top. She can't have *nothing* for her birthday. No. That would be cruel.

Clara's phone number is written out beside the cupcakes, and I gaze at the small piece of paper, acutely aware that I have the real possibility of finding my auntie somewhere in Holland. And if I find Clara, then I might also find Johanna. And I could try to fix this. I could. We might not lose the house if it's someone else's. I might be able to fix whatever has happened to this family. But I don't have a way of seeing into the future. And anxiety stems from the unknown. That's what I read once, anyway.

The possibility of going behind Mum's back to contact her estranged sister fills me with dread. But now there is a new problem. Which is that Mum never came home last night. And that according to her colleague Abdul – who I called in desperation early this morning – she's not worked a shift since last week, either.

Where is she?

I take the piece of paper with Clara's number into the living room, placing it on the floor next to my phone. Then, I lay down on the sofa, pulling the throw partly over me, and I stare at it, like it's some magic crystal ball that will give me the answer.

Should I contact Clara, or shouldn't I?

Pang. A pinch in my stomach forces me to turn my whole body to face the ceiling. I readjust my glasses and sigh angrily. I hate this feeling. I really, bloody, *hate* it. Why did I have to think about it? If I hadn't yesterday made it clear to Luke that I'm a fool who can't have an adult relationship of any kind, he'd be texting me to ask if I've spoken to her yet. And I'd be having to tell him that I haven't had the guts to do it. That my reckless old gut is not playing ball today. That I just can't shake this unrelenting sense of dread, deep down in the pit of my stomach. That I should be blaming Mum for all of this, but instead I'm arranging her cupcakes and card as though nothing has happened.

There's a creature down there, in the innermost pit, I'm sure of it. An unforgiving monster, one that this fool – me, of course –

has created, who nips at my insides everytime I go off course. Or do something that someone might not approve of. Something a bit risky. Something worth doing.

It's her family, not yours. Pang! *You don't know what you're dealing with.* Pang! *You're out of your depth.* Pang!

Mum would die if she knew I was sitting here with her sister's contact details in front of me. I imagine her taking the scribbled-on post-it note out of my palm, a thunderous look on her face. *'I wasn't being serious, Mum!'* I'd protest, like that timid little girl that I was. Except that Mum's not here. And her not coming home like this is completely out of character.

No one can help me now but myself. Except this isn't *quite* my forte. I realised a long time ago – without the help of a therapist – that I've been taught to avoid difficult or dangerous situations. Of course, most parents do this. They subject their children to repeated warnings growing up, telling them *don't do this*, or *don't do that* – or else – in order to try and keep their babies safe. Sometimes, growing up, I would feel like the world was against us. Or was it us against the world? *Beter alleen, dan in kwaad gezelschap,* Mum would say. It's better to be alone than in bad company. But is it? Is it really better to be alone? And if I don't find a way to quieten this monster inside me, will I forever be wondering what if?

I have to do something, before the bailiffs come back. Before this shit gets any worse, and that bitch Debs has even more to talk about. I'll show her who's got *issues*.

Yet I know that if I contact Clara now, we're all going down with the ship. Mum. Me. Clara. There'll be no coming back from it.

It will either make us or break us.

I yank up my socks and cross one ankle over the other, weighing it all up in my mind for the thousandth time. I just need to practice what I've learnt. *You've got tricks for this, Remi.* Tried and tested ones that I've collected from various podcasts and psychology reports. Self-enquiry, mindfulness, meditation, visualisation. I pull out my imaginary pencil and start to write out two sentences, each filling its own patch on the white ceiling.

WILL SOMETHING TERRIBLE HAPPEN?
MIGHT SOMETHING WONDERFUL HAPPEN?

Then, I write out a third sentence, which I've learnt is the most important one.

WILL IT BE THE END OF THE WORLD?

I lay there silently for a moment, pondering that last question. What could be so awful about contacting Clara that could blow our whole lives to smithereens? *Oh, I don't know,* I answer. *Everything?*

So that didn't help. But the longer I wait, the further and further away our painting will be. This house isn't even ours, for goodness' sake. It's now or never.

Instinctively, I lean over from the sofa and pick up the one item that could change everything. I hold the post-it up to the screen, and jab in the numbers. I can't face calling her, that would be far too much for me. So, I start to type.

Hi Clara, I hope this is still your number. This may come as a surprise, but it's Remi, Elise's daughter. Could we meet?

I read it back twice, and before I have the urge to delete it, press send, slamming the phone face down on the cushion next to me. It's done.

Shit. It's really done.

I exhale heavily and slump back into the sofa, feeling the adrenaline slowly building up inside me.

What will Mum think? Have I done the wrong thing?

A sinking feeling starts making its way around my body, and my ears burn red. I start to chant *not the end of the world, not the end of the world* through clattering teeth. I can feel the thud of my heart, the familiar sensation of panic blocking my airways. I try to sit up, but the light-headedness forces me back. My head rocks back and forth in a swaying motion, something that feels oddly comforting, like an involuntary response to help soothe the pain inside me. I consider running upstairs to reach my weighted blanket but accept that the throw will have to do. One arm jerks out to catch the corner and I pull it up over me as far as I can. I screw my eyes shut and do what I've taught myself to do; to count in threes slowly, while imagining a wave crashing onto a shore somewhere. My hand goes up to my necklace.

It's going to be fine. Touch wood touch wood touch wood touch wood. The panic will pass. Six… nine…twelve…

Then, *ping!* A reply comes through.

Remi. You don't know how wonderful it is to hear from you! And I would absolutely love to meet. I'm actually near your way at the moment, if you're still in Langswood? Can we meet at No.77 at 5pm? Clara.

I've done it. We are meeting, and there's no turning back now

Chapter Sixteen

'je vangt meer vliegen met honing dan met azijn'

You catch more flies with honey than with vinegar

No.77 on Langswood High Street is a grand brick building, three stories high with sash bay windows and an Instagrammable front door. Balconies jut out above the bay areas, covered in glorious spring hanging baskets filled with pink begonias, possibly the biggest hanging baskets I've ever seen. A placard that says 1881 sits proudly above the door.

For the nineteen years I've lived in Langswood, I've witnessed this place change names, colours and identities almost half a dozen times. The Merry Crown, The Lion, The Jolly Tankard, some other crazy name that referenced mermaids, and now No.77. To target the many types of people who live in this town, and to survive and thrive as a business, it's become some sort of a hybrid place. It's a swanky cocktail bar at night, full of young professionals who commute into London, and a coffee shop and play café by day. Brunch is served at lunchtimes, sometimes bottomless on the weekends, with unlimited amounts of Italian prosecco. Pimped up roasts are served on Sundays, with things like paprika roast chicken, beef cheeks and bone marrow sauce.

I've spent many nights here with my childhood friends, sat on velvet bar stalls, sipping from overpriced cocktails that we couldn't really afford. When we were in sixth form, we would meet here for our weekly therapy sessions. Not official therapy, of course, but the one that only long-lasting friendship can give you. The best kind of therapy. The one where no one really challenges you, but where everyone goes along with your opinion and tells you what a great decision you made.

It's one of the few places in Langswood where you can wear a bodycon dress and four-inch heels and not feel self-conscious. Except I don't wear those types of things anymore, due to living in perpetual fear of ending up on someone else's TikTok feed, looking like a sausage squashed into a tutu.

The last time I was here was a few months ago on Christmas break, with my old school friends Lacy and Heidi, when we'd been reminiscing about the Zante trip we took in the summer before we started uni. My first trip abroad without Mum. She'd been really unhappy about me going, obviously. The compromise was putting a tracker on my phone, which in fairness to her, did actually make me feel better in the end. It seemed like a good idea for both of us. Sometimes the overbearing Mum thing isn't a disaster, after all.

I only had one panic attack and that was the night before I left, when Mum hadn't spoken to me much, except to tell me that she'd lost five pounds from *the stress of it all*.

Typically, something bad happened. On the second day of the holiday, Heidi had tripped up a step, of all things, in her new red stilettos and severed her ankle so viciously it had to be sewn back on. Who knew an eight-inch step and a four-inch heel could cause such trauma? There wasn't a sexy doctor in sight at the Greek hospital, which Heidi found thoroughly disappointing. TV shows like ER really do create unrealistic expectations.

When Heidi broke her ankle in Zante, her dad Mike had flown straight to Greece to be by his daughter's bedside. Thankfully, they'd sorted out insurance before the trip, but his flight and accommodation, time off work and her subsequent physio and rehab had cost him a fortune. Heidi didn't know he'd had to sell his beloved Rolex watch that his late father gave him to pay for it, but I knew, because Mum had happened to bump into him on the way to the pawn shop, and it was all I heard about every time we passed it on the High Street. I haven't been abroad with my friends since.

When I first came to No.77 in the daytime, I almost instantly regretted it. Bars always look so much grubbier and tackier by day. Now, from my corner table by the front window, I can see the dust on the vodka bottles, the stains on the rug by the door. Some of the tables look sticky, and I can't decide whether it's from too much cleaning chemical, or unwiped cocktail-juice from the night before. My coffee mug has an ever-so-slight lipstick mark on it, and I find myself wondering who those lips might belong to, wondering what their mum is like. Wondering if their mum lied to *them* that she had no family. That they were in fact broke, and not rich at all.

I'd checked my bank balance on the way over here. One-hundred-and-thirty-two pounds and fifty-six pence. Without a job, I live off the allowance that Mum pays in every month, but I realise that is going to change now. My throat feels dry as I realise that I have nothing of my own in savings. Everything has been controlled by Mum, and I've been unbelievably complacent in allowing it. I've not made one penny of my own. I have been acting like an immature, spoilt child.

I take a sip of my velvety Biscoff latte – the one that I'd bought on autopilot without even a glance at the price – in shame. So the house isn't ours. An image of Mum at the bank, pen in hand, lump in her throat, contemplating forging my signature to afford our council tax threatens to open the floodgates in my eyes. Except there's the small, niggling detail that's been lingering at the back of my mind. How would she be securing loans in my name? Don't you need something of value to secure loans against? What on earth do I have of any value?

Trying desperately to distract myself, I spy a group by the child-friendly area where a few toys are laid out on a carpet. There's two women, a bit older than me, having a conversation about which shoes to buy for a wedding. *Should I buy the pink shoes, or should I buy the black shoes?* A little girl, who must be the daughter of one of the women, is playing on the floor with a plastic marble run. I watch as she takes each piece and expertly fits it together with another, testing each fast loop, spinning gear or wiggly slide by dropping a marble down and whooping with delight when it drops out the bottom into the bright red plastic trough. She tugs at the woman on the right, saying *mummy, look, mummy* with a proud look on her face, and the woman nods and replies *wow, that's amazing, honey* without once looking at her little girl, or at the pretty impressive marble run she's created.

I get it; I do. I've seen the mum memes on Instagram. The ones where they get woken up endlessly by their child elbowing them in bed. The ones where they get asked *mummy* twenty times, before the child says *watch this* and then does a shit cartwheel across the floor. A shit cartwheel that they've seen twenty times before. This particular mum is probably so desperate for some rare adult time that she's too engrossed in her conversation to acknowledge her child's masterpiece. I get why mums – or dads – need to do certain things, because they are so sick to death of washing school uniform and being sicked on, and cooking dinners that will be pushed around the plate and moaned about. I get that they need their own lives. Their own secrets.

I get that mothers make plenty of sacrifices for their children. I mean, we're reminded about it enough, aren't we? As if as soon as we're born, we're expected to be eternally grateful, to start the pay-back of birth with cuddles and smiles. On cue, when friends visit. Even if our mother is a lying, selfish twat. Which I'm not saying mine is, necessarily. But I have an auntie, an auntie who is alive. Why wouldn't she tell me that?

A latte steamer hisses moodily in the background.

Am I angry because whatever has happened, she's refused to let me help her? That she's not given me a chance to try and build bridges, whatever this family of ours has done? Am I mad because no matter how hard I try, I can't seem to talk about anything meaningful with my own mother? I lift my glasses off my face and rub my eyes wearily. My palms are sweaty with nerves. Perhaps she's trying to protect me. Perhaps she did the right thing. Which would mean then, I'm very much doing the *wrong* thing, now.

I reach down into my tan suede crossbody and tap my iPhone for the time. Ten past five. Clara is late, and I'm starting to get anxious that she won't turn up. Mum might be home by now. She might have witnessed the full extent of the bailiff's visit, and seen all the missing things, and the fact that her stupid daughter opened the door when she told her not to. I take another sorry sip of my latte.

Where is she? I look out of the window and scan the crowded pavement. Traffic is starting to pile up, the first of the commuters, longing to get home after a hard day's work in the city. Parents are rushing to get their kids to and from those essential but social-life-crushing sports clubs. We're eight short miles away from central London, but the area is so densely populated that it's a good fifty-minute car journey to reach it. Parked cars, nose to nose, fill the side of the pavement. On the other side of the road, a Deliveroo driver sits patiently waiting outside Papa Johns for his next order.

And then I see her.

Her skin is smooth and tanned and just a tiny bit freckly, just like in her Facebook profile photo. She's wearing a navy-coloured, long-sleeved linen shirt, a long denim skirt, and brown loafers with an exquisite gold buckle. She sashays towards me, her curly hair bouncing around her shoulders, her eyes bright and confident. She looks crisp and clean, and I realise there's something significant about her. She looks important, like someone who knows exactly what she's talking about. Mostly – and to my relief – she looks nice.

I rise slowly from my seat, flashing her a little wave, and as she reaches me, without either of us saying a word, she pulls me into a hug, one that feels warm and natural and almost like we've never been apart. With tears in her eyes, she orders a bottle of prosecco and without asking, pours me a glass. I'm sat opposite my auntie in disbelief. Disbelief that I am finally related to another human being that is not my mother. Her accent is Dutch, but her voice is a Van Tam voice. It has the same notes and tones as Mum's, spoken from the same lips, the same face, the same body. We are from the same pack, from the same herd, and I realise that I am now busy picking out all the similarities that we share together, down to the way that her earlobes adjoin to her head.

She doesn't seem to mind my staring, and we silently cheers each other. *To a new start.* We tell each other how much we both look like Elise. And then Clara explains how my message this afternoon felt just like fate. That usually she's in Holland, but today she was in London. That she's a vet, and that she'd travelled here for a one-day conference about dog dentistry.

I tell her a bit about me. About how I found her number – a made-up story involving Eliza, not including bailiffs or Luke or sneaking around in Mum's address book. We talk about my paramedic course at university. And about Mum, all the good bits of course. I tell her about Copperfield. She says that she loves Siberian cats the most.

She tells me that she's missed me. She says that she misses

Elise terribly. That she's thought about us every day. She tells me I have a grandad! A grandad named Fred, who apparently, misses me very much, too.

She tells me she is overjoyed that I look so happy about this. But she is anxious that this is all very overwhelming for me.

See, I think. This lady knows her stuff.

She shows me a picture of Johanna, one where she is smiling broadly. It was from a long time ago, when Johanna was a dancer, Clara says. In the picture she has smooth, straight fair hair and sparkling eyes, and is standing in front of what looks like a theatre, dressed in an oversized, fancy-looking fur coat. It is one from a striking collection that she'd inherited from her noble Dutch family, according to Clara.

She tells me that Johanna travelled the world wowing audiences with her pirouettes and her jives and her Argentine tango. That they'd all moved to the UK when Elise was sixteen and Clara seventeen.

She tells me that, as a child, she'd long to watch her mother, swirling around in an extravagant dress, five shades of her favourite colour pink, melting together like a churning milkshake.

Then, she asks what I know about my grandmother.

So, here we go. To the story, the horrible story that's been etched inside my mind since I was a fifteen-year-old girl. To the reason that I'm here in the first place. I don't present Clara with my two scenarios. The first, where Johanna is an irresponsible drunk. The second, where she's – potentially – a much less irresponsible drunk. I don't want to cloud her recollection. I want to know her scenario. Clara's truth. To add to my list of possibles. I mean, I *feel* like I can trust her. But I felt like I could trust Mum, too.

And so she takes me back. All the way back, to the night it happened. To the hospital. Not in Amsterdam, but in Cambridge. To the very worst night of her life.

To the night that Johanna survived.

Chapter Seventeen

'niemand kan twee heren dienen'

One cannot serve two masters

'So Johanna *is* alive,' I say in a too-high voice. Getting confirmation from a person and not just a piece of paper has made it so much more real for me now. 'I'm sorry, it's just a bit of a shock, that's all.'

Clara takes a sip of water and leans forward, placing her hand over mine. Her nails are short and square and painted an exquisite shade of sage green. I can smell her perfume, honey and pepper with a creamy velvet heart. As her palm lands on top of mine I almost recoil in surprise. If it were Mum, she'd have sat back and sighed, or steered the topic towards some other person's recent plight. *'If you think that's a shock, have you heard what's happening to poor old Connor Dayley down the road? First this, then that. Een ongleuk komt zelden alleen. Misfortune seldom comes alone. Talk about having problems!'*

She most definitely wouldn't have touched me in any way, or showed me any kind of understanding, and I'm not quite sure how I feel about Clara doing just that. My immediate reaction is to tactfully pull my hand back and scrunch it into a ball on my lap, where it can avoid all attempts of affection, but I decide to leave it there and settle for a bit. Perhaps I might learn to like this feeling.

The windows of No.77 are now dark and splattered with chunky raindrops, and inside, the staff are slowly starting their evening change over, from funky pub-slash-café to swanky bar. The nursery mums are quickly being replaced with the school mums, child-free this time, and the coffees replaced with wine. Background lounge music is flowing softly out of the speakers as a man polishes cocktail glasses behind the bar. I take a first sip of my prosecco, which I've not touched since the waiter poured it into my glass two hours earlier. It's warm and flat, but I'm grateful for the acidic tang on my tongue. Crisp green apple with a faint honey sweetness glides down my throat almost too easily for someone who hasn't tasted alcohol in a while.

Clara is sat looking at me intently, her eyes matching the blue hydrangea in the framed picture above her. We've talked non-stop since she arrived, yet what she's told me about Johanna is only just starting to sink in. All the evidence is now clear, but I can't quite comprehend that Johanna is alive and out there somewhere. That my grandmother is out there somewhere. That she's been living a life parallel to mine, breathing the same air as me, for *eighteen years*. That I might finally get to meet her. Or meet her again, should I say.

I've missed so much. Her birthdays, her milestones, our Christmases. She's missed so much. My last day of nursery, my first day of school. My first nativity play. I mean, the nativity play wasn't a huge success, I wasn't Mary or an angel or even a shepherd, but I did have a speaking part as a Person of the World. *What the heck is a Person of the World?* Mum had quipped, but I was happy with my gold hat and blue robe and my line of *what is that star*, except just as I said it, baby Jesus' head rolled off and everyone laughed, to which I immediately ran off the stage crying. Perhaps I'm glad my grandmother missed that one.

'She is alive,' Clara says, taking a deep breath in. 'Except you need to know that she's very much on her second life now.' I feel her squeeze my hand gently. This time it's her who glugs down her prosecco.

'Is she sick?' I ask. I guess that she'll only be about seventy, which is a spring chicken these days, but I'm not sure what lasting effects the accident might have had on her.

'I don't really know where to start,' replies Clara. 'But yes, she's been sick for a very long time. She never really recovered from what happened to her that night.'

'That's terribly sad,' I say. 'It's crazy, isn't it? How one moment of being in the wrong place at the wrong time can change everything?'

'Totally. A simple night of watching Midsomer Murders – Johanna's favourite – turned into a disaster. She'd seen a text from her neighbour saying that her son was sick and did anyone have a thermometer. So, Johanna had popped out to deliver it. Doing the kind thing, as always. She was dressed in her favourite crimson tunic and white trousers with the pearl detail down the side. Considering all her injuries, she was most gutted about ruining those white trousers. That's typical Johanna.'

'I can't imagine many people survive from her types of injuries, do they?'

'Oh no, she was extremely lucky to have got through it. About three months or so after she arrived in hospital, Johanna underwent thoracic surgery and live manipulation of the ribs. Essentially, she had her whole ribcage clamped and reshaped. She was given surgery to reconstruct her leg and her ankle. And she recovered very well from those.'

My head is bobbing as I wince at the thought. Just imagining some kind of manipulation of the ribs makes me pour us both another glass of prosecco.

'And then came a subdural haematoma. A bleed on the brain.

The doctors were monitoring it, but it had slowly been getting worse, and Johanna needed an emergency craniotomy.'

'Oh, the poor thing. That doesn't sound good at all.'

'Not particularly, no. But it's a life-saving procedure,' she says. 'The surgeon creates a temporary flap in the skull, and the haematoma is gently removed using suction and irrigation, where it's washed away with fluid. The section of the skull is then put back in place and secured using metal plates or, in Johanna's case, screws.' The way that Clara is explaining it with such precision and grace, you can tell that she's used to communicating these types of diagnoses.

'Gosh. You must have been going out of your minds.'

'It was a stressful time, yes. Not least because we spent weeks thinking that someone might have done this to her intentionally.' She tucks a falling section of hair behind her ear in can what only be described as a beautiful way. 'Then one day, a man turned up at the hospital.'

'Gerald,' I blurt out. 'Was his name Gerald?'

Clara's jaw goes slack. 'Yes! His name *was* Gerald. How on earth do you know that?'

'So, he *was* telling the truth!' I think of Gerald's poorly face, his sunken eyes on mine. 'He turned up at our door on Sunday morning. It's a long story.'

'Turned up at your door?'

'To tell us he was dying. That he wanted to know if Johanna was OK, before he, well, you know. Before he passed. I've got no idea how he found us.'

Clara twists her necklace gently between her fingers, a bit like I do, except hers is gold, a dainty leaf with an emerald in the middle. 'And what did Elise say? To Gerald, I mean?'

'Not much. She told him to leave us alone and to never come back to the house again. But the way she worded it – *don't come near me or my mother again* – was a massive red flag for me. She wouldn't have said that unless Johanna was alive. Which, of course, she is.'

Clara's lips tighten. 'And Elise told you what, exactly? That your grandmother was dead?'

I pause, not sure that I want to share the story with her. It had seemed so natural sharing it with Luke, someone who doesn't know the family. But it seems strange to talk about it at this table, as if it is something sacred between just my mother and me. I'm not quite ready to share it with her sister just yet. It just doesn't seem fair.

'Kind of. She didn't really tell me much, to be honest. And I never asked,' I lie.

'Right, well. I was angry at Gerald too, at first. But Johanna, she was just so understanding. Whether he could have done better with his motorbike, whether he could have avoided her or not, who knows? But we were just so relieved to have some answers.' She takes another sip from a crystal-cut glass of water. 'And relieved that he had called for an ambulance that night. Whether anonymous or not.'

The relief floods the table, and I feel it's only appropriate to glug more bubbles down quickly, and to refill my glass.

'And you said it was an accident, right? That Johanna was lying in the road before Gerald got to her?'

'Yes. The doctors all agreed that something had run *over* her, not into her. It tallied up with what Gerald was telling us.'

'And she was drunk, was she?' This is the part where I'm expecting her to say that Johanna had been drinking. That as well as a cup of Yorkshire tea, that night she'd sunk four glasses of wine and a vodka tonic. Then, at least part of Mum's story would be true.

But instead, Clara stares at me in a strange way.

'Why would you ask that?' she says. Her demeanor suddenly changes, and she folds her arm across her chest.

'Just wondering,' I shrug, considering making my excuses and fleeing to the toilets now.

For a moment she keeps staring, until her eyes soften, and her hand goes back over mine. 'What I was trying to say earlier, Remi, is that Johanna's injuries slowly got the better of her over the years. It started out with her finding it difficult to concentrate. She's always loved reading – novels, magazines, anything she could get her hands on – but she couldn't seem to finish a book. Then, we noticed her movement slowing. Easy things, things she's done a million times before, like typing out an email or making a cup of tea. She'd be ages doing those things. It was like her life suddenly went into slow motion.'

We both look up as the waiter interrupts us to bring a jug of fresh tap water. Once he's gone about his business, he lifts our prosecco bottle from the bucket alongside us and refills our glasses to the brim. He smells like the end of a long shift, of body odour covered heavily in Dior Sauvage. I gesture at him to bring us another bottle. The bubbles are helping me make sense of all this.

'Then she had a fall,' Clara talks around him. 'A pretty bad one, in a supermarket, while she was out shopping alone. Fortunately, some good Samaritans came to help her, but she became very nervous about going out after that.'

'It sounds like she's been through a lot,' I say. 'Like you've all been through a lot.'

'The thing is, Remi, Johanna has dementia. Vascular dementia. She's had it for a long time. Vascular dementia can cause slowness of thought or difficulty with understanding simple things. It can mean changes to your mood and behaviour. People can feel disorientated and confused and have problems with language.' She pauses. 'And memory.'

It takes a while for that last point to sink in. 'You mean, she might not remember me?'

'I'm afraid to say I don't know.'

'Does she remember you? And Mum? Does she remember Mum?'

'Sometimes she does, sometimes she doesn't. She hasn't seen your mum in a very long time.'

I pause as the waiter returns with our second bottle. The bubbles spill into my glass and I take another few sips. 'OK, so this is what I don't get,' I say. 'So we were all in Cambridge, right?'

Clara raises her eyebrow.

'Then considering the timing, I don't understand why Mum just upped and left with me? Was there a reason why we left so suddenly?'

The freshness of this new bottle tastes invigorating, and I can feel my shoulders drop.

'Your mum wasn't coping with Johanna's diagnosis too well. Your dad had died so soon before and…'

'She moved to work for another NHS Trust,' I finish.

Clara twists her necklace again quietly.

'Sorry,' I say. 'I really appreciate you telling me all the details about the accident. But us moving still doesn't make complete sense to me. Johanna is Elise's mother, so why wouldn't she wait a little? And moving to a different NHS Trust doesn't explain why we never saw Johanna again. Never saw *you* again. I didn't even know you existed until this morning.'

'Like I said,' says Clara. 'It was a really difficult time.'

More tiny bubbles erupt inside my mouth and I realise I'm starting to feel a bit woozy.

'But it's not just that, is it, Clara? Because no daughter would just cut their mother off like that. And no mother would just cut their daughter off like that. And sisters? There's got to be something you're not telling me.'

I offer her a top-up and she waves her hand to signal a pass. 'Remi, I've told you as much as I can. But you need to talk to your mother. There are some things I can't…' she pauses. 'You just need to talk to her.'

'That's exactly what the man said.'

'What man? Gerald?' she says in surprise. 'Well, I'm glad he had the strength of mind to suggest that. Because it's true, Remi. This should really come from your mother.'

I take another mouthful of my glass. 'She cut you off too, didn't she? Or was it the other way around?'

'Remi, I really don't feel I can...'

'Clara,' I stop her. My voice is starting to sound slurred. 'I really am grateful that you're here. That we're here, together. But you have to understand, that I'm a twenty-one-year-old woman and I'm getting really sick and tired of being told to ask Mum.'

The words sick and tired shock me and her both. You can tell she's not used to having to deal with a niece, or a daughter, or anyone of the younger generation, actually. Especially not someone who is so unused to drinking that's she's pissed on a few glasses of prosecco.

'What happened that was so bad, so awful, that a whole family, a family who should have been sticking together through the worst of times, decided to split right apart?'

Clara looks at me like she's toying with the idea whether to reveal something. Then she sits forward and puts her elbows on the table to mirror mine.

'A few weeks after the accident, one of the last times I saw you actually.' Clara's Dutch accent means she pronounces weeks like *veeks*. 'We met in the park. Me, you and Elise. You were wearing the cutest Minnie Mouse sunglasses and a flowery hat. She always dressed you so well, she did. I pushed you on the swing, and you wanted to go higher and higher.'

More bubbles float past my lips and into my esophagus.

'Well, Elise had shown me something that day. It was a letter from the Health and Care Professions Council. They were suspending her.'

'Suspending her?'

'She was convinced that her bosses were out to get her. I kept telling her that she was part time, almost a volunteer, really. That she didn't need the job. But she was devastated.'

She didn't need the money, just the power, my new-found acid tongue goes to say.

'But why would they suspend her? And if she didn't need the job, then why did we move? Because I'm not buying the whole *it was a hard time* bullshit.'

Bullshit. That word just flew right out of my mouth.

'And mostly, why did she tell me that Johanna was dead? Why did she make up some cock-and-bull story about a tram in Amsterdam?'

Shit. There goes the *I don't want to tell her the sacred story* nonsense.

'Remi, I…'

'Look. Unless you're willing to tell me what I need to know, then I really need to get back to…'

'There was an investigation,' says Clara quietly. 'And a news article. A few news articles, actually. About your mum.'

'What sort of investigation?'

'Again, this really all needs to come from your…'

'Mum. From my mum. Yep. Well I'm going. Right now. To ask her about the investigation.'

'Remi!' Clara grabs my arm gently. 'Don't. Not like this.'

I stand up to leave.

'I'm going to ask her right now.' Clara doesn't need to know that actually, I have no idea where my mother is.

'You can't,' she challenges, as if she's regretting letting all this slip. 'She'll know that it's me who has told you this. And you can't tell her that you've seen me.'

'Why?'

Clara's face turns ever so slightly scarlet. 'Because you just can't.'

We stand facing each other, and she takes my hands again in hers. I wonder if she can feel the burning of my wrists or if that's something solely for me.

'If you want to know what the problem is. I can show you. But you will need to come to Holland.'

'Well that's decided then,' I reply. 'Holland here I come.'

Chapter Eighteen

'dat is een pleister op een houten been'
That is a bandage on a wooden leg

I wipe my lipstick mark from the top of the bottle of Pinot Grigio, which smells like green apple and pear with – if I'm being honest – a hint of piss. The newsagents hadn't had an awful lot of choice, but then I wasn't really looking for anything other than the cheapest bottle of white wine that they had. After all, students will drink the most urine-like wine if it's less than a fiver a pop. And seeing as I'm now on a serious budget, I'd chosen not to waste cash on wine that was required solely for the purpose of getting drunk. And I wanted to get drunk tonight. Or perhaps I should say, get drunker. Dutch courage is to be my ally if I have the chance to confront Mum.

The beauty of living in the same place for most of your life is that you know all the backstreets well enough to find a good hiding place to drink your wine from a bag in peace. Behind No.77 lies a small green, surrounded by tall Georgian townhouses with large windows that, like an optical illusion, gradually get smaller as they reach the top. Trees line the green separating the houses from the pocket-sized patch of grass, and I'd settled on a slightly damp wooden bench hiding in the shadows, not too remote that I'd be a goner if someone attempted to murder me, but remote enough to make me feel invisible from the glare of the headlights appearing every so often on the road ahead.

The distant hum of the town feels comforting, and the brown paper of the bag is crinkling softly with each sip. I sit for a while, sipping and slurping, until the wind picks up and the sky does its usual thing that it does so very often in England – it threatens to rain. Again.

The sky has turned a deep indigo by now, so I toss my empty bottle triumphantly into a nearby bin and stride towards the river road, the most well-lit of all places and somewhere that's guaranteed to host a steady stream of cars at any time of the night, to follow the water home. There was a big commotion at this part of the river not so long ago. Crowds had gathered on the Mitre bridge and the surrounding walkways, with people all standing and watching a man in the water, struggling to keep his head above the surface. All of those people – there must have been thirty or more – watched, some even *filmed*, yet nobody had attempted to throw him a life ring, even though there were at least three that were accessible metres from the scene. It was a sorry state of affairs that no one tried to help him, said the newspaper the very next day. One onlooker had *thought that he had jumped in on purpose,* they'd reported. Another said he'd *looked like he was just messing about.* Thankfully, officers had arrived, and the lucky man survived to tell the tale, but it could easily have been a very different story.

Is it easier to assume it was all their fault? Is it in us all, innately, to assume that they probably deserved it?

A raindrop hits my shoulder and I start to walk faster, mulling over my meeting with Clara. I can taste petrol and prosecco and frangipani. Was I rude, the way that I swore like that? Was I too much, interrogating her with my questions? I'm not sure how I expected the meeting to go. But I was sharp, that was for sure. A noose pulls tighter around my stomach, encouraging me to retch. The regret starts to bubble inside me, and I scold myself for not softening my words, for not being more measured. I'd enjoyed our time together. In fact, I was thrilled at how she'd been in the flesh. I couldn't have wished for her to be any nicer, really. Except now I might have ruined it. She probably thinks I'm a spoilt little only child brat who is used to getting her own way. And Clara had told me more about my family in thirty minutes than I'd been told in my whole twenty-one years. Disappointed in myself doesn't even cut it.

The fear of having left a bad impression on my newfound auntie lingers the whole way home. It almost replaces the trepidation of walking into Mum, who has not a scooby-doo that I've just had a drink – or five – with her sister. And apparently, I'm not supposed to tell her.

I wonder what could be so bad that Clara begged me not to tell her?

I pull out my phone and check for a message, but there's nothing at all from Mum. *Good,* I slur out loud. *I bet she won't know what's hit her when I walk in smelling of booze.* She's never seen me tipsy before, well, not since I was fifteen, when she told me Johanna's *story*.

She'll know that I'm by the river. If she's looking of course, which she will be. It's a pity that the *find my iPhone* app only applies to my phone and not hers.

I chuckle sadistically to myself as I stumble over a cobblestone. A few days ago, I regarded myself as a well-travelled, sensible and rational young woman, who wouldn't let anyone pull the wool over her eyes that easily. I wouldn't have classed myself as overly gullible or naïve. In fact, as someone who'd had safety first incessantly rammed down her throat, I'd say quite the opposite. Yet here I am, a laughing stock. The cobblestones are laughing at me. The river is laughing at me. *I'm* laughing at me. The trees are swaying back and forth, taunting me. *Did you do this, Remi? Are you a cover for the real truth, that the toddler somehow tore the family apart?*

'Remi!'

Joyce's voice makes me jump.

'Do you know you've just trodden all over my geraniums?'

I peer back through the darkness and can just make out a trail of sorry, squashed plants. 'Oh bugger. I'm sorry, Joyce. I didn't mean to walk on your border.'

'I've got the bowls club coming over next week! What will they all say?'

'Oh, you've got plenty of time to spruce them up before then.' I hiccup as I struggle to get my door key out of my handbag. The poor geraniums in Joyce's garden are probably glad they're dead. 'It's not the end of the world, is it?' I mutter under my breath.

'Have you had a few sherries?' challenges Joyce. 'Because you know your mum wouldn't like that.' Joyce's silver hair that's set in stiff, wiry curls is glinting in the moonlight. Her eyes sit either side of deep glabella lines that are carved solid from decades of frowning.

I could throw these door keys right at her if I wanted to. But I clench them in my fist instead. 'I haven't,' I say. 'But I am an adult. Is there a reason that you need to know what I've had or haven't had tonight, Joyce?'

'Excuse me?' she spits. 'I guess I shouldn't be surprised by that reaction.'

'Now you're being patronising.'

'Well, that is certainly not my intention, Remi. But it would help if you were to just answer the question.'

'And why should I answer your question?' I hiccup again, turning and sashaying towards my front door, just like Clara had done as she'd entered No.77. 'You know, there's a name for nosey neighbours!' I call back. I could start to quite like this take-no-crap version of myself. 'You wouldn't want to get a reputation for spying on people, would you now?'

Joyce places a hand on her chest dramatically. 'Oh, I do hope your mental health is in order, Remi.'

'And what is that supposed to mean?'

'It's depression, you see. I myself have had it. And it can drive very normal people to do things that are extremely out of character. You know, like drinking, darling,' she waggles a finger at me. 'And living way beyond our means.' A sly grin spreads across Joyce's face. She knows about the bailiffs this morning. She would have been watching the whole thing.

Without looking back, I unlock the front door and slam it behind me, pressing my body hard against the wood. That grin of hers makes me want to vomit.

For a moment, I'm so preoccupied with thoughts of crushing more of Joyce's geraniums that I forget Mum might be home. But the bare walls of the entryway are a grim reminder of what I'm about to face. As silently as I can, I tread lightly through the hallway. I glance into the living room, but the lights are off. In fact, all the downstairs lights are off except for a couple of those plug-in nightlights and the bathroom light that stays on permanently. I lay my keys on the kitchen table, realising that the note is still there.

Do not let them in. I will take care of this.

Part of me considers that, if Mum is indeed upstairs, I could sleep on the sofa again and buy myself a few more solitary hours. Time to sober up. But I have the sneaking suspicion that Mum isn't home.

My phone says it's eight o'clock, not late enough for bedtime yet. I tiptoe upstairs, thinking I might catch Mum in the bathroom or dressing room. But she's not there. She's not anywhere. Looking out the window towards the driveway confirms it. I'd been so busy batting Joyce away that I'd failed to notice that her car is not there. She's not home.

Alcohol churns violently in my gut as I slump down on the edge of my bed, calling for Copperfield. *Where is she?* I ask him when he appears on the windowsill. He swats his tail at me with a dark expression in his eyes. He can sense it, I know he can.

The sound of Copperfield's purr fills the quiet bedroom.

Where the hell is she?

Chapter Nineteen

'een stok zoeken om de hond mee te slaan'
Looking for a stick to beat the dog

It's a few minutes before ten on Wednesday morning and I startle as Copperfield meows loudly into my face. He often does this when he wants attention, or if he's hungry, or if Mum's in one of her *schoonheid begint met schoonmaken* – cleanliness starts with cleaning – deep cleaning moods. The early morning sun is filtering through the curtains and I wince crossly at the light, bracing myself for the inevitable onslaught of nausea to accompany my hangover. I've always hated Wednesdays, ever since they made the school day half an hour longer to fit in an extra maths lesson – I mean, who wants an extra maths lesson? But I'm not usually this grizzly. Perhaps it's the relentless throbbing in my head, or my pumping heartbeat that's doing this really aggravating thing where it tries to escape the confines of my chest like it's in an episode of Gladiators.

I swallow, realising that my mouth tastes like the bottom of a hamster cage. Reluctantly, I attempt to release myself from the depths of my sweaty slumber, the soft cotton sheets clinging to my thighs, feeling a bit like a baby's damp wet wipe. I'm hot and clammy and downright disgusting. Copperfield stares at me in the same way that a judgmental child would do when they think that their grown-up carer should know better. I give him a look of *you're right, I should know better* and lift my pink-painted fingernails up to scratch his chin, but he jumps down and scurries away in revulsion.

Breaking free from my cover, I swing my legs over the edge of the bed, reaching for the curtains and yanking them open with an angry tug. I've never understood how blackout curtains get away with calling themselves blackout, when they don't make anything at all black. A fan sits precariously on my bedside table, pushed aside to make way for books and jewellery and snotty tissues that, had it not been for the last few days, would usually have been tidied away. I desperately need a breeze, but even the simple act of pressing the on button feels like a herculean task. *Ugh.* It's been so long, I'd forgotten what the morning after feels like. A cold flannel on the forehead would be heaven right now. And a paracetamol. Or five.

My clothes from last night are strewn all over the floor, and I realise that I'm completely naked except for one lone earring and a full face of smeary make-up. My mind goes back to the reflection in that mirror all those years ago, to the revolting swirl of black, red and orange that was my face.

You stupid, stupid girl.

I think of Holland. Of my *here I come!* declaration to Clara. Had I really never visited the land my mother came from? The land of *de jongen die meer kaas wilde*, the greedy little Dutch boy who always wanted for more cheese. And *de zeemeermin van muiden,* the vain entangled mermaid. The home of the many frightening folktales and figures that filled my childhood. The place that is fifty percent part of me.

And if I really am going there, then how do I do it with little more than one hundred pounds in my bank?

I could call Aoife. Except she's the sort of person who would lend you a fiver and then add a tenner in interest. Per day, probably. And I can't ask her, anyway. I'm not in the habit of asking friends for money. I'd rather poke my eye out with Copperfield's claw.

But what else? The only source of money that I know of in the house is a jar that Mum calls her Pontoon money – we use it to place bets with, when playing blackjack or shithead – but although it looks large, it's mostly full of copper. I'd hazard a guess that it has five or six pounds in it, max. Which is not enough to get me to Holland and back. Or placate the bailiffs when they return.

Where are my *schimmelpennigs*? Why was I so stupid to assume that I never needed to save anything for a rainy day? What type of person does that make me? Have I become the greedy little Dutch boy? Am I the vain entangled mermaid?

There's only one person who might be able to help me now. I need a car, and not one with an almighty clamp around its wheel.

'Hello?'

'Luke,' I say as he picks up. 'I'm so glad you answered. Luke, look, I'm… I'm really sorry about yesterday. But I did it, I actually did it. I messaged her like you said and I met Clara. She's lovely. But I don't know where my mum is and I'm scared I've opened up a can of worms and I was so embarrassing in front of Clara and I behaved like an old fishwife and I bought a bottle of shit wine and I downed it on a spooky park bench and I walked home in the dark alone and I trod all over Joyce's flowers and I told her she was a nosey old so-and-so and I…'

I take a deep breath.

'I'm worried my mum has found out somehow. That I went behind her back. And I think… I think I'm going to be sick.' I clamber over to the en suite just in time for the watery bile to come pouring out of every orifice.

'Remi!' I can hear from the phone. 'Are you OK?'

'Sorry,' I groan into the mouthpiece. 'Oh Christ. Oh God. I was actually just sick on the phone to you.' That has to be the most embarrassing thing I've ever done.

'Look, it doesn't matter,' says Luke. 'Just when you're done being sick, then open the door, will you?'

'Open the door?'

What on earth is he talking about?

'Yes. The front door. Your house is in Copthall Lane, right?'

With bleary eyes, I throw on some clean knickers and my black and white zebra print dressing gown and look out through the window towards the front driveway. I recoil in horror as I see Luke waiting patiently by the front door. Stumbling down the stairs in an excitable panic, I tighten the chord of my gown over my bare chest, the dull ache across my forehead pulsating with every step. *Luke.* Sure, he's seen me in the mornings before, but he's never seen me this stinky and hungover and harassed.

What is he doing here?

My head is spinning so fast that it takes all my concentration to fixate my gaze on the handle. The door creaks loudly as I pull it open, allowing the outdoor air to come rushing in. It almost makes me keel over. The weather is cool and as grey as I feel. It's overcast – as is usual for England most of the time – and there's a whistle to the wind, the dark clouds sweeping swiftly across the sky like they're in a desperate hurry to escape to the Mediterranean. Luke, in contrast, looks bright and cheery in an orange hoody, white shorts and trainers. He's one of those people who will only wear trousers if it's a mandatory requirement, but who can blame him, with long, toned legs like his? He looks majestic, taller than usual, his clean-shaven skin making his baby-face look more baby.

'What... what are you doing here?' I say.

'I know you told me not to come. But I...'

It's clear Luke is distracted by the house and our surroundings. I can tell by the way he's admiring the brickwork, the lush gardens and the massive chunks of metal on everyone's driveways. 'This road, this house... I mean, wow,' he says. 'It's mental around here, like. You didn't tell me you lived in a castle.'

The way he says castle like *cassel* undoes a tight knot in my stomach and I usher him in, glancing around for Joyce, who I know will be on high alert to my activity. I've never been to Luke's family home, but he'd mentioned a run-down housing estate and a neglected town centre a bit like Verborough before. And by the tone of his voice, I can tell that Langswood is very different from where he grew up. I imagine a mid-terraced maisonette with peeling paintwork and a concreted front lawn, where Luke, his parents and his two siblings would sit together around one small table. Where all the spaces and the nooks and crannies would be stuffed full of their most treasured things. I imagine a house not big enough to have lots of empty rooms and lonely corners.

Luke steps onto the entrance rug and suddenly I'm grateful that our house is as big as it is. I leave a space between us, pulling the cord of my dressing gown even tighter over my now cold but clammy torso.

'Did you drive down here? Where did you park?'

'I borrowed Jaz's car. It's parked there,' he points to a pimped-up Honda Civic sat politely on the roadside, right outside Joyce's house. 'Why? Is it alright there?'

It's not really alright there, I think. I'm tempted to ask him to move it further down the road, maybe somewhere not right outside her house. After last night, it will only fuel Joyce and her prying mind. But, I realise, I don't care if she knows about Luke. I don't care if the whole street knows about Luke. I don't even care if Mum knows about Luke! And anyway, I need that car. There are more important things to think about now.

I smile at him weakly. I think I'm still drunk.

'Are you OK?' he says with a concerned look on his face, taking in my disheveled appearance.

'Not really,' I say. 'I feel about as good as I probably look.'

'You're not hungover, are you? I have to say, you look quite cute hungover.'

'Cute?' I reply with a hand held subtly over my mouth, not wanting to poison him with my hamster cage breath. 'Go through there will you? I'll be back in a minute.'

I push Luke towards the living room and scramble back up the stairs into my en suite bathroom, to run the cold tap and splash my swollen face with water. I do a quick brush of the teeth, an underarm wash and then grab a pair of linen trousers and a white shirt from my wardrobe and shove my mid-sized body into them, tying my hair back into a pony and swapping my high-street glasses for my designer ones. Back downstairs I find Luke where I left him, in the living room looking all serious, sat forward on the sofa with his hands clasped together.

'I have to admit, I was shocked when I saw it was you. How did you get my address?'

'Aoife gave it to me,' he says. 'I know it's a bit presumptuous, just turning up at your Mam's house like this… but the way you were on the phone the other day. I know you said you didn't want me here. But I just got the sense that something was wrong.'

I look away, pretending to fluff the cushions.

'Are you moving?' he asks.

'No, why?'

'Oh, just, the house… it's a bit bare, like. Looks like you're getting ready to leave.'

I sense the knot tightening again in my stomach. I really don't have time for twenty questions, and I most definitely don't want to discuss the traumas of the other morning. I'd been working hard to put horrible-man-one and horrible-man-two far into the back of my mind. 'Mum was just… having a clear out,' I say. 'And actually, I'm glad you're here. As there's something I need to ask you.'

'Aye. And what's that,' says Luke.

Except I can't do it. I can't ask to borrow his friend's car. I can't ask for the however much it will cost to get to Holland and back in petrol. Or for money for a hotel. I have never had to ask anyone for money, except Mum of course, and it feels criminal, like asking for a few hundred pounds could be classified as coercive and controlling behaviour, punishable by a lengthy jail term.

'Is it about your gran?'

'Why would you say that?'

'Well, to tell you the truth. There's another reason why I came to see you.' He gestures at me to sit down beside him.

'Do you know Bradley from football? He's on your paramedic course, in the opposite class to you, I think. Anyway, yesterday a few of us were at his place studying together, and he told me he'd been researching failings in the ambulance service for his dissertation. He had a case study on his desk, like a *what not to do in this scenario* type thing. The case study included a statement from some anonymous guy.'

'Right,' I say. 'Well, we do sometimes use case studies in our lessons, I suppose.'

'Yeah. But what was weird, is that when I asked him about it, he said that his lecturer had given it to him, but with clear instructions to keep it to himself. He specifically told him not to show you, Remi. He actually named you, like. Which I thought was really odd. So I sneaked a picture of it when he wasn't looking.'

He takes his phone out of the pocket of his shorts and shows me his screen. There is a picture of a printed document, a bit blurry, but the words are legible. I zoom in to read.

This is the statement of (name deleted), an emergency medical technician, dated (day and month deleted) 2005, in reference to the case of an individual who we shall call 'Paramedic A', who has been accused of a serious breach of protocol and patient care.

At approximately 9.45pm, I was dispatched to attend to a fifty-three-year-old female patient in (undisclosed location). I was provided with very little details in terms of what might have occurred prior to my attendance.

I met Paramedic A upon arrival. I was ordered to stay near the ambulance, whilst the paramedic in question went to the patient. From the outset, the paramedic's tone was unnecessarily harsh and dismissive. She crouched down in the road next to the pavement and I remember her saying, 'For crying out loud. What the hell's wrong with you?'. Those were her exact words. The torch she was holding had revealed the lady's matted hair and her dirtied face.

The lady made a deep, gurgling sound. She slurred 'I'm OK,' or something to that effect. Then, she writhed around on the concrete, struggling to get on all fours. Her clothes were covered in mud and gravel and her hands were scratched and bloody. Her mobile phone was laying a few feet away from her, face down, on the grass verge.

Paramedic A told the patient to get up. She tucked the torch under her arm, reaching towards the phone and picking it up. Then, she said it again. 'Get up. Now.' The lady attempted to follow Paramedic A's orders, but as she struggled to lift her head, she fell further towards the floor. Paramedic A told her to get up again, louder this time, in a tone that said she wouldn't repeat it.

The lady mumbled into her chest. She muttered something like, 'It's just...' and then she complained of what she said felt like a crackling sensation under her skin, as she attempted to swallow down a frothy red liquid that I could see was bubbling inside her mouth. 'It's blood,' she said quietly. 'I can taste it.' By this time, I was getting very worried for the patient. But Paramedic A took the lady's arm and aggressively pulled her towards her, to a standing position, so that they were now side by side in the road. It wasn't difficult for the paramedic to lift her, for the lady was only a slight little thing. Paramedic A's behaviour was extremely unprofessional and unkind. I could only describe it as though she were taunting her. 'Just what?' she asked accusingly, as she dragged the lady towards the ambulance. The lady winced as she clutched onto her arm. Her ankles were giving way underneath her. 'Woah, there,' the lady said. 'You're hurting me.'

'Walk with me,' Paramedic A instructed impatiently. The lady attempted a step forward and wobbled. She moaned something quietly, something muddled and incoherent. Her head was bowed, and her tangled blonde hair was falling into her face. But instead of slowing down, the paramedic started to move faster, forcing the lady along with her. 'Walk with me,' she ordered. The lady had walked then, leaning into Paramedic A for support. I was willing her not to let go, as I knew for certain that she'd fall if she did. As they reached the back of the ambulance, the lady let out a long, pained wail. I dropped my clipboard then and stepped forward in a hurry. 'Here, let me help you,' I shouted.

But Paramedic A had gestured at me to move. 'You can help by moving out of the way,' she said. I did as I was told, not knowing what else to do. I just remember biting down on my tongue hard as I stood silently, watching. So much so that my tongue was bleeding afterwards.

When they eventually got inside the ambulance, she let go of the lady's arm and pushed her forcefully onto the observation bed. 'Sit there,' she said. The lady's face crumpled, and I could tell she was finding it hard to sit. She opened her mouth wide to breathe, groaning as she tried to readjust herself on the stretcher. I jumped inside and tried to reason with the paramedic, urging her to start tests and administer treatment, but she totally ignored my advice. I felt helpless and extremely concerned for the patient's welfare. The paramedic started shouting then. 'Stop moving, will you?' she said. 'Stay there!'

With the lady's Nokia phone in one hand, the paramedic searched slowly through the patient's contacts, like she was looking for someone in particular. When she found what she needed, she pressed call. I could tell someone had answered, as I could hear his muffled voice at the end of the line. Her tone was thorny and cold. 'I have your wife here,' she said. 'I have her here, in the back of my ambulance.' He must have said something in reply, something like, 'are you sure?' because she said, 'Oh, I'm sure alright,' and then she closed the ambulance doors and turned to look at the patient, whose bloodshot eyes were moving slowly around in her head.

The authorities will have the recording, I assume. But the way she said it, it was like she was trying to make a point. She was acting as though it was all the patient's fault. She told the person on the phone that his wife was drunk. 'As drunk as a lord,' were her exact words. She accused the patient of wasting our time. It was strange, considering that my first conclusion was not that this patient was drunk. It is my opinion that I do not believe the patient was under the influence of alcohol at all.

Once she'd finished the phone call, all I wanted to do then was to get the patient to hospital. So, I opened the doors and climbed into the driver's seat, beginning the twenty-minute journey, where, shortly after our arrival, the lady had a cardiac arrest.

PART TWO - HOLLAND

Chapter Twenty

'voor iemand de kastanjes uit het vuur halen'

To pull the chestnuts out of the fire for someone

Mum was a dancer when she was younger. I can tell by the way her calf muscles look when she reaches for the best glasses, high up on the kitchen shelf. And, by the way she moves around the house in a deliberate way, so gracefully, landing every step with a soft foot and not a hard one. Her toes have these horrible, bulbous bunions on them. But that's the only horrible part about the way she looks. She has the hair of Medusa, and the beautiful face of the Greek goddess before Athena turned her into a hideous monster. Sometimes, when she thinks I'm not looking, I catch her fingers tracing the air like she's remembering a routine.

We've never danced together, there is rarely music at our *kleine bijeenkomsts*, and I was never encouraged to join a dance class or a theatrical club, even though lots of my friends did. I wonder why, now, as I watch a jumbo jet crossing the clear blue sky, trying its hardest to disturb the serenity. Its white linear vapour trail follows obediently behind as I try to guess its destination. Greece? Japan? America? I wonder about all the places that Johanna would have visited to dance. Would I have been a good dancer too?

My head rests heavily on the seatbelt as I hum the tune of Tiny Dancer, which is playing quietly on the stereo, and gradually my breathing slows. When I wake, the clouds have come over and I realise where I am – sat in the front passenger seat of Jaz's car, next to Luke, driving through what looks to be a Dutch village called Veldhaven according to the car's interactive map.

For a moment, I'd forgotten that we were on the way to see Clara. And a grandfather, according to my newfound auntie. I try to erase an image of me rooting around in Mum's private document box, but it's playing on my stomach. I really hate that I did that. I could have stuffed the title deeds back in Mum's box unread and gone back to my typical ceiling staring, the thing that seems to fix everything. Except the ceiling won't solve a debt on our heads. Or a mother that's gone missing. Luke's picture of some statement that no one wants me to see had forced my hand, and it turns out that asking for something like borrowing a bit of money and a car comes quite naturally when you're desperate.

I need to know what everyone has been hiding from me.

And more importantly, why?

'What is she doing, Luke? Just upping and leaving and then ignoring me like this? Is she doing this on purpose? Is she trying to torture me?' I'd said as we'd been getting ready to leave.

'Do you think we need to call the police?' had been his reply. He'd been less than impressed when I'd told him about the visit from the debt collectors – something I felt I couldn't hide any longer – and I'd found myself getting defensive.

'No,' I'd insisted. 'The last thing I want is to involve the authorities and have us being the talk of the town. Again. Mum would absolutely hate that, and we all know who would love it. It's totally out of character, though. I mean, I get that we had that argument. And we don't argue that often. Or should I say, I don't often argue back.'

It's true – we rarely have a loud shouty argument like we had the other night. Just one-sided disagreements that end in me apologising and Mum tutting and walking away. The next day, she'll do something extravagant – buy me something lovely or take me somewhere nice – in an effort to prove that she is a nice mother after all, and perhaps I was being an ungrateful little child. And perhaps I should think about that.

'But is our argument the reason why she's not come home? Do you think she's intentionally avoiding me? Either this Gerald guy turning up has really hit a nerve… or it's the money thing… or, she's found out about me meeting with Clara. Oh God, Luke. Do you think she knows about Clara?'

'I'm sure she doesn't. But she'll find out eventually, Remi. You've got to be prepared for that.'

I'd realised then how unprepared I was for any of this. How unprepared I was for any of the more difficult parts of life. If this is what real life is like, of course. If real life is just constant handfuls of crap being lobbed at you from different directions, crap that seeps into your pores, crap that you can't wipe off. I'd been training to attend to these handfuls of crap on a daily basis as a paramedic, except that they were happening to other people, not to me. Had I assumed that crap only happens to other people? To people who don't live in Langswood? Or that I had this innate ability to avoid it if I chose?

Had I really been that ignorant of it all?

I can taste the bland, insipid chicken soup I had at the service station for lunch in the hollows of my cheeks. I try to stretch but I can't seem to relax my shoulders, which are up by my ears, stiff and locked in a hunch position. I decide to look out the window instead, to take in the panorama of the Dutch countryside that is stretching out for miles around us. My only experience of the Netherlands had been the proverbs painting, with its brown houses and bleak landscape filled with funny-looking figures. Yet the real Netherlands looks nothing like this to me. It's flat, that's one rumour that's true. Is flat landscape boring? Better than looking at one side of a hill. And it's definitely not bleak. The countryside unfolds like a carpet, the empty meadows stretching far and wide until they reach different wooden structures. The sky here feels bigger than back home. I almost feel free.

I open the window, expecting to smell what calm smells like. I would like to feel calm, but a huge blue bottle fly rushes in, and I have the sudden urge to throttle it. I want to bash it and hit it and crush it and then toss it out of the car where it came from. But when it's landed on the dashboard and the time comes to fulfil my fantasy, I find that I can't do it. I leave it to Luke to shoo it out of the car. *You lucky, bloody fly*, I think. *How do you escape so lightly?*

I fold my arms crossly while Luke drives in silence, with the quiet sounds of the radio whining in the background. The Dutch landscape is hopeful, except the wind whistles miserably as we pass. Now, the clouds look furious. Am I as angry as they look? Is everyone angry today? Is Mum angry with me? Am I the reason for everyone's anger?

Or is it really all to do with Johanna?

'Go faster.' I tell Luke. 'We need to get there faster.'

I feel satisfied when I see his foot pressing down harder on the accelerator, and soon we are driving through a town, where there are tall houses for the tall people who inhabit them. The tall houses make up for the horizontal land, I decide. Some houses feel as though they are leaning ever so slightly towards us, like they're wanting to whisper us a secret or two, and in the windows, I can just make out lamps and bookcases and the occasional sleepy cat watching the world go by. I imagine steep, vertigo-inducing stairs and rooms painted in deep reds and warm ochres. I'm imagining the conversations that might be going on in these houses as Luke nudges me to tell me that my phone is ringing.

'Aren't you going to answer it then?' he says, pressing his thumbs on the steering wheel as though he was imprinting them in clay.

'Oh, gosh,' I mutter, reaching down into the footwell and rummaging urgently through my brown Coach leather handbag, the one that Mum got me for Christmas to match my brown Coach boots. I press the green tick before it registers whose name is on the screen.

'Mum?' I say after a while. 'Mum, is that you?'

'Remi,' she says in a voice that sounds quiet and distant. 'Remi, I...'

'Hello?' I repeat, but the line is crackling, and I curse as I realise I can't make out any more of what she's saying. 'Sorry, Mum? Can you hear me? Mum?'

I pull my phone away from my ear to check that I have a signal, but as I do, the line goes dead. And it's then that I realise she can locate me, on the find my iPhone app. She can see that I'm in Holland.

I could have turned it off, but I didn't.

'She knows!' I say to Luke. 'Oh my God, she knows.'

Luke throws me a surprised look, and then grabs his phone from the central compartment and chucks it onto my lap. 'It's OK,' he says. 'Try calling her back from this.'

'Thank you,' I say, my hands trembling as I start to punch in the numbers that I need. But when I press call, her phone goes straight to voicemail.

And then a message appears on my screen.

I am fine. I will be back in a few days. But when you get there. There is something I need you to do for me.

Chapter Twenty-One

'men kan geen vuur in de ene hand en water in de andere dragen'

One cannot carry fire in one hand and water in the other

'We're almost here,' says Luke, leaning forward to read the badly weathered road sign. It's in Dutch of course, but I can just make out the words *mile* and *flower picking*. Thank goodness I wasn't named Gerte or Femke, or I'd look a right fool for not being able to string the simplest of Dutch sentences together. Good job that, according to Mum, the Dutch speak better English than we do. Clara can most definitely speak excellent English, most probably from the years of living in the UK.

Luke sniffs quietly, a distinctive sniff that he's done at least fifty times since we left for Holland. 'Are you feeling better, now you've heard from your Mam, like?' he says, and then he does it again, and I wonder how I'd not detected it before, and if perhaps I'm not the only one who suffers with repetitive bodily actions. It's not annoying, but it's like that thing that once you see, you can't unsee.

'I don't think I'm feeling any different, really,' I say. Which is true. 'I mean, she's alive, at least. But then I never assumed that she wasn't.'

He twiddles his thumbs to bring the colour back to them. 'Still no guesses as to where she is, then?'

'No. No guesses at all.'

'And what did the message say?'

'Just that she knows I'm on the way to see Clara. No *how are you*, or *so sorry I've been ignoring your calls*. Just *there's something you need to do for me*.'

Luke takes my hand now and squeezes it softly as we pass a flock of sheep, grazing contently. He looks as though he wants to say something, but perhaps he doesn't know quite what to say. I decide to pull my hand away, and busy myself cleaning my glasses on the corner of my shirt.

'I'm sorry,' I blurt out. 'I should never have said you couldn't come to Langswood.'

I want to say that I didn't think he'd care that much when I said no. And that I never expected him to come, anyway. And that I'd wondered if he just felt sorry for me. Or was using me for sex. Or for lifts to football. Or for the fact that my mum has all this money. Or, should I say, had all this money.

But that would all sound a bit silly considering that he'd agreed to drive me all the way to another country – he'd got a mate to bring down his passport – in a car that he'd borrowed from Jaz, *and* is using his student loan money to pay for the petrol and anything else that we need along the way.

'You didn't want me to meet your mam, did you?' he says.

'Why do you say that?'

'I can tell. Except it's probably easier if you just accept that your mam — and in my case, my dad, too — is a disaster. It's a lot easier for me, anyway. And I really wouldn't care, Remi. Problem families are my forte.'

'Look,' I say, sucking in my cheeks. 'If this is going to work.

You, driving me here like this. Then we have to be on the same page, Luke. My mum is a lot of things… but she's not a *disaster*, OK?'

'Whatever you say. But can you please understand that I'm not just here to drive you, Remi? I'm coming into Clara's house with you. You know that, right?'

Damn it. Of course I didn't know that.

'Yes. Of course I knew that,' I say.

Luke nods suspiciously, and I wish I'd have insisted that actually, I'm an independent woman, one who doesn't need a chaperone. The last thing I need is someone else making me feel like a child.

Or perhaps I'm being too harsh. Maybe I do need someone to shut down my *I'm perfectly fine on my own* narrative? After all, isn't that what all the Hollywood girls want? Someone to put their finger to their lips and say *shut the fuck up, I'm coming, whether you like it or not*?

Our eyes focus back on the road, where we make a left turn and then follow along the canal through a village. Shabby-looking bicycles have been left scattered along the streets, with baskets ready to be filled with bread and flowers. Or perhaps young children. Except there are containers for that, large rectangular containers attached to the front of some of the bikes, old enough to look like they belong in the second-hand shop at the local dumping site. Small brick houses with steep, triangular gabled roofs sit on one side of the canal, while expansive green fields fill the space opposite. I can see windmills in the distance, standing tall over the open land, and the tall spire of what looks like an old church. As we turn another corner, we pass a tulip field that could only be described as idyllic, with flowers of all the colours of the rainbow, and I realise why Clara had chosen to move back here. The Netherlands is not the topsy-turvy world that I'd imagined. It's actually quite beautiful.

Another canal appears and I see Clara and Elise, building little boats from sticks and leaves and running along the bank to watch the water carrying them fast away. I see them skating on the ice in the winter. Our car lurches forward and I continue to stare at the water, which is murky enough that you wouldn't want to paddle in it. Two ducks bob along, their brood of golden-coloured ducklings following in an almost perfect line behind them. I wonder how long it will take them to break the chain that is family. Days, weeks, months? Or are they in it for life?

'Look,' says Luke, pointing at an ornate ceramic nameplate adorned with old-fashioned wildflowers that reads *Bloemenhuisje.* We're here. We're at Clara's house. The Van Tam family cottage.

Except it's not a cottage. From afar, it looks more like a manor house, or one of those estates where they film things like the Traitors or Made in Chelsea or some grand murder-mystery type programme. Our tyres kick up gravel as Luke turns the wheel sharply and accelerates onto a pathway with a private property sign fastened to the gatepost. Probably wise to have that there, as it looks like somewhere that you'd burgle, if you were indeed into that sort of thing. The sun is out now, the last of the daylight showing itself almost like Clara has arranged it on cue, and the whole place comes to life like a beautiful Instagram story. It is blooming just like the tulips were in the fields that surround us.

The honey-coloured stone that encases the building is bathed in a warm, orange glow. Its picture-perfect thatched roof, with two symmetrical slopes on each side, is fringed with moss and wildflowers, and its windows are framed by perfectly worn wooden shutters painted a soft shade of blue. The soft shade of blue shall be my next bedroom wall colour, I decide. Wherever that bedroom might be.

We park on the empty driveway and step out of the car, where it's quiet except for the gravel and the soft creaking of a windmill in the distance. Clara appears from the front door, dressed in a soft pink shirt dress and waving to us excitedly like she's been waiting for this moment for a very long time. Her skin tone and the shape of her eyes and mouth look even more like Mum's than I'd first realised. Her wave is even the same. I'm relieved that the guilt of being close to her seems to be reducing the more I see her.

She runs over to our car like an adored puppy let off its leash. We exchange a hug and I introduce Luke – who I know she assumes is my boyfriend judging by the sly grin on her face – and then we follow Clara through a charming well-stocked front garden and down a pathway of weathered stones to the front door. We wait patiently as she opens the huge thing – pushing and pulling a few times until she eventually manages to prize it from its doorframe – and then we duck as we step under a beam into a traditional downstairs boot room. I'm hit by the strong scent of aged wood and farmyard animals. It's not musty, but it's a smell that gets right under your nose, like the prawns from the sandwiches that had been left in the utility. I decide that I won't let it ruin this beautiful old house, and that I shall just have to accustom myself to it. I breathe in and out a few times to prove it.

The boot room leads into a large, grand kitchen, made softer by farmhouse chairs and stripy cushions tied around the seats. Dark wooden beams that look like they've seen better days cover the low ceilings.

'*Komen*,' says Clara in her interesting accent. Her Dutch is loud and a bit phlegmy, like she's hacking up spit, but in a ladylike way. She gestures through to a living room, or a snug maybe, adorned with expensive-looking vintage furniture, with elaborate silk rugs covering creaky floorboards. Clara sits herself down on a flowery pouffe with tassels around the base.

'Sit, *sit*. You must be tired after your long drive.'

I yawn, almost on cue. It has taken almost five and a half hours to get here.

'Thank you,' I say, handing her a small bunch of flowers that we'd picked up at the service station where we'd got the soup.

The flowers look far less impressive than any of the ones we've seen in the passing fields or indeed, in her front garden, but she looks pleased, and Luke smiles as we take a seat together on a small, upholstered sofa. I find myself hoping that she doesn't offer me tea.

She doesn't. Instead, she starts talking about dogs and the fact that she'd had to put down two almost identical-looking cocker spaniels this morning. One was riddled with cancer, the other had collapsed after eating something poisonous in the woods. Discarded drugs, the distraught owner reckoned, who was adamant he was calling the *politie*. Both beautiful dogs were no older than four. It's part of the job, she says, but putting something to sleep, especially something with so much life left to live, never gets any easier. She tries not to remember their names.

We talk about Luke's teenage spell at the Manchester United Academy, Clara's love life, or, in her words, her lack of one, and my borderline obsession with animal print. Everything that we didn't come here to discuss. I wonder if I should remind Clara of our contract. That I'd come to this house if she told me how the accident changed everything. But it's clear that, for now, she's avoiding the topic of family. I suspect that she's nervous, judging by the way her gaze keeps flickering away from us and around the room. Meanwhile, I'm avoiding asking Clara what I really want to know. And, what Mum wants, too.

There's something I need you to do for me.

'Would you like a beer?' asks Clara, clutching onto a can. 'I hope you don't mind Grolsch. It is either that or Heineken. Or Amstel. We only drink Dutch here. Seeing as our ancestors were brewers.'

So it's true. A simple Van Tam Google search had revealed all I needed to know about my great, great grandparents. If only it had been that easy with Johanna.

'Brewers, really?' says Luke. 'That's pretty cool, like.' He takes the can and flicks it open, then takes a long sip of his beer, and I wonder if he does indeed think it's cool, or if he's just saying that to impress her. Mum told me that's what men do. They say things they don't mean to impress you.

'Yes,' says Clara. 'Apparently, it all started with a former spice trader who returned to Amsterdam with a bold vision – to create a beer that captured the exotic tastes and flavours of his travels. The family expanded the brewery to Rotterdam and introduced a more – how do you say it – a more palatable lager like the Bavarian-style beers that we see today. They sold the brewery before Johanna was born to a rival company for a very large sum, but it wasn't without its problems. There were rumours they were investigated for illicit absinthe production, or something like that.' She takes a long sip of her lager. 'But what do we care, hey? It made us millionaires, didn't it?'

I glance at Luke, surprised that Clara would put it this way. I feel obliged to put my beer can in the air, in an agreeable way. I will not tell Clara about the house, or the bailiffs, or the fact that Mum and I are quite clearly not millionaires. Not anymore, anyway. Instead, I decide that it's a good time to address one of my questions.

'If our family were brewers,' I say. 'Then why does Elise hate people drinking so much?'

Clara looks surprised by my question.

'It's just,' I continue. 'I noticed in the picture of Johanna that you showed me that she was holding a bottle of wine. I guess… it's very different to Mum, that's all.'

'Oh,' says Clara. 'I think I know what you mean.' Her tone is soft, but with an undercurrent of despair that she's doing a terrible job of disguising. I wonder then, just how much she misses her sister.

'It's… complicated,' she says at last. The heavy silence that comes next speaks volumes about the loss she must feel in her life. Perhaps she's felt the same emptiness that I've felt all these years. Perhaps she lays staring at the walls like I do, imagining the living ghosts of her past.

I nod in disappointment, aware that my expectations for my newly discovered family member are unreasonably high. She might be trying to help me piece our family back together, but I've known her for less than forty-eight hours, and I know better than to ask a personal question like *was your mother a borderline alcoholic or not?* Except she must know what I'm thinking, because she answers that exact question without me saying a word out loud.

'Johanna didn't get drunk often. She was a free spirit, a Dutch girl at heart who believed that everything was perfectly fine in moderation. She never got mad at us for drinking as teenagers. In fact, she encouraged it, sometimes. *Better to do it at home, where I can keep an eye on you,* she'd say. There were times when she would get a bit, how do you say it? Merry? Sorry, my English is not what it used to be. But nothing different than what most people do.' She throws me a kind look and I force a weak smile in return.

'There was this one time I remember, when we were picking her up from an evening dance competition. It was in England, we were all there, waiting in the car for ages… but she turned up so merry, that our Pa locked the passenger door and wouldn't let her in the front seat. He was furious with her for making us wait so long, and they had this blazing row… and then he told her she could walk home. Well, she turned up at home two hours later, with scratches all over her from where she'd fallen into the bushes. I mean, it could have been pretty bad, but the sight of her, it was funny, to be honest. Elise took a picture as evidence of the state of her. The next day, she laughed and laughed about it. Her friend Maureen thought it was the best story ever and brought it up at nearly every party we had after that. Pa even learned to laugh about it, too. But Elise, well, she never forgave Johanna for it. She said it was a careless thing to do.'

My mind goes back to Langswood, to Mum's story. *Carelessness is why we are alone.*

Clara pushes a loose curl behind her ear. 'I know, I know. In hindsight, it wasn't the best thing for Pa to do. Elise should have been furious at Pa for driving off and leaving Johanna like that. But Elise never gave Pa a hard time, only Johanna. Whether it's fair or not… I think kids just have higher expectations for their mothers. And your mum, well. She doesn't forgive and forget easily.'

She leans forward and puts a comforting hand on mine, as is Clara's usual touchy-feely style. 'If she ever gave you a hard time about drinking, I'm sure she was just scared of what it might do to you. Like any parent would be. Elise was always… cautious, would probably be the best word to describe her. The opposite to Johanna, really. Has she ever shown you the Dutch painting by Pieter Bruegel the Elder?'

I pull back, surprised that she would mention the painting.

'Oh, yes,' I say. 'My dad bought her a huge framed replica to hang in our entryway. It was a push present apparently, her reward for birthing me.'

Clara's blue eyes crumple at the corners slightly. 'Go on,' she says.

'Well, it's always freaked me out a bit, if I'm honest. But Mum has always been obsessed with that painting. And, with those Dutch proverbs, or whatever they are supposed to be.'

'Always,' agrees Clara. 'Though I've never felt a connection to them, personally.'

'Who is Pieter Bruegel the Elder?' asks Luke politely from his seat, as if he should contribute something to our conversation. 'Should I have heard of him?'

'Bruegel was a sixteenth-century painter, most famous for his landscapes and peasant scenes, but The Topsy Turvy World, or the Upside-Down World as it used to be called in English, focuses on people, on normal village life. It is supposed to show the stupidity and foolishness of humans, told through over a hundred proverbs which he has drawn as villagers, acting these famous sayings out.'

'You mean like *never believe someone who carries fire in one hand and water in the other*? Or *he who eats fire, craps sparks*?' I say.

Clara wags her finger at me knowingly. 'Exactly. My favourite is the symbol of a globe standing on its head. To show that we live in a world where nothing is as it should be. It really is a fascinating painting.'

A weird one, I think.

'You're right,' I say instead. 'And proverbs are important, right?'

'Well, proverbs can be useful,' Clara nods. 'Except there's always the danger that they can oversimplify complex situations, and lead to misguided actions if blindly followed without considering context.' The room falls silent and Clara's face drops. 'My apologies. Sometimes my English can be a bit formal. My father ensured that I learnt the proper way. Anyway, what I'm saying is, is that they're generalisations. And generalisations can be dangerous. They can stop you from having an open mind.'

'Sounds a bit like my dad,' says Luke. 'He sees the world in black and white, does Dad. Like when I told him I was going to study marketing at uni. *What do you want to do that namby-pamby course for?* is what he said. His idea of success was to become a carpenter or a mechanic... not someone who designs brochures and eats sushi for lunch.'

Clara forces a laugh. As she turns her head, I notice a Gucci earring in the distinctive shape of a G. She replaces her can of beer and offers Luke another, which he declines on the grounds that he's my designated driver.

'Would you like another, Remi?' she asks. I shake my head and take a slow sip of the full can in my hand. Dutch beer is stronger than English beer, Mum had warned me.

'Are you sure? It's almost the witching hour, after all,' she says, flicking another loose curl out of her face. 'Growing up, my favourite time of day was the witching hour, as Johanna would call it. Around five o'clock, she'd have a glass of wine and put some music on and we'd all dance around the kitchen table. It was her happiest time. If it was summertime, then even better. She was a retired dancer by then. She'd call me over and brush my hair with her hands, like I was her adored puppy. She'd do that even when I was in my twenties, even though I'm taller than her and my hair had turned from a silky mane into a wiry mess. I never worried about her drinking. I've never worried about my mother Johanna in my life.'

I watch as she peels open her can with her exquisitely painted fingernail. 'The only person I've ever worried about is Elise. And of course, you, my dear Remi. I've often worried about you.'

'Me?' I say. 'Us? Why?'

Clara's curly hair is now tucked neatly behind her ears, and I notice for the first time that she has a line that runs down the middle of her front tooth, like a tiny flaw in her otherwise perfect smile.

'I mean, I probably shouldn't tell you this,' she says. 'Of course, I don't like to talk badly about anyone. Especially not your mother.'

Luke glances at me in a concerned way.

'No, please,' I say. 'I've never heard anyone talk to me about my mother, good or bad. But, tell me. Is it really all that bad?'

Clara's pause goes on for a second too long, and then she lets out an almighty laugh. 'Oh, Remi, you are just as funny as I thought you'd be! Luke – is she always as adorable as this?' Her dress moves like the current as she glides over towards the windows to close the blinds on the evening sun.

Luke sniffs another of his funny little sniffs, and then he laughs loudly along with her. He really is trying to impress her, it seems.

'Elise was… how do I put it? Bossy, is that the word? Yes. She was extremely bossy when we were growing up. And I was what you'd call the follower sister.'

Bossy? My mother? Never! I almost say. But I hold it all in, as I should do, of course, in allegiance with my closest family member. Even if she has lied to me. Multiple times, it seems.

'Oh, it was all my fault, mind you. I was happy to follow. When we were small, even though we're not twins or anything, the head teacher of our school strongly advised our parents to separate us and put us in different schools, to allow us to flourish as individuals. That's what they do with all the siblings who are close in age, they'd said. But Johanna was adamant that we stay together. We were better together, she'd insisted. We complemented each other. We came as a package. For all those years, I couldn't escape the sister thing. And somehow, even though I came into the world a year before her, Elise swiftly emerged as the dominant one, finishing my sentences, deciding what we'd wear and who we'd be friends with. Defending me against bullies at school. What I didn't realise is that, whilst she was shouldering it all on the outside, she was struggling on the inside.'

'What do you mean, she was struggling?'

'Let's just say, I've always imagined Elise with a permanent set of invisible tinted glasses. Perhaps she was born with them, who knows? Not rose-tinted ones, but grey, smeary ones. Ones that need a good clean. If we see yellow, Elise sees mustard. If we see orange, she sees brown. Does that make sense, Remi?'

I nod, realising what Clara is saying. She's saying that my mother is a pessimist. She's a cynic. A doubter. A worrier. Which means that she struggles to accept that the world is not against her.

'But was she OK?' I say. Had I ever asked Mum if she was OK? 'Perhaps she was just scared,' I say out loud.

'Of what?' asks Clara.

Scared of judgmental neighbours. Scared of dying men. Scared of perfect mothers and of perfect sisters, I think. *Scared of a daughter who sometimes hates her.* There are so many things to be scared about.

'There was nothing to be scared about,' says Clara. 'We had a wonderful upbringing, Remi. Some of my best memories are of me and Elise imagining ourselves as Disney princesses. We'd grow our hair long and swap costumes and share shoes. I was usually Ariel and she was Cinderella, and Johanna was always Aurora.'

'But anxiety can stem from many things,' says Luke. 'And being a worrywart doesn't make you a sceptic.' He nudges me, as though he's aiming that at me, and I scowl at him crossly.

'You are right,' says Clara. 'So, you're not just a pretty face, then,' she smiles at Luke.

He smiles back and I can sense a bond growing between them. I should feel pleased, but every time Clara talks negatively about my mother I get this horrible feeling of betrayal inside me. I was not there, during their childhood and therefore I shall not take sides.

'Well, I made you a promise, didn't I, Remi?' Clara sways over to the living room door. 'I have things I promised to show you, I know. So. Shall we?'

We rise to our feet, placing our cans on the table in front of us. 'Do you think now is a good time to tell Clara that you don't know where your mam is?' whispers Luke.

'No,' I hiss. 'Not yet, anyway.'

We follow Clara through the living room and out to the large glass conservatory, which has a much more modern feel to it than the rest of the house and wonderful views out to the fields. The conservatory is filled with rubber fig leaves and towering ferns. Clara points out to the garden, towards a small, converted outbuilding. 'There,' she says.

I glance at Luke, not quite sure what she's getting at.

'There's a workshop above the garage. It's mine and Elise's

study. I used it to store all my veterinary papers, and Elise, all her university coursework. And some other bits and bobs, you know. Perhaps you might find something in there.'

My eyes scan the old building. The way she says the word *perhaps* makes me feel suspicious.

'What might I find in there, Clara?' I ask. I feel bolder after a few sips of Dutch beer. 'What's going on?'

Luke stands protectively between us. Perhaps the beer has got to him, too.

'I just think, Remi. That after all these years, now that you've realised…'

She stops and I wonder if she's having trouble translating.

'Well, I just really do think that you deserve to know,' she says, as she hands me a small set of keys. 'It'll be inside the desk, the mahogany one, with brass handles and drawers on the left-hand side. Open the top drawer and there's a red folder. It will be in there.'

Luke flashes me a strange sideways glance, then he takes my hand and we walk slowly together towards the study. Luke's palm feels as clammy as mine.

'What the…' I whisper to him, unsure how to finish the sentence. My other hand goes to my neck, feeling for the smooth outline of a small, wooden circle. What secrets are to be found in the Van Tam family outbuilding that, apparently, I deserve to know?

'Whatever it is, I'm here, OK,' he says.

Touch wood touch wood touch wood touch wood.

As we reach the garage, we place one of the keys in the lock and force open the door to reveal some stairs. We tread the stairs carefully, until right in front of us, appearing almost as if in a film set, we see the mahogany desk that Clara was talking about. The old desk with its rich wood is marred with scratches and ink stains, and dust flies around the room as I cough heavily. I imagine Mum here as a child, her small hands running along these very walls, her feet treading the creaking floorboards. I can see her and Clara imagining it as a den, or a fairy house, or a pirate ship. I can see her sulking up here when things weren't going her way. I can see her crying up here in secret like I would do in the utility room at home.

I inhale sharply and let go of Luke's hand, stepping closer to the desk, reaching out to touch the tarnished brass handle of the top drawer. The smell of animals and old wood is even stronger in here and I'm having a hard time trying to alter its composition inside my nose, from a terrible smell to one that I can endure for more than thirty seconds. I rest my nostrils and start to breathe in and out through my mouth, as though I'm a poorly person who is lacking in oxygen. I can tell that Luke is doing this too by the heavy sound of his breathing.

Pulling the drawer out slowly, I see an instant flash of red. The folder is there, as Clara said it would be. It feels heavy, like it's full of papers, and I wonder whether I'll have to sift through documents to reach what she wants me to see. But as soon as I open it, I realise that won't be the case. What I'm looking for is right here in front of me.

There are two newspaper cuttings, stuck together on a single piece of A4 paper. As my eyes scan the date, I can see they're from November 2005. Eighteen years ago. I focus on the first one and read.

The Telegraph

Paramedic banned for misdiagnosing 'hit and run' motorbike crush victim

A Cambridge woman with near-fatal injuries was misdiagnosed as 'trashed' by a paramedic, who turned out to be her own daughter.

At a hearing on Wednesday held at the Health and Care Professions Council (HCPC) in London, paramedic Elise Van Tam was found guilty of five counts of misconduct for the mistreatment of her mother, Johanna Aaldenberg, and handed a three-year suspension. Ms Aaldenberg suffered a brain injury, tears to her liver, a collapsed lung, 12 broken ribs, a broken ankle and fractured vertebrae after a motorbike ran over her while she was collapsed in the middle of Petworth Close in Cambridge in July of this year.

After an anonymous call to the emergency services, an ambulance arrived to find Ms Aaldenberg crawling around injured on a grass verge. Elise Van Tam, the lead paramedic attending the scene, accused her mother of being under the influence before forcefully walking her into an ambulance.

The list of failings found by the HCPC includes neglecting to properly assess Ms Aaldenberg's injuries, taking her to a general hospital as opposed to a specialist trauma unit, failing to make any sort of diagnosis and providing an inaccurate statement to police. These failings led to Ms Aaldenberg being left on a stretcher outside of the Fenland Hospital accident and emergency unit for over an hour, where she suffered multiple cardiac arrests.

It is unclear what caused Ms Aaldenberg to be collapsed in the road, however prior to the incident, her daughter Clara confirmed she had been suffering from transient ischaemic attacks (TIAs). These mini strokes are caused by a temporary disruption in the blood supply to part of the brain. They can cause speech and visual disturbance, loss of movement in the body and slurring.

Elise Van Tam was reported to the HCPC by her paramedic colleague who attended the incident and whose name we cannot identify. Both parties declined to comment.

The Cambridge Mail

Paramedic who called crush victim drunk is suspended

A blundering paramedic who mistook her critically injured mother for a drunk has been suspended.

She rang the woman's husband – her own father – from the ambulance to say his wife was 'drunk as a lord'. In fact, she had suffered a brain injury, 12 broken ribs, a lacerated spleen, a broken ankle, a collapsed lung and multiple broken vertebrae.

More than three months after the accident, the extent of the brain injury has yet to be fully established, but a neurologist categorised it as 'significant'.

The 53-year-old victim was found lying on a grass verge with life-threatening injuries by the ambulance in the summer of 2005. The paramedic failed to identify any of her injuries and forced her to sit unaided in the ambulance. It was only on arrival to hospital that her life-threatening injuries were discovered.

The paramedic was suspended for three years after being found guilty in her absence of five charges of misconduct by a health and care professions council hearing in London.

Panel chief Laura Crick said at the tribunal: 'This was an extremely serious incident where the patient sustained significant traumatic injuries. These should have been identified, despite the fact that she may or may not have consumed alcohol. We can only apologise for the way the victim was treated, and we are taking steps to ensure that something like this cannot and will not happen again.'

The words burn into my eyes like stinging nettles. Johanna never let my mother down. It was the other way around.

My mother is a cold-blooded liar.

Chapter Twenty-Two

'iemand een rad voor de ogen draaien'
To turn a wheel before someone's eyes

Every word hits me as if it's a mallet to the head as I read over the newspaper articles for the third time. It's all there, in black and white, on this flimsy piece of paper in front of me. Elise Van Tam and Johanna Aaldenberg are there. My mother and my grandmother, if only by a different name. Her married name, surely. No wonder I'd gotten nowhere in my internet searches.

The words cross into each other as I read them, smudging together like an age-old graffiti wall. Each time I get to a headline, it feels like a fresh wound is ripped open inside me, and I realise that no amount of re-reading can make it sound any less dramatic. The paramedic daughter who mistreated her own mother. The paramedic daughter who told her father that his wife was drunk. *Drunk as a lord.* When in fact, she was dying.

Except she didn't die, like in Mum's story. But I can understand now why she wanted me to believe that she was dead. Bit by bit, it all comes together in my mind, as if I've spent years cutting a piece of paper with scissors to finally pull it open and reveal the snowflakes. I can feel the weight of eighteen years of lies, scaremongering lies, on top of me. Bloody hell, Mum. *Bloody hell.*

The old mahogany desk looks like the perfect thing to smash right now. I imagine bringing my clenched fist down hard on it, the satisfying crash of wood splintering under my anger. But as I stand here breathing in the farmyard and the wood and the old paper and the truth, I realise the futility of it all. I am horrified by what I've just read. Ashamed, even. Yet at the same time, I feel strangely defensive against these articles.

How can I feel like that when she did something so wrong? How can I want to defend her?

The need to see Mum feels stronger now somehow. Had she planned for this all along? To leave, once she knew that I was onto the truth?

And if something bad *has* happened to Mum, am I the only one who would care?

'What does it say?' asks Luke, who's stood frozen, like an awkward accessory, across the other side of the room.

'Honestly?' I reply. 'Honestly, Luke. I don't even know how to explain it. Here. You'll have to read it yourself.'

He steps towards me, and I pass him the piece of paper.

'And there's more.' I gesture towards the bulging red folder. On top of what looks like hundreds of pages of word documents is another newspaper article, this time with a prominent picture of Mum in the centre. She's in paramedic uniform, an oversized midnight green shirt and trousers, black boots and a softshell jacket, and she's looking straight at the camera and smiling, under the headline: *Incompetent paramedic fails her mother by mistreating her as a drunk.*

'I'm so sorry you had to find out like this,' says a voice from the doorway. Clara avoids looking directly at me, instead choosing to stare down at the bare floorboards like she's attending a burial. She pauses for a moment, then walks quietly over to the mahogany desk, to the red folder and pulls a fourth newspaper article from the pile. 'You don't need to read the article. But I thought you might want to see the picture.'

I take the cutting from her hand and stare at the woman on the page. This time it's a full, clear headshot of her. Her skin is a beautiful shade of porcelain, with a sprinkling of sandy-coloured freckles spread wide across her sky-high cheekbones. A mane of smooth blonde hair flows gently past her delicate-looking shoulders. Her wispy fringe falls softly on her forehead, just above a set of thick laughter lines that frame her glittery, pale blue eyes. Eyes just like Mum's. Eyes just like mine. Johanna really is as striking as I'd imagined, and the sight of her is the final straw.

'Can we get out of here?' I throw the article back at Clara and put my hands up to my cheeks, digging my nails in hard, like I need to feel something sharp. Luke fumbles with his own A4 piece of paper and drops it clumsily, and I watch it fall to the floor, then kick it away so that it disappears under the mahogany desk. 'I just really need some air.'

I skulk out of the study and stomp down the stairs, with the two of them shuffling behind me like anxious assistants following their primadonna. I get as far as the grass lawn, where hastily I pick a shady spot and lay down flat on my back, with my hands on my belly and my face towards the clouds, imagining that the sky is my ceiling. The sun is coming down as fast as the blood is draining out of me.

Clara takes a seat next to me on the grass. Luke follows suit, attempting to cross his legs like a schoolchild on the class carpet. He settles for crossing his ankles instead.

I give my very best *I'm not in the mood for talking* impression and for a while, we all stay there in silence. I close my eyes, listening to the flutter of tiny wings, as butterflies and bees start to make their way home for the night, and I focus on calming myself.

'We used to meet outside like this, on the grass, in the park,' says Clara eventually. 'You'd be wanting me to swing you round, or practise cartwheels with you, and I'd bring you one of those chocolate eggs with the surprise inside.' She picks up a blade of grass and runs it carefully between her fingers. 'One of the very last times that I saw you, we met on the grass like this. It was a couple of weeks after the accident. That's where Elise showed me the letter that I told you about.'

'The one that said they were suspending her?' asks Luke quietly.

'Yes, from the HCPC. They're a regulator, they're the ones that set the standards and investigate complaints. The letter was to inform her that she was being investigated. It said that they'd placed an interim order on her, preventing her from practicing. That it was in the public interest, because it looked like there had been some serious mistakes in service user care.'

I stay quiet, swallowing down the words *serious mistakes* like huge shards of glass.

'She was angry,' says Clara. 'She thought that they were out to get her. She even suggested something absurd, that me or Johanna had something to do with it. She was given twenty-eight days to respond to the letter with her observations, and then it went before the council and the case was heard. Even though none of us attended it in person. Elise wasn't required to show.'

'No,' I say, as Clara tries to touch my arm. 'Please, no one touch me right now.'

'Of course,' Clara says. 'I know this must be so difficult for you.'

'So, how did the press get hold of the story?' asks Luke.

'When she was struck off... well, that's when the press started taking interest. I guess it's not a usual thing to happen between a daughter and her mother.'

I feel like I would like Clara to stop talking, but I get the impression that whatever is coming out now has been waiting to erupt for a very long time. Her tone is now bright and brassy. She can't be enjoying this, surely?

'Anyway,' she says. 'A journalist turned up at Pa's door one morning, wanting to speak with Johanna. To get pictures and quotes, you know. Johanna refused to give any comment, of course. She knew the story was about her daughter, and she wanted no part of it.'

The grass is itching my back. *Thirty-three. Thirty-six. Thirty-nine.* I am staring at the sky through closed eyelids, counting black holes and invisible stars and lucky get-away flies with my monster running havoc inside me.

'The colleague who reported Elise. Were they in the ambulance, too?' asks Luke. I think back to the statement he brought home on his phone from university. The *what not to do* case study example that no one wanted me to see. Was everyone in Verborough laughing at me? How had they even let me onto the course?

'Yes,' answers Clara. 'They were second in command to Elise that night. It was a difficult situation, but it was the right thing for them to do. If they hadn't reported her, then perhaps the hospital staff would have, anyway. Johanna could very easily have died and there needed to be someone held to account.' She holds her hands up in the air. 'People are just programmed to want to have someone to blame, of course.'

'To make sure that it didn't happen again, like?' says Luke.

'Precisely. But Johanna didn't want this for Elise. None of us did. Of course, we were terrified at the thought of what *could* have happened that night. It was a huge mistake, one that could easily have ended in disaster. There was a part of me that was extremely angry. Especially as she didn't tell me...' Clara trails off.

'She didn't tell you?' I say, finally with enough breath inside me to speak again.

'Not what happened at the scene, no. I didn't find out until it came out in the press. Even Johanna didn't tell me. But on reflection, why would Elise have told me the finer details? She just kept repeating that she thought Johanna was drunk. That I know what Johanna is like. I was sure that she must have been traumatised by it all, but… I'm her sister, you know.' Clara lets out a miserable sigh.

'And she really hadn't been drunk, not at *all*?' I say, with hope in my voice, hope that perhaps there *was* some truth to Mum's story, and that it wasn't as clear cut as the newspaper clippings had made out.

Clara shakes her head gently. 'The doctors all agreed that she must've had a mini stroke, most likely while she was crossing the road, or perhaps just moments before. And that she'd lost her balance and fallen. Maybe she'd fainted, or she'd knocked herself out. They weren't sure how long she'd have been lying there for, but the motorbike – Gerald – didn't knock her down. He just didn't see her.'

I think of Gerald, of his insistence that he didn't know she was there. The cancer-riddled old man who turned up on our doorstep had been telling the whole truth. It was Mum who had not.

'I never forgave that man for not staying with her and going to her side. I don't know how someone could be so selfish, so *cruel* as to do that. And the not knowing what had happened to her. Me and Pa were going out of our minds with all these questions in those first few weeks. It was agony, and he caused that. But I do understand it must have been difficult for him to come to terms with. Except I think he deserves all he gets.'

I roll onto my belly to seek solace in the musty-smelling earth, resting my body on my elbows. It feels heavy, even though I've not eaten anything proper in three days. Apart from the soup. 'So, the magazine articles, is that what tipped Mum over the edge? Is that why we moved away?'

'The truth is Remi, I didn't understand it. Johanna was getting better. We were all devastated for Elise and what it meant for the family. But we agreed to put it aside, to move on with our lives. The newspaper articles came and went. People found a new thing to latch onto. We didn't want Elise to leave and we especially didn't want it to affect our relationship with you.' She picks at another blade of grass, only this time she flicks it away aggressively.

'We loved having you in our lives. You were the light that we all needed, especially for Johanna – you two were inseparable when you were together. But Elise, she couldn't cope with it all. Her face had not only been in the local papers, but the national papers too. All her colleagues knew about it. The blundering paramedic who mistreated her own mother.' The way she says it, suddenly the grass has turned to daggers, and I have the urge to get up. 'It was an awful time, for *all* of us, and when you moved to Langswood we were devastated.'

I think back to the neighbours' chat that Eliza showed me yesterday, to the fact that some of them had been introduced to Clara with all the diamonds. 'But you came to see us in Langswood, didn't you? So, why didn't you ever come back?'

Clara swings her legs from underneath her and stands up too, brushing the loose grass from her dress. 'I needed to know where you were, that you were safe and settled somewhere. That Elise was, well, that she was OK. But that day. I realised why she'd invited me to see you. It was a goodbye.'

'A goodbye?'

'Oh yes. Elise made it very clear to me that I couldn't come again.' Clara starts walking towards the house, then. 'And then… well, hang on a second, will you.'

She ventures inside, and Luke pulls me into him. 'You were the light that everyone needed,' he says, brushing my fringe out of my eyes. 'I can believe that, alright.'

I'm still unsure that I want to be touched. But his breath feels warm and his aura feels strong and sturdy and reassuring all at once. He's a neutral. He's safe. And I can also get rid of him at any given moment. I cannot do that with these expanding women family members of mine. You can't just get rid of family. It's not as easy as that.

Almost as soon as she's disappeared, Clara is back. 'I think it's time to give you these,' she says.

I turn to see her holding a small antiquated box, covered entirely in a deep burgundy velvet. She fiddles silently with the brass clasp.

'I found them a while ago, when I was having a clear out. OK, I'm lying. I stole them. But you'll see why when you open them.' She hands me the box, which feels unexpectedly light and soft.

'I never dreamed that I'd be able to give them to you,' she says, with a glint in her eye. 'There was a time when I thought that, if I ever saw you again, that giving them to you wouldn't be the right thing to do. But here we are. And I believe it's the right thing to do now.'

Her gaze is intense, and it goes on for a lot longer than I feel totally comfortable with. I feel the need to look away, but I can't. Somehow, she's taped my eyes to hers.

'Thank you,' I say. I start to undo the clasp and she quickly pushes her hand onto mine.

'Promise me you won't open it until tomorrow, though. I think there's been enough for you to take in for now.'

Not quite feeling the strength for any more surprises, I decide to follow her advice and hand the box to Luke.

'How do you feel about staying here tonight?' says Clara. 'It's late, it's a long drive back, and I want to take you to see your Pa tomorrow. Would you like to see your *grootvader*, Remi? I know he would be ecstatic to see you.'

My grandfather. I'd almost forgotten about him, in all this mother-filled pandemonium. 'I would love that more than anything,' I reply, my eyes now filling with tears. Clara was right. It really had been a lot for one day.

'But what are we going to do about Mum?'

'What do you mean?'

'I'm just… I'm not sure where she is. And I'm… I'm worried about her, Clara.'

Luke looks at me like he's expecting me to tell her the story. I know I need to tell her about the bailiffs. How can I fulfil Mum's request if I don't tell her about the bailiffs?

'Well, there's one more thing,' says Clara.

'And what's that?' asks Luke.

She takes my hands in hers, her blue hydrangea eyes still stuck on mine. 'If you're willing to trust me, Remi. Let's talk about it tomorrow.'

'Looks like we don't have a choice,' I whisper to Luke.

Chapter Twenty-Three

'hij kijkt door zijn vingers'
He looks through his fingers

At nine o'clock, we lay on the sofa bed next to the old kitchen, and Luke holds me, sporadically kissing me on the forehead. Clara's ceiling is covered in white painted wood planks that I'm turning into a maze. I am comfortable again now with his displays of affection, out of the public eye. His skin smells of peaches and baby oil. This house smells of Holland and he smells of home.

'Did she mean it, do you think? Did your mam mean to treat Johanna that way?'

A few days ago, I'd have said no. Of course not. She would never treat anyone that way.

But now, I say nothing.

Instead, I close my eyes, and dream again of a body, shackled to the ocean floor.

Chapter Twenty-Four

*'als de vos de passie preekt,
boer pas op je kippen'*

When the fox preaches passion, farmer, watch out for your chickens

I wake under the warm blankets that Clara had lovingly washed and prepared for us. I recognised another similarity between her and Mum as we tucked ourselves in last night – a need to sleep in clean, expensive bedding. The house is silent except for the hum of the refrigerator and two ticking clocks, the incessant and irritating *tick tock, tick tock* preventing me from getting anymore shut-eye. They're on a constant cycle of interrupting each other, like sisters, each one fighting to be heard.

It's early, I can feel it's early, and although I'm eager to get this day started, and excited to meet my grandfather – I still can't quite believe that he exists – I decide I don't want to be awake enough to think yet. Not about what I discovered yesterday, anyway.

I scrunch my eyes up tightly and imagine being somewhere else, on a summer holiday maybe, willing my nose to smell coconut and mango and salt water. But the musty smell of the cottage is too overpowering to shake off. And as I turn to reposition myself towards Luke, a muscle cramp strikes without warning.

'Owww.' Feeling pain, I bury my head into the pillow so as not to cry out in anguish. I struggle onto my side, and then suddenly, there goes my right leg, too. I'm writhing around in the bed now, thrashing about, trying my hardest not to wake up Luke, but it's too late for that, and his eyes flicker open.

'Woah,' he whines, sitting bolt upright and turning to face me. 'Shit, Remi. What's wrong?'

'Cramp,' I moan through gritted teeth. I throw the cover off me to grab at my legs, but as I bend to reach them, the feeling of them being on fire only gets worse.

'Oh, holy shit, that's painful, that is,' he whispers. 'Hang on in there.' He mimics my wincing expression in a show of solidarity.

'Uh huh,' I stammer, feeling like a complete and utter moron moving about like this, but having no way of doing anything about it. Then, as fast as the pain came on, it subsides, and I go still, holding my wounded calf, breathing hard and heavy, not daring to open my eyes yet.

'Has it stopped?'

'I think so. Really sorry about that,' I pant.

'What are you sorry for?'

'For waking you up. And for looking like a complete hypochondriac fool.'

'You were in agony, Remi. I'd rather be awake.'

'It was just a muscle cramp, Luke.' I don't tell him that my chest had gone tight and that familiar feeling of choking was upon me like a noose.

'They hurt though. Really hurt. Has it gone now?'

'Yes, I think so.'

'You want some water?'

'I'm fine.'

'Remi, for goodness' sake. Just please, take some water.'

'Sorry, yes. I'll have some water, then. Thank you.' I take an appreciative sip from the cup that Luke passes me from the coffee table. *Agony.* I wasn't in agony. Agony is what Johanna must have felt when she was walked into the ambulance with a body smashed into a hundred pieces. My mind goes straight to her, to the hospital and to the suffering she must have experienced. Is she still in agony now?

Luke rolls towards me and gives me a bear hug, as if sensing what I'm thinking and wanting to squeeze the negative thoughts out of me. I keep my arms by my side, with my calves still twitching, appreciating the heaviness of Luke over me. He catches me glancing at my phone, which is lying face down on the tasseled pouffe, with Mum's message somewhere inside it.

'She's not called again, no?'

'No.'

'Not even messaged you?'

'No,' I say. I hadn't told him what Mum's message had said. Or, what she wanted me to find and take from Clara's house.

'Did your mam ever talk to you about your dad, when you were young?' says Luke. 'I mean, I know you're really angry, Remi. And you have every right to be. But it sounds like she had a lot to deal with.'

I rest my head on Luke's chest, feeing calmer now. Is he feeling the need to defend her, too? Is this what he does with his dad, actually, even though he pretends he doesn't?

'Shit happens. That's what she'd say. *Het leven gaat niet altijd over rozen.* Life is not always beautiful. You can't fill in the well, after the calf has drowned. The damage has already been done, and you just need to get on with it. Dwelling on things is an example of weakness, and showing weakness makes you an easy target.' I reach out my arm and grab at my glasses, pushing them clumsily onto my face. 'So no, apart from telling me the story of how he died. We never spoke about my father.'

'And how did he die? If you don't mind me asking?'

'He dropped dead on a tennis court, a heart attack at thirty-eight. No warning signs. No clear ones, anyway. He was playing sport, doing what he loved. I like to think that it was always meant to happen that way. And that death likes to steal the good ones early for himself. That's what Mum said, anyway.'

I turn onto my back, this time being the one to take Luke's hand and then gently curling his fingers around mine. 'Mum always told me that she thought she was having a boy. But that thank goodness she didn't. That boys are more likely to drop out of school, and more likely to look for trouble. That they're much less sensible. And much more likely to die in a car crash. Or I guess, have a heart attack on a tennis court.' Luke lets out what sounds like a nervous chuckle, and I smile at him earnestly.

'I took that as a compliment, of course. But I longed for a man in our lives. A brother would have been great. But a father – even better. I used to imagine what it would be like, if he were alive. I'd imagine waiting in the kitchen for him to get home from a work trip to Europe. Mum would have his favourite dinner – toad in the hole – ready and warming in the oven as he unlocked the door and threw his bags down, exhausted from a long journey. That night, we'd all hang out together on the sofa, feeling happy that our small family was back together again.'

'Nice,' says Luke. 'Nice.'

'I'd imagine Mum and Dad leaving for holidays together, while I house-sat with my make-believe nanny and grandad. I'd be so excited for them to come back, to tell me which restaurants they'd been to, what the beaches were like. If they'd swam in the pool. If they'd found a good place for seafood paella. I'd picture their car pulling up and me running downstairs ready to greet them, fluffing the cushions as I went. Mum would be so happy to see the cushions fluffed. They'd step into the house together, Mum in her jeans and a nice top and Dad in his loud Hawaiian shirt. Mum's toenails would be painted bright purple. Her hair would be bouffant at the front but flat at the back where she'd dozed on the plane. She'd flip flop across the floor, her body sounding like a belly dancer because of all her new jewellery, bangles all clanging together as she put her handbag down on the kitchen table. She'd be bright and cheery and happy to be home, but she'd instantly complain about the cleaning. *I bet this floor hasn't been mopped, remember to do the corners next time.* She'd go straight to the kettle, fill it with water and flick it on. *Make us all a cup of tea*, she'd say. Then, she'd roll her suitcases into the utility room and would have a wash on before the water had even boiled. Dad would laugh and tell me to ignore her and give me a big bear hug, like a man of six foot even though he was only five foot five. *It looks very clean in here to me*, he'd say. *Do you like my new sunglasses?* Not really, I'd think, but I'd lie for his sake. He'd hand me a duty-free bag with a giant Toblerone and a bottle of Davidoff Cool Water perfume inside. *Thanks for looking after the place*, he'd say. *We had a wonderful time, but I'm glad to be home.*'

'He sounds nice, your imaginary dad,' says Luke.

'He is,' I smile. 'So is my imaginary mum.' The guilt seeps in as I realise what I'm saying. 'But you're right. I guess she did have a lot to deal with.'

'Well,' says Luke. 'She's made a few mistakes, for sure. But I bet she *knows* that, like. I'm sure she's sorry. I'm sure she has her reasons and that. And I'm sure she hid it from you because she loves you, Remi. I'm sure she's not the villain that the newspapers painted her out to be. Maybe she told you that your gran had died because she just didn't know what else to tell you? I mean, it's a bit of a crazy story to get your head around, right?' He pulls my hand up to his lips and kisses it softly. 'How about we open that box that Clara gave you? Maybe there's something nice inside?'

I pretend to act surprised, like I've forgotten the box exists at all. Except I'd slept with it tucked under a cushion, like it needed protecting, like it was the most valuable thing on earth.

'What do you think is inside it? It doesn't feel very heavy.' I sit up against the back of the sofa bed, taking the box from its hiding place and clutching it tightly with one hand, and softly stroking the burgundy velvet with the other.

Is this what Pandora's box feels like?

I feel my mouth start to water, so I swallow the liquid down and adjust my glasses so that they're pressed firmly onto the bridge of my nose. I fiddle quietly with the brass clasp until I've worked out how to unlock it. The little box flips open with surprising ease, revealing a densely patterned silky material on the inside lid, like satin. Sitting neatly in the main compartment are a series of white envelopes. As I flick slowly through them, I can see that they're numbered from one to eight, starting with one and ending in eight as if Clara has ordered them for me. It feels so neat and organised that I almost expect to find a set of instructions alongside them.

Luke sits up sharp beside me and I shuffle my body right up to him, so that he can clearly see what's inside, too. I decide I want him to read them with me. Better than him asking me to repeat them.

'I don't know why,' whispers Luke. 'But I thought it might contain something else, like. I didn't expect more paper, did you?'

I shake my head quietly.

'Do you think they're letters?' he asks.

I take the envelope numbered 'one' and turn it so that the name and address is clearly facing me. 'Well, they look like letters,' I reply. 'Except they're not for me. They're addressed to Johanna.'

'And hang on a second…' I pull a folded envelope from inside the outer envelope. 'This one is addressed to Elise.'

Confused, I start to open the second envelope with our home address on it, tugging at the paper to release it from its casing. Then, I unfold a lined piece of A4 paper, with small, neat handwriting written in blue fountain pen, and I read it aloud. Thankfully, it is in English.

Dearest Elise,

My heart is extremely heavy as I put these words to paper. It has been six months now of you not returning my calls, although it has felt like six years. I can't quite comprehend the situation we are now in and it grieves me to know that circumstances beyond our control have driven such a wedge between us. I have considered just turning up at your door, and not leaving until you open it, except I respect you enough not to resort to that. So, I am writing to you instead, in the hope that you will – please Elise – just let us back in.

I admit, I have no memory of that night, so perhaps it doesn't haunt me like it does you. But I am alive, I am not dead. It was a mistake, a misjudgement. I know you've never much believed in mistakes, but they do happen, Elise. I understand the press articles were very difficult for you. I also know the tribunal put you under a lot of stress. But running away from your family, a family who loves you, will not solve anything, in my book.

I have had so many proud moments in my life, Elise, but one that stands out above the rest is when I had you and Clara. *Mijn prachtige dochters.* My beautiful daughters. I feel so lucky to have been blessed with you both. They always say that the early years go so fast, and it is true. It goes in a flash. Never have I experienced something so exhausting, so exhilarating, so emotional, so entertaining, so expensive as children! It has been one heck of a ride, and one that I am so grateful to have been a part of.

I did not believe it was possible to strike lucky for a third time, but then darling Remi came along. The gentlest, most sweet-natured baby. Before she arrived, when we knew you were having a little girl, I would sit and imagine all the adventures we were going to have together. I was so excited to become a grandmother. What an absolute privilege!

For those first few years, I had the honour of watching Remi grow and seeing her develop her own unique personality. Me and Pa were in awe of her curiosity and her courage to try new things. She is such a whirlwind of energy, as any three-year-old is, of course, but her imagination knows no bounds. She has the natural ability to transform an ordinary moment into a magical escapade. If you are with Remi, you know it will be an interesting afternoon!

Most of all, she has a gentle heart, always sharing her cake with me or giving Pa a cuddle when his knee has been bothering him. I long to hold her in my arms again, to play with her, to feed her, and do all the things that a grandmother should be doing. I have to be honest, Elise, and say that I do not understand why you have chosen this route. I have never tried to cast blame for what happened. You are my precious daughter and I love you with every fibre of my being.

I do understand that we all deal with things differently, though. Perhaps you could start by writing back?

Your loving mother,
Johanna

Johanna. For the first time, I hear her voice out loud.

Six months without seeing me. At three and a half, six months would have been a seventh of my whole little life. I fold the letter and place it back in its two envelopes, laying it carefully on the quilt cover in front of me, as though it's been marked as *exhibit A* in a police investigation. Luke looks at me and nods. Slowly, I take another envelope from the box. This one is marked *two* and has a pretty stamp on it, covered in part by a big black postal blotch. Again, it is an envelope within an envelope. The paper inside smells of almonds and old grass.

Dearest Elise,

Me and Pa thought about you both on Mother's Day. We wondered whether Remi's nursery would have made you a card? I do hope so. How is she doing at nursery? I assume she's at a new nursery… did she settle in OK? I bet she had no troubles whatsoever, she was always very popular with her little friends here. Very soon she will be starting school, I bet she is so excited to be a big girl (like she always said she wanted to be)!
I would love to know which school she will be going to, and what her uniform will look like. Would you consider me and Pa coming down to see her on her first day of school? We could work around you, we wouldn't be a bother. We could even sit in the car to watch her walk in, if you don't care to see us.

Please?

Your loving mother,
Johanna

With a clenched fist, I press the second letter and its envelopes face down on the cover next to the first. I'm still taking the words in as I dive towards the one marked *three*. The third letter feels bulkier, and I realise there's a small birthday card attached to it. Taking it apart, I see that the card has a little brown bear on the front, holding six pink balloons. As I open it, out drop two crisp fifty-pound notes. The letter is written in red ink this time, with a small hand-drawn birthday cake and six candles in the top right-hand corner.

Dearest Elise,

Happy sixth birthday to Remi! I've enclosed a birthday card and have popped some money in there, too. I'd love for her to be able to buy herself something nice that she wants.

I wonder if she likes the same things as you did, Barbie and My Little Pony? That poor Barbie whose hair you chopped right off! I've still got some of them in the loft somewhere, I'm sure of it. Perhaps I could ask your Pa to dig them out for Remi.

I dream of the day that I could give Remi a present in person again. I see so many lovely things in the shops, little girls' accessories, beautiful princess outfits, there are so many more things in the shops nowadays compared to when you were small.

My friend Pauline - do you remember her – received the sweetest little 'Best Grandma' necklace for her birthday the other day. It doesn't matter that she goes by Nanny, not Grandma, but she was wearing it when I saw her this morning for coffee. I have to admit, I had a little cry on the walk home. Not that I begrudge you, for not sending me gifts for my birthday. I've never been precious about material things without meaning, you know that. But her grandchildren had picked it out themselves from the shops. Pauline's daughter – their mum – had said they were so excited to choose it and to give it to her.

I understand you may not agree, but I believe that children need their grandparents. I know you are a very capable (and brilliant) mother, but at least let us take the pressure off you having to care for her alone! We could babysit, I'm sure you could appreciate some time off. I know how hard it can be to juggle work and childcare. And what would happen if, God forbid, something happened to you, Elise? Do you have a next of kin where you are? What would happen to Remi?

Your loving mother,
Johanna

I stare solemnly at the letter, reading over the *Happy Birthday* part again. *Six.* That's three whole years since we'd left and moved to Langswood. The card and money being inside this envelope, means I never did receive it like Johanna had intended. My belly starts to ache with resentment.

'What *would* have happened to me?' I say to Luke. 'What if I'd walked downstairs one day, to Mum, collapsed dead on the floor?' My hot and clammy hands are still holding the letter, crumpling the sides.

Luke touches my shoulder with his lips, something that feels better than it should do, considering the mood that I'm in. Placing the letter down as *exhibit C* I pick at the next envelope. Except Luke stops me.

'I think I need to tell you something,' he says. 'Before you read anymore.'

Chapter Twenty-Five

'de vis begint te rotten bij de kop'

The fish starts to rot from the head

'My mum has been stealing from my trust fund?' I say, shaking my head. 'But how would you know that?'

Luke's face turns peach, just like his scent. 'Last night, while you were taking a shower before bed. I spoke to Clara. I'm sorry Remi, but I just felt like she needed to know the real reason that we're here.'

'Which is what?'

'Well. It's the fact that two bastards turned up at your house while you were alone and started removing things. It's the fact that those things were in your name. And that your mam is struggling with money. Which means that you're now struggling with money.'

'She's not struggling with money, Luke. Not everything is about money.'

'Remi, I know it's hard to fathom. And I know you're trying to see the best in people, and that you don't want to think your ma is struggling. But she must be. There's no other explanation for it. And that's what we're here for, isn't it? For Clara to help clarify things for you? And to find your grandma, and to stop you from losing your house?'

'So, what did you tell her?'

'That you found the deeds, and that your house belongs to Johanna. And that your mam has been loaning against your name.'

'Christ, Luke.'

'Like I said, I'm sorry, OK. But this is all just so...' He struggles to find the right words. 'I mean, who is protecting *you* in all of this, Remi?'

I stare at him with fire in my eyes. *I do not need protecting*, I want to say. *If anything, I need freeing.*

'I asked Clara if she knows where the money is from. Because clearly there's money and if it's yours, then you have the right to know.'

'And what did she say?'

'That you have a trust fund. Set up by your great grandparents, Johanna's parents. The trust fund was meant to be accessible to you when you turned eighteen. Elise had control of it, so I guess that...'

'You guess that she hid it from me, is that what you're going to say? And now, she's stealing from it. Is that it?'

'Yes. I think that she is, like.'

'But why would Mum need to be loaning against my trust fund? She's from the same rich family as Clara is. Which would mean she'd have her own trust fund, surely?'

'Maybe the house was her gift? From Johanna, I mean.'

'But the house is not in Mum's name. If it was a gift, wouldn't Johanna or the grandparents have put it in Elise's name? I know what Mum has done, Luke. I know she made a big mess of Johanna's accident. I know she kept Johanna from me because of it. But it's not as clear cut as Mum just deciding to steal from me. Something is not adding up.'

'Well, perhaps you should talk to Clara about it,' he suggests.

But I don't want to talk to Clara about it, I want to say. I want to talk to Mum. Except that's just not possible, is it, even if she wasn't somewhere else, running away from me, running from the conversations that we should have had all those years ago. My mind goes to Mum's message. The one that asks me to do something for her.

The message that asks me to find Johanna's will. And to take it from Clara's house.

Perhaps she is a thief. Perhaps she was desperate, and she was borrowing, like I am borrowing from Luke. But whatever she was doing. If she thinks I'm stealing something on her behalf, then she's got another thing coming.

I may have this crazy urge to defend her. But I am not my mother's daughter.

Chapter Twenty-Six

'hij kan de kerk nog niet in het midden laten'

He cannot leave the church in the middle

The fourth letter from Johanna to Elise is written on paper from a notepad, with floral outlines coloured in purple around the borders.

Dearest Elise,

It's been seven years now. Double figures for Remi! Ten years old, can you believe it? I know that I can't. Is she tall, Elise? I imagine her with lovely thick hair, like you and your sister. Clara misses her a lot, you know. She tells me that she writes to her too, except she keeps her words in a diary, rather than send them directly to you like I do.

I guess you might wonder why I do it? Why I continue to write, when I've not heard one word back? Clara asked me this, too. But the answer to me is simple. Because I know that if I stop, I've lost you both. And if you don't have hope, you don't have anything. You see, I do hope that one day, you will change your mind. I understand it is unlikely, though. I feel it is even more unlikely, as each year passes. Pa told me just as much the other day. *It's been seven years. Why would she change her mind now*, he'd said. But there must be something I can do.

I lie awake at night, you see, wondering what that might be. Was I a terrible mother? Are you doing this to punish me? Do you hate me for the accident? Was it me who ruined your life? I can't stop asking myself though, if any of these were true, why you didn't just come to me and talk to me about it? Why you couldn't give me a chance to explain?

Remi doesn't have to choose me or you, Elise. She doesn't have to make a choice. She shouldn't have to make a choice. If you don't want to see me, that is your decision. But Remi can come to our house. We don't even need to communicate, if that's what you want. Perhaps I have been selfish in the past. I am sure I have not been the perfect mother. But can you see how you are being selfish now?

I promised myself I wouldn't beg. But this is breaking my heart.

Your loving mother,
Johanna

I close the letter and hold it shut.

'Just say it,' I mouth to Luke, who's sitting in tense silence beside me.

'Say what?' he says.

'That you think my mum is a terrible person.'

The ache in my chest threatens to suddenly choke me. 'You think she's a horrible, horrible person, don't you,' I say, as my voice cracks and a tear runs fast out of the corner of my eye.

Luke goes to speak, but the words won't come out of his mouth. Instead, he lifts envelope numbers five, six, seven and eight out of the box, quickly unwrapping the paper packages for me, almost like he has decided that he can't stand this misery much longer and this all needs to come to an end, sharpish.

I set them up in my hands in order and start to read again.

Number five is a postcard, with a picture of a white exotic-looking building and bright mosaic tiles, and *Isle of Wight* written in the bottom right-hand corner.

Dearest Elise,

I often wonder what Remi likes to do on the weekends. I know she will be past the bedtime stories, and the trips to the swings at the park. Perhaps she's into video games now? Does she know what she wants to be when she's older? I wonder if she ever asks about us. I know Pa is feeling it, too. This grief... the grief of losing Remi is overwhelming, and I'm trying not to feel angry or confused. But I just cannot help it, Elise.

Part of the reason why I write these letters is that I do not want Remi to think that we did not care. That we never tried to contact her. That we never tried to see her. I'd like to think she knows that I write to you. Please just give it a chance. We are starting to become desperate.

I will come to your door if that is what we have to do!!
Your loving mother,
Johanna

Number six is written on illuminous yellow paper, a bit like a larger version of a post-it note.

Dearest Elise,

We finally did it and came last Saturday. I am not sure if you were in or you just chose to ignore us. We knocked quite a few times. But Clara noticed a neighbour was loitering around, and to save any awkward questions, we left without wanting to cause a nuisance.

I know there is no automatic right for us to see Remi. I have to be honest with you and say that I have very much looked into what is the law. I read somewhere that people use what's called a 'professional mediator'… perhaps something like that could help us get past this? I do not want to take this to court, and I believe I am too unwell to even contemplate it, anyway.

Please tell Remi we want to see her. Please tell her that we love her more than ever.

Your loving mother,
Johanna

Number seven is on plain old brown paper, with a tea stain down the middle.

Dearest Elise,

Pa and I spent an hour today talking about you and Remi. I am very aware that I am going to have to accept the situation and stop writing.

So, I wanted to tell you a few last things.

My main wish is for you both to be happy. We talked about how proud I was when you chose to work for the ambulance service. Your desire to help on the front line was admirable, to say the least. We talked about how tragic it was when Samuel passed. How awfully hard it must have been for you. I am so sorry that it happened to you, Elise. We talked about Remi and her beautiful outlook on life. You could see her brightness even as a three-year-old child. We talked about how happy we are that you have each other.

I daren't tell you that you are sensitive, Elise. But being sensitive is often a great quality to have. You may feel the bad times more than other people, but that's the same for the good times, too. If only we could continue those good times together. I feel so lucky to have spent three precious years with Remi. My only wish is that I could be allowed some more.

I know you blamed my casual drinking on a lot of the problems you had when you were a teenager. I know you were teased a lot about my being on the television, about my skimpy outfits and my dancing with someone who was not your father. I want you to know that I understand all of this and I feel awful about all of it. I feel especially awful about what happened to you.

I'm so sorry that all these things happened to you.

Your loving mother,
Johanna

The final piece of paper, letter number eight, is on paper marked with a *Fred Aaldenberg* letterhead printed in gold.

Dearest Elise,

I am pretty tired now, and Pa's wrist is hurting from writing all of this down. This is the most talking I have done in a long time. I still don't know if you have been receiving any of my letters, or if you read them at all. For all I know, you could have moved to the Caribbean.

Remi will be fifteen now. I would love to think that there's still hope, but it shan't matter anyway, now. This is to be my last letter. My memory is almost gone, and there is no time left for us, and that makes me so incredibly sad. I will miss writing to you. But I want you to know that I feel very lucky to have spent the time with you that I have. Thirty-two precious years with you, and three precious years with Remi.

A couple of words of advice, if you'll allow it. Don't sweat the small stuff. Live each day like it is your last. Try not to overthink things. Let bygones be bygones.

Look after each other. You have one life, so live it.

Your loving mother,
Johanna

I can't speak. Instead, I fold the pile of envelopes and letters up and place them all back in the box.

'So, not only wasn't she dead. But she wanted to see me,' I say to Luke, after the tears have stopped flowing and my heart has moved back into my chest.

'It sounds like she was desperate to see you.'

'But Mum wouldn't respond to her. Why on earth wouldn't she respond to her? I just don't understand why?' I feel nauseous, like the heady smell of old envelopes will forever be ingrained on my fingertips.

'Pride,' says a voice from the doorway. Clara invites me to take a tissue out of a box she's holding in her hand. The tissue feels soft and luxurious, much like the tissues at home in Langswood. 'Sometimes, people don't care whose house is on fire as long as they can warm themselves in the blaze.'

I have the vague sense that I've heard that line somewhere before.

She takes a tissue for herself and pops it neatly into her pocket, and I notice that the largest solitaire diamond that sits on her middle finger looks like an upside-down teardrop. I can't make out if the rainbow sparkles are coming from the ring or from the outsides of my eyes, which are still brimming with tears.

Clara puts her hand on her hip as she speaks. The belt around her waist spells *CD* in large letters, which I guess must stand for Christian Dior. I wonder if she knows that Primark is a store that sells cheaply priced clothes, and not a swanky law firm founded by Pri and Mark.

She lowers her head in a sympathetic way. 'It's not easy to hear that your mum might not have done what is best for you, growing up. I can't relate, I have no experience in that. But Elise was happy to take the house. She was happy to take Johanna's money. And eventually, she was happy to take yours, too, Remi. Luke has told me what has happened.'

Luke sniffs and then swallows loudly. I'm still annoyed at him for doing that without my permission. Even if his excuse was that he was doing it for me.

'She was happy to allow Johanna and Fred to separate, so that Johanna could stay in England, in the hope that Elise might change her mind about allowing access to you. Yes, that's what happened, Remi. And yet, when it came to paying back her mother, Elise wouldn't do it. What Johanna wanted more than anything was to see you. And it didn't happen. I'm so sorry, Remi. I'm sorry that your mother did this to you.'

A lawn mower starts up somewhere outside. I'm starting to think that Clara doesn't like my mother very much. Not very much at all. I wonder if Johanna only allowed Mum the house as a bribe. And whether she didn't like her all that much, either.

'Clara,' I say. 'Where *is* Johanna? I know you said she's got dementia, but if she's alive, then…'

'You'd like to see her? Of course, Remi, of course!' says Clara. She mutters something in Dutch, twisting her necklace a bit like

I would, except that she does it in a more excitable way. 'Don't worry, we are getting to that in good time. We will go to see Johanna. But first, I want to take you to your grandfather. He's just around the corner, you see. And he is desperate to see you! I'm just so glad it's you and me now, Remi.'

Clara comes closer to me as the air between us shifts.

'You see. We were never meant to be apart.'

Chapter Twenty-Seven

'iets bedekken met de mantel der liefde'

To cover something with the cloak of love

Why does my mum want me to steal Johanna's will from Clara's house? I've come up with two possible reasons. The first reason is that she's named as a beneficiary, and she wants a copy of the will to prove it when Johanna is gone, to save our house, get back our belongings, and to pay me back the trust fund money that she borrowed. The second reason is that she suspects that she isn't. And if she isn't a beneficiary, and neither am I, then quite frankly, we are fucked.

Clara insisted she made us all lunch before we leave to see Fred. Apparently, she has had professional chef training in France alongside the very best Michelin-trained chefs, but Thai food is both her speciality and her preference. I don't particularly feel like eating much today, especially not anything spicy or rich, but there's something about Clara that is hard to say no to. Perhaps it's a cultural thing, but we're in her house and it is only polite to take what is offered, after all. Plus, there are questions I still need to ask her. And she is the only one who can reunite me with my grandmother, after all.

We learn about the Dutch dish of *kipsaté met pindasaus* – chicken satay with peanut sauce – as Clara expertly tosses noodles and bok choi together in a gigantic wok on the stove. She seems cheery, much cheerier than yesterday when she was busy revealing all the disastrous mistakes that my mother had made. She pours herself a glass of white wine, which looks Mediterranean by the picture of an Italian villa on the bottle. I walk past her to fill up my water from the sink. Her thick, curly hair smells of coconut and soft chamomile. She gestures at me and Luke to sit, and we crash down into the not-so-soft wooden dining chairs and wait patiently for our lunch like teenagers after sports practice.

Clara lays Chinese-style bowls out in front of us on the old dining table, which looks like it may have been expensive once, but is now a faded patchwork of scratches and water stains. The room fills with the smell of rich soy sauce and sesame oil as she spoons noodles into our bowls with a huge ladle. These new smells are a welcome replacement for the mustiness we've been putting up with. She hands us each a fork and encourages us to tuck in. By the smile on Clara's face, it looks as though she's enjoying serving us like this.

For a while, we eat in silence. Luke looks to be enjoying his noodles, and I decide I'd like to cook for him when we're home. Perhaps I could make him one of Mum's special apple pies. I see his eyes fall onto a picture of Clara with a cat, where she's dressed in her white veterinary uniform. It's next to a picture of Clara doing a high kick dressed in a pink leotard and with her hair tied up in a bun, and then another, of Clara holding a huge glitter ball trophy in front of a banner that says something in Dutch. She looks ecstatic in that picture. It strikes me that there are no pictures of anyone else in this house. They are all of Clara.

'What made you become a vet?' asks Luke.

'That is a very good question, Luke. It's a difficult one to answer, actually.'

'Is it because you love animals?' I say.

'Kind of,' replies Clara with a laugh. 'Except no one ever asks a doctor if they are a doctor because they love humans. I have no pets. I am not going to be that cat woman at home as well as at work.'

'Fair enough. I'm allergic to cats, actually,' says Luke. I shoot him a look which says *is this why you've been sniffing the whole time?* Copperfield had been all over him at the house before we left, but he'd not said a word to me about allergies.

'Sorry Remi, I didn't want to break it to you back in Langswood. And Copperfield is a very cute cat.'

So, Luke is not anxious like me at all. He's just allergic to my cat-hair-infested cardigan.

'I guess I became a vet because it was what my grandfather would call a proper profession,' carries on Clara. 'I wanted to be respected. And to make a difference. I would say that I am clever. And I also have a weird fascination with death. That last part is a joke, by the way.'

She spoons a huge piece of bok choi into her mouth.

'Putting a pet down is always a horrible experience. Accepting that death is an everyday occurrence might sound like something you get used to, but trust me, it never gets any easier. Every death hits you in a different way. And you might think that death is the worst thing that can happen. But often, it's not. Sometimes, it's the poor ones who survive who you can't stop thinking about. Sorry, Remi. I know that you're in training to be a paramedic. There are lots of brilliant things about being in the healthcare profession. It's a wonderful job, really.'

I feel I would like to be like my auntie. I would like to be respected. And I would like to make a difference. I wonder whether I'm clever.

'My biggest worry is that I'll make a mistake,' I say. 'A

mistake like Mum made.'

'You won't,' says Clara. 'And if you do, it's OK to hold your hands up and say *I did it. I made that mistake.* What's worse, is being like your mother, and trying to pretend that it's always somebody else's fault.'

Luke chokes loudly on his noodles.

'When she unknowingly put incorrect information on a tax form, it was the accountant who was useless at their job. She was so stressed about it she didn't eat for two days. *Did I know you can go to jail for not paying your taxes?* When she got the timings wrong and missed her flight to San Francisco, she insisted it was the plane's fault for boarding twenty minutes early. When she fed everyone out-of-date salmon and we all got sick, it was the norovirus-carrying neighbour's fault for popping in and passing it on. If only Elise would relax a little. Even if that does sound patronising – and I'm trying not to be.'

It does sound patronising, I decide. And ever-so-slightly mean from her sister. But perhaps Mum deserves it.

'You will be a great paramedic, Remi. But a paramedic's salary won't support the house that you and your mother live in, unfortunately.'

I'm not sure how much I want to support the house that my mother and I live in. Perhaps I'd like a new house. A small house where we can't lose each other would do just fine.

As we finish our food, Clara tells me that she can help me. She tells me that this big house isn't her only house, and that she also has a flat in Battersea, right next to the Power Station which has been turned into a sleek shopping mall with restaurants, as well as a house in France, where she does all her excellent cooking.

I want to ask her why she has so much money, and why Mum doesn't. I want to ask her why she has this house, and why Mum doesn't. I want to ask her why she looks happy, and why Mum doesn't.

'I will let you into a little secret, Remi. My grandparents – your great grandparents. They lost all their money once. They had to work very hard to get it back again, and this made them think very carefully about where all that money went when they were gone. I think they will be delighted to give some more of that money to you. I know you will take care of it.'

She wants to believe I am not like my mother, except I have never before had to take care of money in my life. How do I know that I am a good keeper of coins? Am I the sort of person why is honourable and strong-minded enough to keep coins long enough for them to become *schimmelpennigs*?

'Tell me. What did the bailiffs take that upset you the most?' she says.

I don't have to think twice about this. 'The painting,' I say. 'I want Mum's painting back.'

Clara is frowning. 'Fine. The painting. I will help you get the painting back. But this is all for you, Remi. I am doing this only for you.'

'I know,' I say, and I move to kiss her on the cheek, like a good niece would do. Except her cheek feels prickly this time. And I can't quite work out why.

Chapter Twenty-Eight

'hij hangt zijn huik naar de wind'

He hangs his coat to the wind

My grandfather's house is set back a good way away from the roadside, much like all of the houses that we've passed on our journey here. The quiet country lane is lined with tall, willowy trees, with large detached houses all reached by long winding driveways, hidden behind thick, lush greenery. The road, in contrast, is narrow, and a lone cyclist pedals quickly past us, the rhythmic whir of their wheels aligning with the sounds of bees and birdsong. Cyclists move extremely fast here in Holland. As soon as we see him, he's gone, so much so that I wonder if he was even there at all.

To enter the Van Tam / Aaldenberg estate, you must pass through a white wooden gate, then follow a gravel driveway which leads you into a private garden that's filled with bushes and shrubs and rocks and raised beds, with patches of luminous colour, all divided by a paved pathway that delivers you to a green front door. The house is a double-fronted, two-storey building, with green shutters at each window that don't quite match. Elaborate lace curtains hang on either side of the downstairs windows and potted plants cover the windowsill. Some of the plants look healthier than others, and the bushes look a little bushier than they're meant to be.

Our car comes to a rolling stop and we all step out in unison, me clutching my velvet box, Luke fiddling in his pockets with some loose change. Clara takes the lead, a position that suits her. She starts striding towards the house with a smile that says she's glad to be here. She knocks twice on the door loudly, and then swiftly unlocks it with her own key, like she's done this routine a thousand times. Luke and I scuttle into the house behind her, our heads bowed in apprehension, taking in the warm scent of masculine cedarwood and eucalyptus. It smells nice, this house. My tummy reacts as it detects a faint trace of toast, like someone has been making grilled sandwiches with butter.

'He never answers the door,' says Clara. 'But don't worry.' She gives me a harder-than-intended but still somewhat comforting shove in the ribs. 'He knows that you're coming.'

We flick off our shoes and follow her down the hall, past a room with a large stone fireplace and a mantle adorned with antique clocks and unidentifiable houseplants. The walls are painted in soft, muted colours – warm taupe, buttery yellow – and the furniture is a mix of well-loved vintage pieces and things that you might see in an Ikea flatpack showroom. A plush sofa in a faded floral pattern is visible from the doorway, with a lump carved out where a person's bottom has so often been. Two wingback chairs flank the fireplace, with a patchwork quilt thrown neatly over the back of the comfier looking one.

The hall leads onto a narrow corridor, one side housing a large ornate floor-to-ceiling mirror, and the other, lots of different sized framed paintings. Most are seascapes or landscapes, some are dancers in black and white, but at the very end of the corridor sits a framed Ajax shirt with the number nine in the centre, and lots of black squiggles, which I realise must be signatures of the team. Luke looks enthusiastically at the shirt as we pass, like he never expected to find a fellow football fan here.

We carry on together, past a door revealing what must be the dining room, which houses a large oak table in the centre, surrounded by colourful mismatched chairs. An empty magnum of champagne sits proudly on top of the table, with a candle poking shyly out of the top of it. The back room we discover is the lounge, and it's beige, similar to our own, except it has touches of exquisite copper and gold. Fred is sitting in an armchair, a shabby, well-worn thing, with a sleeping dog laying at his feet, a beautiful golden cocker spaniel, whose shiny coat matches in perfectly with some of the fixtures and finishes.

I immediately consider that his face looks good for being in his seventies. His smooth brown skin and crystal-like eyes make him look much younger than his years. His hair is grey but it's that good shade of grey, that bedazzling silver shade mixed with streaks of smoky dark brown. He's resting his big hands on his round tummy, his golden jewellery glinting in the spring sunlight that's now streaming through the windows. He has an expensive-looking watch on his right wrist, one that wouldn't be out of place at one of our house parties in Langswood. His frame is plump but solid, cuddly but strong.

The TV is blaring out a football match and I can see by the clock that it's at ninety-three minutes. A team in white and red scores and the big man flies out of the chair, saying something in Dutch with his arms punching the air like an enthusiastic school boy. The cocker spaniel goes flying up with him, dancing around his feet like he's sharing in his glee. I don't support football much, but I smile at watching them celebrate like that. I'm mostly charmed to see that he looks happy. He holds out the remote and clicks the tele off. Then, Clara starts to talk for him.

'The match was played on the weekend, but he likes to watch the highlights on repeat. It's Ajax versus PSV. A little like the London derby, but with Dutch teams, of course.'

Clara approaches Fred and kisses him on the cheek as she helps him to stay upright. He's a bit crooked, hunched over and wobbly like he could easily fall back into his chair with a thud. He looks a little apprehensive about seeing us. But he takes the time to straighten out his knees and then he turns his body towards me.

'Remi,' he says softly, as he pulls me in for a bear hug. His silky golf shirt feels soft to the touch and a strong but pleasant scent of vanilla and hay reaches the very top of my nostrils. I know I must feel rigid with nerves, but he squeezes me tightly anyway, almost too tightly that I go to drop my velvet box. Eventually he pulls back from our embrace, and we lock eyes, not awkwardly, but slightly clumsily, and he holds me there while a huge watery tear falls from his eye, one so unexpected that without thinking, I go straight back in for another tight bear hug. It's quite a few seconds before we pull apart again.

'Sit, sit, please!' says Clara, gesturing for us to take a seat on the small blue sofa across from Fred. Feeling a little overcome, we both gladly follow her instruction, and we perch three in a row on the sofa like birds on a power cable, close but not quite touching, each of us preoccupied with our own private thoughts about each other. *I wonder if he thinks I'm beautiful. As beautiful as three-year-old Remi was.*

I wonder if he hates my mother.

'It's a lovely house you've got here,' says Luke, eager to start up the conversation, so that I don't have to. 'I'm Luke, Remi's boyfriend.' He puts his palm on my thigh and squeezes gently. I immediately go stiff with nerves.

'It is so fantastic to meet you, Luke,' says Fred quietly. He says fantastic like *fantashtic*, his voice smooth and crisp, each word shaped with a careful precision. He leans forward, holding out one of his huge hands and encouraging Luke to shake it. As their arms move vigorously up and down, a figure appears in the doorway and I turn to Luke in surprise. 'Jasper,' says Clara, pronouncing it as *Yasper*. 'Would you be ever so kind as to make my niece and her boyfriend a drink, please?' She winks at me. 'And another cup for my wonderful Pa, of course, too.'

'You have a butler?' thinks Luke out loud, watching the figure nod and then disappear off towards the kitchen.

'Jasper helps Pa around the house a bit, doesn't he, Pa?' Fred's slippers are folded down at the backs. 'And he drives him places. It's company for him, really. Except that he supports PSV.'

'Could be worse for you,' says Luke. 'Could be Sunderland.'

'True,' smiles Fred, reaching for his tea. The way his smile lines crease makes his face look more weathered, but still kind. He takes a sip from his white porcelain mug. I assume Sunderland are rivals of Newcastle, or something like that.

'Pa's got bad knees, you see. And hips. Bad everything, to tell you the truth. His body is shot, he wouldn't mind me saying that. Don't get old, will you? We don't recommend it.'

He shuffles uncomfortably in his seat and Clara reaches out for a cushion, which she carries over to her Pa and stuffs gently behind his back. The dog moves to Clara's leg and she bends down to give him an affectionate scratch under the ear. 'This is Bart. Short for Bartholomew. I have to say, I've never had another *Bartholomew the dog* come into my practice before. We can all blame Johanna for that.' He barks an appreciative woof and this time, she moves his floppy ear aside and kisses him on his cheek. 'Perhaps you might like to tell Pa about yourself, Remi?' she says, looking at me. 'I'm sure he'd love to hear all about you and your life back in England.'

I tap my feet nervously against the carpet, worrying that there's nothing interesting in my life to tell. Fred takes another sip of his tea and then nods his head obediently.

'I would,' he says. 'But first, I'm curious to know what it is that you're holding there in your hand, Remi?'

I look down at the little burgundy chest that I'm still clutching tightly in one fist. Clara sits herself back down beside me, and now she too puts a palm on my thigh, squeezing lightly. I glance at her and then Luke, feeling claustrophobic under their grasp. It's as though they're both holding me here, shackling me to the sofa, and I wonder if they're just as petrified as I am to be front row in this unexpected family reunion. Perhaps it's now me who is supporting them through this whole affair. It sure feels like we're in this together now, anyway.

Fred flashes me a friendly smile, a reassuring *you can tell me, I won't judge* kind of smile. So far, he's only spoken a few words, but then we are speaking in his second language, after all. I sense a look of *let's have a chat about it and drink some tea*. I've only been with him for five minutes, but I decide that I like my new grandad.

'It's a box that I'd been keeping for her. I gave it to her, yesterday,' says Clara to her father.

'And what's inside?' asks Fred.

'Envelopes,' I say. 'Envelopes, with hand-written letters inside. Letters from Johanna to Mum. About me. About trying to see me, anyway.' I flip open the clasp of the box and display the envelopes to the crowd, like I would have done as a child in a classroom show and tell. 'There are eight of them. One of them you helped to write, actually.'

Fred peers over into my box and lets out a heavy, understanding sigh.

'I'm not going to lie, they were extremely difficult for me to read. But I'm so grateful that Clara kept them for me. I… I don't know what Mum was thinking.' I nudge Clara with my shoulder, and she nudges me softly back.

'What I don't quite understand, though,' says Luke, focusing his gaze on my auntie. 'Is how you found these letters in the first place. If they were addressed to Elise, and Remi never knew about them, then… how did you get your hands on them?'

I flick through the envelopes in front of me, some addressed to Elise, some addressed to Johanna. An envelope within an envelope.

'Elise didn't keep the letters, Luke. She returned them to Johanna. Johanna had told me each time she'd written a letter to Elise. I had a suspicion that Elise might return them, so I made it a priority of mine to pick up the post from the post-box on the driveway, on my daily visits to the house. I realised that Elise was returning them, because I could recognise her handwriting. It's almost identical to mine. I warned Pa to look out for her handwriting, too. The objective was to intercept the letters, before Johanna could know. And that's what I did. I knew that Elise had read them, as the letters were returned opened. But I couldn't bear for the devastation… for the upset it would cause to Johanna. To know that her words… that they'd failed. If Johanna had hope, she had something. I put them all in a box and kept them for a day when we might be reunited with Remi. I wanted you to know that your grandmother cared. I wanted *proof* to show you, one day. I had hope, too, that the day would finally come. And thank goodness, it did.'

She puts her whole arm around me now, and I let out a raspy sigh, feeling a comfort that I didn't realise I needed. The hurt is there, deep within my belly, and I know now that it will never, ever leave me. That it's been tattooed into my soul.

'We were stuck between a rock and hard place,' says Clara. 'We were absolutely desperate to have you back in our lives. But the situation was out of our control, and we didn't want to rock the boat with Elise. It broke all of our hearts. But especially Johanna's.'

I take a big shaky breath and disguise it by sipping at the tea that Jasper has put in front of us on the table. Since our meeting a few days ago, Clara hasn't been clear about where her mother is. I knew she was suffering with dementia, and now, that Fred is here, and Johanna is there. I'm assuming she means in England. We could have spoken about it on the car journey over to the house, of course. But assertiveness is something I'm still working on.

'I understand how you must feel about my mum, Fred. I'm so sorry that she did that to you all. But I'd really like to repair the damage that's been done, somehow. Do you think I can see her?' I say, chewing at my lip. 'I know Johanna's poorly. But I'd really love to see her, finally.'

'Please, do not apologise, Remi. None of this is your fault,' says Clara.

Saliva threatens to block my throat. 'I appreciate you saying that. But I just feel awful about it all.'

Fred looks like he would like to speak. But Clara talks over him. 'The only person who should feel awful about any of this is Elise. And she is not here, so… would you like something stiffer? This feels like a celebration. It's not every day that you get to see your long-lost grandchild, is it Fred! Fetch us a bottle of champagne, will you, Jasper? I'd like to make a toast.'

'That's awfully kind,' I say. 'But the truth is, I don't really drink.' My cheeks turn pink, remembering the raging hangover that I was suffering from a few days ago. 'Well, not usually, anyway.'

'But how will I get to know the real you?' asks Clara with a grin. 'I'm kidding, of course. It's something my grandfather would have said.'

Bart goes to sit at Clara's feet, and she pats his belly fondly. 'Now there's a saying in Dutch, *nu komt de aap uit de mouw*. Legend has it, that a few hundred years ago, Dutch sailors returning from long voyages would occasionally attempt to smuggle monkeys into the country, using them to settle their bills at their local drinking taverns. The monkeys brought lots of eagle-eyed customers to these taverns, people eager to see these monkeys, exotic animals that they had never seen before. The sailors would hide them inside their coats, but sometimes, the curious monkeys would give the game away by poking their heads out of the smuggler's sleeve at the dock gates. Your great-grandfather would tell me that this is what alcohol did to people. It brought their monkey out of their sleeve. I mean, he was right, of course. I'd tell you anything after a few glasses of wine. Would you like a biscuit, anyone?' She holds the biscuit tin out to us.

A biscuit that looks identical to a custard cream sits like a sign from God at the very bottom of the container. I pick it out carefully, and bring it to my mouth, appreciating the scent of rusks and vanilla that now reminds me of hot coffee and biscuits on the sofa with Mum.

Mum.

'Does your mum still like a drink, Remi?' asks Clara.

Fred coughs loudly and I'm so stunned by the question that I don't immediately understand it.

'Oh, we all do, sweetheart. Apart from you, of course. Like I said, Johanna was very lax with it when we were younger. She took the Dutch view that if we were around it early, then alcohol isn't a privilege. The Dutch are, on the whole, quite responsible with their drinking, you know.'

I turn to Luke and he nods towards Fred, who is now full-on glaring at Clara, in a *what are we talking about this for?* kind of way.

'I bet you're good at science, like your mum,' Clara carries on, oblivious to Fred's stare. 'She was brilliant at science. She should have got top marks, but she took her exams ever so seriously, got a bit overwhelmed by it all in the end. She ended up with a pass, which is still very good, of course. Her maths exam, however, well, she'd been out the night before and was probably still drunk when she sat it in the morning. I'll never forget the look on Johanna's face when she found out.'

'Mum was drunk?' I say.

She pauses, only just now considering that perhaps she shouldn't be telling me this. Fred is gawping at her in a strange sort of way, and I wonder if he always hangs his mouth open like this, or if he's just shocked by what Clara is saying.

'I just,' I say. 'I really don't understand. Mum hates drinking.

She's never allowed alcohol in our house. She went mental at me for getting drunk when I was younger. Absolutely mental! She told me...'

I pause, knowing that the truth is sitting on the tip of my tongue, quickly unravelling itself, but that I really don't want to have to say it. Especially not in front of Fred, anyway.

'She told me not to be like my grandmother, not to be careless, not to put myself into these situations where I didn't have total control. *Negligence will be rewarded with disaster*, that's what she said. Johanna was the drunk. And I was never to remind her of Johanna's death.'

Fred puts his hand to his forehead as though he's feeling for a temperature.

'Her death?' he says quietly. 'Elise told you that Johanna had died?'

I want to pretend that she didn't, actually. I want to pretend that we are the nice side of the family. But I can't do that, either.

'Go on,' says Clara, perched now on the edge of her seat. She's quietly rubbing her hands together like she's coming to the climax of a novel that she herself is the protagonist in. 'It's OK to tell us the truth, Remi. You should never feel bad about it. None of this is your fault, remember?'

'Yes,' I say. 'OK. Well. She told me that you were plagued with illness, Fred. And that you had died too.'

I watch his expression fall, at the same time as Clara's face lights up like she's spotted a dolphin out at sea. In Fred's eyes I can see in pictures the enormity of what Mum has done.

I am so embarrassed. I am so ashamed.

'I'm sorry,' I whisper. 'I'm so sorry, Fred.' My body moves upwards in a hot indignant sweat. My velvet box drops miserably to the floor, scattering my little envelopes like unwanted post dropped haphazardly through a letterbox. 'I don't care about saving the house or the money or the lies or any of those things, Clara. I just need to know where my mum is. And

I want to see Johanna.'

'Remi,' says Luke, trying to console me. But I push him away.

Fred rocks back and forth to get the momentum to move out of his chair. 'Remi, dear. Please. I did not mean to upset you.' He grabs at my arm, but I swing it quickly out of the way.

'First, she's a pathological liar. Then, she's a blundering paramedic. She blocks all access to me, denies me of a family who loves me... and now she's a drunk, too? Is that what you're saying?'

'She's not a drunk, Remi,' says Clara. 'My sister is a lot of things, but... well, she just couldn't handle her drink as well as others might have been able to. And there was an incident, with you, after your dad had died.'

'What kind of an incident?' Luke says for me.

'Elise was in a terrible place mentally. For your husband to die when your baby is young, it's just a dreadful situation for anyone. She had a few too many drinks one night. And she dropped Remi down the stairs.'

'She dropped me down the stairs?'

'You were OK, thank goodness, aside from a few deep cuts and bruises.'

I think of the scars on my face, of the saying I was told. *Zodra het hek van de dam is, lopen de varkens in het koren.* When the gate is open, the pigs will run into the corn. How I'd been told I was a curious child. How I'd been made to feel that the scars were my fault.

'Drink became the enemy,' confirms Clara. 'Her life became all about control. Vulnerability became failure. The topsy-turvy world had turned against her. Johanna was drinking occasionally. She didn't see the harm. But Elise couldn't be rational. They argued about it, and Elise took her drinking as some sort of an insult. Johanna told her that she had every right to have her own beliefs. But that she should learn to give herself a break. And that she shouldn't project those beliefs onto everyone else, because people have the right to live the way that they want to live. Without judgement.'

'And what did Mum say?' I mutter.

'That if Johanna had any respect for the two of you, then she wouldn't be touching that bottle. She went completely into herself after that,' says Clara. 'She became a nervous wreck. She alienated herself from the people around her. It was like everyone was out to ruin themselves. And I warned her, that her assumptions and opinions would become your facts. I asked her, did she want you to live a life looking through a foggy window?'

'And what did she say?' asks Luke.

'Better that, than a glass casket.'

The pain in my belly starts to worsen, and I cover my whole face with my hands. I imagine Mum as a young, frightened widow. I imagine Mum as a mean, over-bearing monster. Which one is she? Or is she both all in one?

Am I a fool for loving her?

Fred grips one arm and Luke grips the other and together they lead me to the safety of sofa. Luke rubs my back as Clara runs for a glass of water.

Three. Six. Nine. Twelve. Fifteen. Shit. Eighteen. Shit.

'Remi,' says Fred eventually, after I've stopped howling and I've managed to get my breath back. 'Will you come with me? I've got something I want to show you.'

I nod, wiping my nose with the sleeve of my top. Clara looks nervous at the thought of her father leaving the room without her or Jasper. But I reassure her by taking his arm in mine. He shuffles his feet along the carpet, and we move down the corridor with the paintings and the framed Ajax shirt, and into a neat and tidy garage. He points at a little child's bike, which is a cute red metallic colour with a worn brown leather seat.

'This was Elise's bike,' he says, softly. 'When she was about five or six years old, we took her bike out onto the old motorbike track, the one that had been left derelict for years and where everyone learnt to ride.'

I'm surprised to learn that Fred can speak very good English after all.

'Elise was so excited about her brand-new red bike. I stood watching Clara on her scooter, while Johanna was trying to teach Elise how to ride her bike without those little wheels that help you balance. Johanna stood over Elise, holding the handlebars so that the bike was upright, talking her through the process. I could hear her telling Elise not to panic, to keep pedalling and not to look down until she applied the brakes and came to a stop.'

I stare at the bike, imagining Mum as a little girl, a girl who was willing to give things a try. A girl who didn't know all the dark truths about risks yet, or about losing things she loved. Not real things, anyway.

'We were all encouraging Elise from the side-lines,' says Fred. 'And she was so excited to show us that she could do it. But Johanna pushed her too hard and she sped off, wobbling from side to side until she came crashing down on the pavement, grazing her elbow and knee. Blood was pouring out of her, and poor little Elise started to cry. We all went running over to her, and I remember Johanna lifting Elise up off the floor, trying to get a look at her poorly knee. But Elise was having none of it. She wrestled herself free, picked up the handlebars of her bike and pushed it at Johanna as hard as she could. Johanna was a little disappointed, but she never said a word about it. She just went back to dabbing at Elise's knee. Later, at bedtime, I'd asked Elise why she'd thrown the bike at her mummy like she did, and she'd told me that she'd wanted her to hurt, just like she was hurting. I'd told Elise that it was OK to feel upset, but that hurting her mummy wasn't the answer. Except I didn't really understand it at the time. Now, I realise it's what all kids do. They want you to feel the hurt, just like they do. Because they don't know how to process their anger.'

Fred fiddles nostalgically with the handlebar of the tiny bike.

'I guess what I'm trying to say, Remi, is that Elise has never really learnt how to process her anger, or perhaps any of her feelings, really. Which is why we are where we are today. After Samuel died, things spiralled. Then the accident became the straw that broke the camel's back. It's not right that she told you lies, Remi. It's a crying shame that we couldn't be a part of your life. But have you considered that she is just a mother, trying to protect her daughter, in the only way she knows how? That she is a paramedic, someone who has seen hundreds of people die. That she has made mistakes. But that she has also helped thousands of people to live.'

'You know,' I say, after I've considered his observations and a few moments have passed. 'Mum told me something once. It was another of Bruegel's proverbs that she loves. *Niemand zoekt anderen in de oven die er zelf niet in is geweest.* No one looks for others in the oven who has not been in there himself. It was the only saying of hers that has really stuck with me. And I believe that it's true. Because to imagine wickedness in others is a sign of wickedness in oneself. I know you're trying to protect her, Fred. But, now that I'm here. Now that I've met you. To tell me that you'd both died when you hadn't? To tell me that it was all Johanna's fault? Well. That is just nothing short of evil.'

Fred shuffles quietly on the spot. He looks downcast, and then he checks over his shoulder, as if to make sure that we're alone.

'I understand that, Remi,' he says. 'I do. But when we're alone again, there is something that I need to explain to you.'

We start to make our way back to the others in the lounge.

And then he mouths, *be careful.*

Chapter Twenty-Nine

'hoge bomen vangen veel wind'
High trees catch a lot of wind

We walk back to the lounge together, arm in arm. He seems much older when he's on the move, a little sicker maybe, and I wonder what other health problems he might be dealing with aside from his bad bones. I've heard many times from many different sources that stress can be a silent killer. The bags under his eyes look more prominent from this angle, and I do hope he's getting enough sleep. Perhaps I'll ask Jasper what he's feeding himself.

The sun has disappeared from the windows and the room seems a lot darker now. Luke and Clara are sitting together on the blue sofa, looking intently down at each other's phones, like they're trying to work out some sort of a plan. The plan, I soon discover, is how to get to Johanna's nursing home without us getting lost. I feel relieved that finally, she has given us the address.

'Put the postcode that I've given you into the navigation system,' Clara is saying to Luke. 'That will take you pretty much straight to the door of Johanna's home. It is too late to leave for

England now, so you will stay another night at my house, and then you will leave in the morning.'

I blink twice, pushing my glasses hard against my nose. If it were anyone else, I would consider the use of the words *you will* instead of *you can* or *you could* as somewhat arrogant. Or perhaps even mildly threatening. But confidence – that sort of admirable, Dutch confidence that I have been lacking in forever – seems to come so naturally to Clara.

'Jasper will drive Pa,' she says. From the lounge, I can see the front half of a Rolls Royce sitting proudly on the driveway. The distinctive figurine of a woman – that I was told by a car-loving, Cartier-wearing neighbour is called the *spirit of ecstasy* – has her arms outstretched as if she's ready and waiting to leave, her flowing cloth billowing behind her like wings.

'And what about Mum?' I press.

'I will leave this afternoon to find her. I have a plan to pay the debts, Remi, and to get back your precious painting. I want Elise to know that we can start again. That even after all she has done, she can still be a part of our family. No bad feelings, is that how you say it?'

'No hard feelings,' says Luke.

I wonder what use it would be now to have Mum as a part of my family. Do not waste your efforts on the incompetent cow. Isn't that what Mum always told me?

'You would do that, for us?' I say.

'For you, Remi. I would do that for you. Let's leave now. You two go ahead and sit in the car while I grab some things. I'll see you out there.'

She throws us a set of car keys and we move out of the lounge, back down the long hallway and to the front door, shoving on our shoes without bothering to tie the laces. 'You got this?' Luke asks me hopefully, as he yanks his white socks further up his ankles one by one. 'You did great in there, Remi. I'm really proud of you, like.'

'I've got this,' I mouth back, forcing a smile and showing him a positive thumbs up.

Clara's Mercedes smells of damp dog and grass, even though she doesn't have a dog, or in fact a cat or any sort of living animal that could have set foot in the car. It's a scent that gets stronger and less palatable the more times that you happen to smell it. Pulling my seatbelt tightly over me, I put my velvet box – the contents of which Luke had scraped back up off the lounge carpet while I'd been in the garage with Fred – down on the floor by my feet. I relax my shoulders, feeling relieved that it's just Luke and I for a moment. He tears open a packet of salt and vinegar crisps that he'd had stashed in his pocket, and crunches through a handful noisily. Usually, this noise would drive me insane, but somehow today, the crunch is a satisfying sound.

'Why did you tell Fred that you're my boyfriend?' I ask him. It comes out more accusingly than I intend it to.

Luke shrugs, resting the crisps in his lap and running a salty hand through his hair. 'Because I believe in honesty, I guess. When you've grown up without it, it's important.'

'Because your dad used to lie to you a lot?'

'He used to tell me that I was just like him. But I'm not.'

'I get that,' I say. 'Believe me, I know what it's like to not want to be like your parent. I used to think that Mum was someone who told me everything. Everything except select things, it seems.'

'Is there a problem with me saying that I'm your boyfriend?' says Luke. 'I didn't mean to cause any problems for you, if that's what you mean. If it gets back to your mam, like.'

'Honestly?' I say. 'I liked it.'

He looks at me then and grins, and I want to grin back. But instead, I lose myself to the window, and to the bushes and the shrubs of Fred's front garden. This should be a significant moment for Luke and me. I feel terrible for not being able to give him more than a three-word reply. He's just made it very clear that he wants to be my boyfriend, that he *is* my boyfriend, and all I can manage is *I liked it*. I should be feeling ecstatic. But it's like I can't quite process it yet, because I can't yet allow myself to feel happy, until I've finally broken free of this fear. This fear of the world being just like those vile little Dutch figures, who are forever running through my head.

'What's on your mind, Remi? I mean, I know it's a silly question. But my stomach is tying in knots and it's not even my own family. You must be nervous, right?'

I play around with my fringe, pushing sections apart and then pulling them back together again. 'A little, yes,' I lie. 'I mean, I'm worried about meeting Johanna. I'm worried about what I'm going to say. Whether she will even know who I am. And of course, I'm pretty terrified about seeing Mum again. About admitting to her that I know everything.' I pull my clothes away from my body and adjust my waistband that now feels tight.

'I'm worried that Copperfield has been home alone for a while now, and that he very well might have escaped. Or that I didn't leave enough food and water for him. And that we've definitely not drunk enough water today. And that I never thought to bring any flowers or anything to give to Fred. And that I don't want to look like a cheap granddaughter. I'm worried that my student house is so mouldy and spider-infested that it's been making me and Aoife ill. And that I could very easily fail my last year of university. And that even if I pass, that I will hate my job when I get it. And I don't know if we even have enough petrol to get Jaz's car home, anyway. And I hate that I've had to ask you for money. And…'

'Shhhh,' says Luke gently. 'I knew I shouldn't have asked.'

'I'm sorry. I'm so, so sorry about all of this. You really didn't need to do this with me. I mean, we're right at the end of our final year, this is just extra stress that you really don't need, Luke.'

I tell him what a useless girlfriend I'd be. I tell him that I don't feel OK. That I'm a nervous wreck. That my default setting is panic. And that maybe I'm never *not* going to be a nervous bloody wreck.

I tell him that if I don't say *touch wood* exactly four times, then I have to start all over again.

I tell him that he is everything. That he is good-looking, talented, laid back. I ask him why the hell he would want to be with someone like me. I tell him that I'll drag him down. And what about after Verborough? We come from opposite sides of the country. I tell him that it's not going to work.

Luke listens to all of this whilst crunching through his crisps. He doesn't look particularly upset, or worried, or bothered.

My legs feel numb and I grab at them, squeezing all the blood out of my calves.

'Fred said something just now,' I say, desperately changing the subject. 'Something strange. He told me to be careful. Listen, I…'

'Stop,' says Luke. He scrunches up the crisp packet and takes a deep, pained breath in before turning his face to me. I take in his strawberry-coloured lips and his speckled, browny-blue eyes. His blonde hair is messy in a sexy kind of way, and he's so handsome to me that in any other circumstance, I'd be losing my train of thought, imagining his hands on me and his mouth on mine. But the panic is still there. We can both feel it.

He clicks our seatbelts off and pulls me into him as close as he can, wrapping his hands around my face. He brushes my hair away from my neck and leans down to kiss just under my ear, and then he whispers, 'Let's just sit for a moment, shall we?'

It feels sensational, his breath against my neck. He pulls back slowly, guiding my head towards his shoulder, and for a couple of minutes we stay there in silence, me resting on his body, watching the sun reflect off the dashboard.

'Can I just tell you a few things, Remi? Before you decide if this boyfriend girlfriend thing is going to work or not?' he says. His hand moves to my cheek, and it feels warm and heavy and reassuring.

'That bird you saw fly across the windscreen yesterday. When you screamed and I had to do an emergency stop on the motorway.'

I go to speak, but he interrupts gently.

'It was *never* going to hit us,' he sighs. 'It was absolutely nowhere near us. But I love that you were looking out for it like that. I love that you look eight times over your shoulder before you pull out of a parking space. And that you won't move on amber even if there's no one crossing the road.'

He kisses the top of my head softly.

'I love that your handbag resembles a medicine cabinet. I love that you'll go to five different supermarkets if you can't get hold of your favourite ginger shot. And that you won't open nuts in public, in case someone nearby is allergic.

'I love how you'll tell me off for drinking milk past its sell-by date, even if it smells fine. I love how you put newspaper inside my wet football boots in the hall.'

I let out a snort in between sniffles, holding tightly onto my tears as the world around us passes by. I'm conscious that we, ourselves, should be already moving, on our way to find the women who made me. But I will myself to just let me have this moment.

'I love that you print all your boarding passes and store them in a folder. And how we have to agree on a designated meeting spot if we're anywhere new. I love how you remind me to stand behind the yellow line at the train station.'

He exhales slowly, and I feel the softness of his breath on my face. 'I love that you are smashing your paramedic course even though it wasn't your first choice of career. I love that you eyeballed me in halls until I came to ask your name.'

'I did not,' I smile, poking at his ribs. 'You were definitely the one eyeballing me.'

It had started like a true cliché; meeting on our first day of university, checking into rooms diagonally opposite each other. I'd felt that instant heart flutter, and then I'd felt the flutters become trembles, and before I knew it, they were multiplying into full-blown flaps. It was someone else's sick-fest, but it was mine and Luke's movie. I'd watch him from across the hall as my heart danced with the swirly wallpaper.

I'd guessed I was just a convenience at first, I was diagonally across the hall for goodness' sake. He'd come home tipsy from a night on the town and we'd meet in our shared kitchen for a midnight snog. I could tell it was him by the way he drifted down the hallway, occasionally stopping to pull up his socks. He would smell of beer and peppermint Tic Tacs. Then one night, he came home sober, and that was the first time he put his hand down my shirt.

'Probably,' he laughs. 'But I also love that you are doing whatever it takes to try and put your family back together. *You* ran after a strange man who turned up at your door one day, Remi. You went to meet Eliza. You got in contact with your auntie. And now you have found your grandmother, and you will find your mam, too. It is all because of you, Remi. So, don't you dare ask why the hell would I want to be with someone like you.'

He nudges my head off his shoulder and comes back to face me. 'And as for other sides of the country. Well, is it a good time to tell you I've been offered a placement year with a marketing agency in London?'

'What? You can't be serious!'

He grins from ear to ear as I throw my arms around him tightly. And then it happens. The panic steps aside, just for a moment, to let a *fuck yes* come jumping through. A wave of relief rushes over me. Whatever happens, I've got Luke. And this time, I don't feel at all like getting rid of him. He doesn't suffocate me. He makes me feel free.

'I love you, Remi,' he says gently.

'I bloody love you too,' I say, grabbing his face and giving him the best kiss that my body can give right now. It's a grateful kiss, but a sensual one nonetheless. 'And please. Don't leave me on my own with Clara. This whole *be careful* thing. There's something about her, don't you think?'

Luke is nodding. 'We need to work out what Fred's warning means. I have a feeling, that there's something Clara isn't telling us.'

Chapter Thirty

'de vis wordt duur betaald'
The fish is dearly paid for

Clara is driving and tapping along to a song on the Dutch radio as we make our way back to the house. She seems jolly, much too jolly for someone who is now tasked with finding and reuniting with their estranged sister and reminding them of all the shit that they've got themselves and their adult only daughter into. It's almost as though she is excited about the prospect of saving us. Possibly a little too excited.

Luke has his eyes closed next to me, and I wonder if he's tired, except he must sense that I'm watching him and so he opens his eyes and shakes himself slowly back to life. I had already decided before we'd got in the car that I am not waiting for Luke to ask any more questions on my behalf. The skin on my wrists is less red and raw than it was yesterday. I feel as though I'm turning a corner in starting to trust my own instincts, and my instincts are telling me to play my auntie at her own game. If she is so outspoken, so loud and so confident, then so must I be.

'How will you find my mother?' I ask Clara.

Clara stops tapping and twists the dial to turn the radio down. 'I'm not one hundred percent sure, Remi. But I have a good feeling I know where she is. I lived in the UK, remember, and I still travel there often for work, so I know it as well as anyone. And sisters have this sixth sense thing after all. I don't think she'll like it, though, me turning up unannounced. When we met a few days ago, I didn't want you telling Elise because I was worried that she'd convince you not to see me again. But now you're here, that doesn't matter anymore. She can't brainwash you anymore, Remi. I can keep you safe now.'

'Right,' I reply. The air in the car has grown hot and congealed. I feel as though Clara has got the wrong end of the stick, somehow. Yes, I am extremely angry and upset with my mother. If her head was a coconut, I'd be throwing hard, wooden balls at it like they do at a coconut shy and I'd be extremely satisfied with the result. But the more that Clara says these, quite frankly, over the top things like *I can keep you safe now* and *we were never meant to be apart*, the less safe I feel.

'I think it would be better if we come with you.'

Clara looks at me sternly in the rearview mirror. 'No, Remi. That is not possible. Your priority is visiting Johanna.' She does this thing with her face, then, like she is about to cry. 'She is dying, Remi. You must see her, before it's too late.'

Her voice chokes up on the word *late*, and I can tell – even though I'd wondered all this time why Clara is here, and Johanna is there – that the sadness is genuine. I can't stand to see a person cry. Are we all held in eternal suffering by what happened to Johanna? Will my wish of seeing her come true before she dies?

'OK,' I say. 'I'm so sorry, Clara.' The thought that Johanna could pass away before I get there is too awful to consider. 'But if that's the case, then shouldn't we leave today?'

'Johanna's home doesn't allow visitors today, Remi. I will let them know that you will be there tomorrow. And in the meantime, I've got a little surprise for you. I really hope you're going to like it.' Clara is smiling again, her eyes wide in the rearview mirror. It strikes me then, just how much she resembles me. Is this what people experience of me? Staring too long, too hard, too strange? I wince in embarrassment as I avert my eyes to the roadside.

Soon, we are pulling up to the estate that is Clara's house, which looks even bigger and grander this time around. I'm used to the sight of big houses and wealth, but this house has so much space around it that it feels criminal to deprive it of people who could inhabit it. The land could house a whole village, let alone just Clara. I think of her rattling around the estate alone, and feel grateful to see in the distance a gardener pruning the hedges along the perimeter wall.

'I'm going to leave soon,' Clara says as she unpacks a leather holdall bag from the boot. 'I've got a car picking me up for the airport in thirty minutes. So please, treat the house like it's your own. Use anything you want to.' She looks me up and down. 'I can lend you some clothes if you like, Remi?'

My clothes smell of noodles and stale, days-old Chloe perfume, and I feel grateful for something new to wear, except I imagine Clara's wardrobe is full of too-tight waistbands and hard-to-wash materials and the fact is, I don't know her. I don't know if she'll be mad if I drop something on her chiffon tunic. Or if she'll be offended that I don't love her flared trousers with the old-fashioned embroidery down the side.

'Thank you,' I say. 'That would be great.'

Clara tells us that we won't be sleeping on the uncomfortable sofa bed tonight. I disagree with her that it is uncomfortable, but as we approach the lounge, I see the sofa bed gone, folded back to its chair-like status with the blankets folded on top.

'I had my cleaner come in and prepare while we were gone. I didn't want to overwhelm you yesterday, but,' she pauses, clasping her hands together triumphantly. 'I'm so excited for you to see it, Remi.'

'See what?' blurts out Luke before I can answer.

'Your room,' she says with a smile. I'm still holding the velvet box tightly in my hands. Fred's *be careful* warning is buzzing loudly in my ear, so much so that I flinch as Clara tries to take my arm.

There's a large portrait of her on the stairs, standing tall in her graduation gown, holding a certificate in one hand and some sort of pin in the other. Curly locks just like Mum's hair flow out from under her cap, her eyes shining with accomplishment. Johanna and Fred are standing on either side of her, placing a loving hand on their daughter's shoulder. Mum is nowhere to be seen. This may be the ancestral home of the Van Tams, but it's like Elise has been erased from the family altogether. I wonder if that is Clara's doing, or someone else's. I wonder if that makes me sad, or angry, or whether I don't really care at all.

We reach a room at the end of the hallway, with a white wooden door and a large, golden bee as a doorknob, and I feel glad that Luke has followed behind us. This doorknob is completely different to all of the others along this corridor of rooms. I think of Eliza, of her kindness not to judge me, even as the scandal of the decade was bearing down on the cul-de-sac that day. I hope my *issues*, like the neighbours had called them, didn't intimidate Eliza as much as I think they did. I saw her, avoiding eye contact with me. But I'd like her to be my friend again, if she'll allow it.

Luke is carrying the few items that we brought to Holland. He's sniffing again, and I wonder if actually, the sniffing is indeed a tick and not the allergy that he claims. Clara sniffs too, but hers is more like a deep breath in, and then she reaches for the bee handle and opens the door victoriously to a bedroom that's huge, even bigger than my bedroom back in Langswood.

And then I gasp. And Luke gasps. A stale smell of old carpet comes wafting towards us from out of the room.

My eyes go immediately to a large, white canopy bed made

neatly with a pale pink bedspread and covered in cushions of various sizes and shapes – diamonds, hearts, clouds. The walls are painted in a light lavender colour, with one accent wall featuring a childish mural of sea creatures. The whale has googly eyes and the dolphin is waving at us with its fin. Fairy lights in the shape of little stars are wound around the curtain rail, and a rug shaped like a giant flower sits in the middle of the room.

There are no toys, but there is a gigantic, open-fronted dollhouse. On the bottom floor of the dollhouse, a miniature kitchen holds a table with two tiny chairs. A staircase winds up from the bottom floor to an assortment of bedrooms, a bit like a mini dormitory, where little beds house odd-looking mice, ones with no faces but with different colour dresses on. Fake books and cupcakes and hair brushes are scattered on the floor around them. There's even a little bath in the bathroom.

Clara encourages us to step forward so that we're closer to the canopy bed, which is when I notice a framed picture of me and Clara. I am roughly three years old, and I am wearing a pair of Minnie Mouse sunglasses. The same Minnie Mouse sunglasses that she described I was wearing in the park, one of the very last times I saw her. The same Minnie Mouse sunglasses that are now displayed on top of the bedside drawers.

This bedroom is a child's bedroom. But I am not a child.

This bedroom was meant for me.

Luke locks eyes with me, and I stare back at him. He's mouthing something but I can't make out what he's saying, and I'm terrified that Clara will notice, so I do what I so often do when I am lost for words – I look up. The ceiling in this expansive but claustrophobic room is dotted with little stick-on glow in the dark stars. They're not yet glowing, because it's not yet dark, but I feel like I remember having these in my bedroom at home at one point in my life, at a point where I was afraid of the night, when all the devils came out to play. Now, instead of soothing me, these stars will be keeping me up all evening, like a frightening reminder of Clara and her strange obsession with me.

She'd been waiting for this moment for eighteen years, I can tell. Was this room meant for someone else who didn't materialise? Was Clara mourning the loss of me, or is it something bigger than that?

Clara walks towards me and kisses me on the cheek. Her skin that a few days ago felt soft and comforting now feels more than prickly – it feels spiky and hot. Luke grabs my hand protectively as she does it. I drop his hand and instead, grab hers.

Luke goes to say something, but I throw him a look to stop him.

I don't pull away from Clara, even though I want to. I am the master manipulator now. I need her to feel that I want her. For the whole of my life, I did want her. Even when I didn't know she existed. But now, I'm not entirely sure what I want from her. All I know is that I might need her. I need to keep her onside. Until I work out what is really going on. Until I see Johanna. Until we find Mum.

'Do you like it?' she asks. 'I know it's perhaps not to your taste, now you're older, of course.'

Her eyes are not boring into me anymore. They are looking at the doll's house, at the two chairs sitting on either side of the tiny table. One for me, and one for her. One for me, and one for Elise. One for Elise, and one for Clara. One for me, and one for Johanna. One for Johanna, and one for Fred.

Who are they for, those tiny chairs?

'I'm touched,' is all I manage to say.

Clara squeezes my hand, then nudges my shoulder like she'd done at Fred's place. Her face is shiny and taut. Where before she looked slim, now she just looks gaunt. Her glow has gone entirely. That new toy feeling is dead, and I feel as though I want my old toy back.

'I am so happy, now I have finally got my Remi back. I always knew you'd come back to Holland.' Then she directs at Luke, as if I'm not listening. 'I always knew Elise would make another big mistake. Well, her loss is my gain, sweetheart.'

Sweetheart. The way she says sweetheart sounds almost callous. Does she forget that this is my mother she is talking about? My mother who has raised me, mostly single-handedly, into adulthood? My mother who is lost? My mother who is widowed? My mother who is as insane as her sister seems to be?

'My taxi is almost here, Remi. I just have one more thing that I need to talk to you about. Perhaps we could do it alone?'

Luke is shuffling uncomfortably beside us, not looking as though he wants to leave. But I nod at him, and reluctantly he agrees.

'OK,' he says. 'As long as you're OK with that?' His eyes search for a sign that I want him here. But I remain placid and composed, and so he turns and walks out, grabbing at the bee handle and closing the door behind him.

'Remi,' says Clara softly as she sits down on the bed. 'I want to talk to you about the painting.'

A bunch of unsightly little faces appear in my mind. The grimacing, gluttonous faces that so often haunted me in my dreams. *De zeug trekt de stop uit het vat*. The sow pulls the bung from the barrel. Negligence will be rewarded with disaster.

'I know it is so very important to you, and I am going to England to try my hardest to negotiate with whoever took it, to return it at once. My plan is to contact the bailiffs and explain that they never should have taken it, because the painting was never yours or Elise's in the first place. If I can prove to them that the painting is actually mine, then they are legally required to give it back. However, I will need something in writing. Something that says that the painting isn't yours. We can backdate it, to make it look as though it was signed a while ago. Then, once I've had the painting returned, I will give it to Elise, and we can rip up the signed agreement. It's all quite simple, really.'

It is interesting, this mix of hot and cold from Clara. The way her voice can drift from grating and hard to song-like and easy.

'I mean, I'm not sure what you want with a cheap copy of an ugly Bruegel painting. It probably wasn't worth their while to take it. But I understand you said it was a gift to your mother from your father. And while I'm at it, I can set your mother up with some money to get the rest of your things back. It will all be OK, I promise you. I will fix it for you, Remi. All I ask in return is that you enjoy your new room now you're here to see it.'

The line on her front tooth glistens in the sunshine as she smiles. She leans over to pick up some papers that have appeared on the bed next to her.

'But the painting is Mum's,' I say, as she ruffles them in her hands. 'The men said the debt was mine. But the painting isn't mine, it's Mum's, so they should never have taken it in the first place, anyway. I tried to tell them that, of course. But they didn't listen.'

Clara's face is full of sympathy. 'I'm so sorry this happened to you, Remi. How scary it must have been, dealing with that all on your own.'

She touches me again, and it's like every time she does so I'm put under her spell and there's nothing I can do about it.

'I'll tell you what,' she says. 'Why don't you write down what you can remember of the bailiffs' details here?' She hands me a pen and orders me over to the bedside table. I do as I'm told, kneeling down and trying to remember what their identifications said. The bastards that told me they were genuine *certificated enforcement agents*.

'And then... and I know this is a bit naughty. I wouldn't normally do this, but we really want to get this painting back for your mother, right?'

I nod robotically.

'Well, then I want you to sign it and we're just going to say that it's Elise's signature. They will never know.'

She slips a piece of paper under my pen.

'I'm going to put my signature here,' she signs it in the right corner.

'And then we need hers here. Do you know what your mum's signature looks like, Remi?'

The paper has typed writing on it, but there's a large post-it note covering most of the text, and a cross where I need to sign. I hesitate, trying to process how this would all play out. It all makes sense, there's no denying it. And what choice do I have but to trust her? Without her, Mum has no chance of getting her painting back. Not in the immediate future anyway, and by then, who knows where the painting will be?

Without Clara, Mum's painting is gone. I can almost feel my dad's tears falling out of the sky.

'Thank you,' I say, taking the pen and scribbling a signature slowly. It's more of a squiggle than anything, but it looks vaguely like hers. *Elise Van Tam*. The mother who lied to me. The mother who hid my family from me. The mother who is now broke and hiding out in an unknown location, waiting for me to find Johanna's will.

'That is fantastic, Remi,' says Clara. 'You really are such a good girl.'

'No,' I say. '*You're* the good girl.' It comes out with a hint of sarcasm, and I can't tell whether I intended it or not.

She looks at me in a strange way.

'You know, doing all this for me, I mean.'

Clara smiles, and then she's gone, and I tell myself that I have taken my chance on happiness, in the hope that Clara will get our things back, and that she will soften my mother. And that I can visit Johanna. And we can start being a family, for once and for all.

Chapter Thirty-One

'dat gaat hier niet gebeuren'

His herring does not fry here

It's two o'clock in the afternoon in Holland. Clara has left to get on a KLM flight to England, and Luke has now returned to the bedroom. We're sitting on the pink bedspread of the white canopy bed, eating grapes from Clara's fruit bowl, being careful not to get any juice on the fabric.

As soon as Clara had gone, I'd tried Mum again. She hadn't answered, and I hadn't left a message. But I knew what I'd wanted to say if I had. That I hate her for running away like a coward, and for not telling me where she's gone. And for getting us into a financial mess, that we now have to rely on her sister to get us out of. A woman who I've known for all of five minutes. A woman who, on first meeting, I thought I was going to love. But who now, quite frankly, intimidates me.

I'd felt bolder now I'd made a big decision about the painting on my own. It was all going to work out, and very soon, Mum would be thanking me. I would finally have the respect that I deserve.

'Do you think this is weird?' I ask Luke. 'This room. Do you think it's a bit strange that Clara has a room like this in this house? And that there are my Minnie Mouse sunglasses on top of the bedside drawers?'

'It's disturbing, that's what it is,' he says. 'I mean, a spare room for a niece or nephew? Fine, like. But she's gone to more effort here than any parent in their right mind would do for their own child even. And it's so *childish*,' he says. 'And you're not a child.'

'That's exactly what I was thinking,' I say. I turn the framed picture of me and Clara, so it faces away from the bed. This room is definitely weird, but part of me is so moved by the amount of love and attention-to-detail that has gone into it that I can't quite hate it. Clara really *was* thinking of me for all those years. What if I'd found a long-lost auntie who didn't want me? What would I have done then?

'It's nice,' I say. 'A bit creepy, but it's nice all the same.'

Touch wood touch wood touch wood touch wood.

'I don't get why we're staying here tonight, anyway,' says Luke. 'Even if we can't see Johanna tonight. Why do we need to stay here? We should be driving back to England now. Making sure we're there, ready for tomorrow.'

'I know what you mean. I'm not one-hundred percent comfortable with waiting, either. And it feels weird being in this house on our own.' I tie my unwashed hair into a bun on the top of my head, pulling at the greasy roots as I do so.

'Do you think she's trying to stall us?' says Luke. 'Stall us from seeing Johanna?'

'But why would she do that? She's trying to help us, Luke.' I wander over to the window, the googly eyes of the whale following me as I walk. Outside, I count ten little poles with young trees attached to them, like naughty children, the poles trying to keep them upright. It's true that in nursing homes like Johanna's, visiting times can be strict. Ill patients need their rest, but Luke's right that we should be making our way back already. Except I know Clara wants me to experience this room, and that she'd be upset if we went against her wishes.

'We can make it look like we stayed here, couldn't we? She'd never know, right?'

I shrug.

'Do you think Clara has any friends?' asks Luke.

'What do you mean?' I say. I wonder how many friends I could say I had, really. Aoife is one, but perhaps she'd say she's just a housemate. Eliza? Copperfield? Do cats count?

'She strikes me as a bit of a loner,' he says. 'Living here alone, in a massive, musty old house with a kid's room and no kids.'

'She's not completely alone,' I say. 'Look.'

I point out towards the garden. 'She has someone out there, tending to those trees. And she said she had a cleaner. It's not like she doesn't have people around.'

Luke follows my gaze. 'Perhaps the gardener would tell her if we tried to leave early,' he says, and I wonder if he's a bit scared of Clara, too.

'Maybe we wait until he's gone. And then we hit the road.'

The gardener is standing at the top of a long ladder that is resting against a tree trunk. He's holding a medium-sized set of sheers and carefully pruning the leaves from the branches, dropping sections as he goes. I watch him prune some more twigs from the bigger branches until he turns, so he's facing in our direction. His khaki t-shirt is tight around his broad shoulders. His jaw is square and strong. I squint, trying to make out his features more clearly. His face looks familiar.

His face looks *very* familiar.

And then I go cold.

He's Phil. Or is he Grant? Whatever he is, he is a bailiff. Or should I say, he's clearly *not* a bailiff. What's clear is that he was at our house a few days ago, with a sign around his neck saying he was a certificated enforcement agent. And now he's here, in

Clara's garden, chopping at her tree.

I gasp loudly, bringing my hands to my face.

'Oh my God,' I say. 'Oh my fucking God, Luke.'

Before I know it, I'm running past him on the pink bedspread, out of the room and down the stairs to the front door, turning the knob to access the man in the garden. I want to scream at him, to tear him down from the tree and claw at him until he tells me what the hell is going on. But it won't open. I wiggle it and I tug at it, but it doesn't matter. The door is locked. Hard.

I scramble from the hallway into the kitchen, to the conservatory and towards the back door. I turn and twist the handle, but that too is locked firm. None of the doors will open. And there are no keys to be seen anywhere.

Clara has locked us in.

I've only felt this kind of panic a couple of times in my life. Once was when I got lost at the fairground as a child, and a creepy old man asked me to get into his car. The other was when I was held underwater by a rip current in Hawaii. Both times I thought I was going to die. It's the kind of panic where your mind and your body seem to separate – suddenly your mind, the part that really doesn't want to be there, is locked inside an iron case of a body, and you're stuck trying to think your body away from whatever terrible predicament you're in.

Move this leg. Move that arm. Run. Swim.

You become somewhat of a captain, desperately trying to control your vessel and get the hell out of there. Except I can't seem to get out of here. And I can't seem to think, either. I've been trying the doors, but they just won't open. I've been looking for keys, but there are none. I've blinked one hundred times and this situation hasn't changed. I've not disappeared. I've not woken up from this horrible dream and thanked God that it was all just a terrible nightmare.

The conservatory seems to be getting smaller and darker. The walls are swaying. I stare into a nearby mirror, and suddenly, I have six eyes, three noses, and my mouth has disappeared completely. Luke must have heard my panic because suddenly his arm is around me and I'm shouting at him to break the window.

'She's... she's lying to us Luke!'

'What the hell, Remi? What's happened, like? What's wrong?'

'That man!' I shout, running towards the kitchen and pointing out of the window.

'What man?'

'The man outside. The gardener, or whatever he bloody well is! He's the same man who was at ours a few days ago!'

'What do you mean, he's the same man?'

'I mean Luke, that he's one of those bastards who tricked his way inside our house in Langswood! And now he's in Clara's garden, pruning her tree!'

'What the...'

'I need to get to him. Now. I need to get to him and get him to tell me what the hell is going on. But all the doors are locked. And there are no keys. There's not one bloody key anywhere and Clara has done this on purpose! There's no other explanation for it! You can't get locked in a house from the inside unless someone has locked all the doors on the outside.'

Luke tries the handle. Sure enough, it doesn't budge.

'Oh my God,' he says. The colour is draining fast from his face. 'I knew it. I knew there was something dodgy about that woman.'

The air is dense, and my breathing is shallow, that sickly mouldy smell sticking to my skin like a piece of clingfilm. The more I try to focus, the cloudier the room becomes. I should have known that there was more to Clara than meets the eye. She doesn't want us to leave this place. Did she not think I'd recognise that her gardener was at our house a few days ago, forcefully removing our things? Or does she think I'm that naïve that I'd trust her, anyway? Does she think I'm still that child, the three-year-old who ran to her and let her push me on the swing? Does she think that I'm *stupid*?

'I'm not stupid,' I say out loud to Luke. 'And I'm not naïve. Or maybe I was naïve, and I should never have come here in the first place. But I need to get to that man.' My foot kicks at the door. Usually, I'd have started counting by now, but my monster is telling me that it's had enough. If it projectile vomits all over this house then so be it.

It takes Luke a couple of seconds before he starts grabbing at the door with me. But it's no use.

The door is not going to open. We're stuck.

Chapter Thirty-Two

'als de hemel valt, hebben we allemaal een blauwe hoed'

If the sky falls, we'll all have a blue hat

'Look for the will,' I say, panting. My toe is throbbing, and it's safe to say that, although we've tried our hardest, we're not very good at breaking down manor house doors of any kind, even glass ones. Or, at finding keys.

'Mum's message. You know, the thing that she wanted me to do for her? She told me to look for Johanna's will.'

'Why the will?' asks Luke.

'Because Johanna is dying, maybe? Because she wants to know if she's in there? Because she wants the will from her extremely dodgy sister who locks people in houses for fun?'

'But this house is massive. Looking for a piece of paper, we could be here for days, like.'

He's right. This house is massive, and it could be absolutely anywhere. And I don't even know what a will looks like. But we need to find it. The pipes start to rattle as warm air surges through the old house, as though it knows we are about to embark on a hunt for its secrets.

'Shit,' I say. 'Shit.' I take off Clara's itchy red cardigan that, like a kind auntie, she'd lent me right before she'd left for England, and I slump over the kitchen counter. It feels disgusting to be wearing her clothes right now. The tap is dripping, and I watch as small teardrops fall angrily into the sink below.

'Well, what are we going to do, then? There are no keys to escape anywhere. And I know this house is big, but I'm claustrophobic.'

I reach into my bag for two paracetamol tablets, and gather enough spit inside my mouth so that I can swallow them down without water. 'You know. For a moment, I did consider whether Clara hadn't meant to do it… if she'd locked the front door on autopilot, and she'd just forgotten that we were inside.'

'Yeah, right,' says Luke, letting out a long, exhausted sigh.

Luke is sniffing again. I'm touching wood again. My necklace has been rubbed more in the last few days than in the last year, probably. Luke doesn't want to touch me, now. And I don't want to touch him, either. We're stuck, in the middle of Clara's kitchen, with our *issues* and our quirks and our shit families circling us like hungry seagulls. I keep drifting from an adult to a child to an adult back to a child again. I am trying to think like an adult. But I am chained up like a child.

Then. 'Hallo?' says a deep voice from behind the door. '*Ben jij daar?* Remi? Luke? Are you in there?'

It's not instantly recognizable, but I'm pretty sure that the voice is Fred's. I hear a hopeful key in the lock and suddenly the door swings open, and Fred is standing there with a sour look on his face. It's a look that says he knew this would happen. *Did* he know this would happen? What is he doing here otherwise?

'Fred! Oh Fred, thank goodness!' I cry. He goes to shuffle inside, but I wiggle past him. Now I'm free of the house I'm walking fast through the garden.

'Remi!' shouts Luke in a concerned voice from the kitchen.

'Stay there,' I tell him. 'I don't want you following me, OK?' With two of us approaching him, he'll no doubt try to run away. Except luckily for me, I can see he's now strapped firmly to a large tree trunk and has no quick means of escape.

'Excuse me!' I say as I reach him. 'Pardon! *Entschuldigen Sie!*'

The man swivels his head around to face me, and I can tell by his eyes that I've spooked him. *Good.* He wriggles and starts to untie the strapping around his waist.

'Tell me everything, or I will report you to the police for blackmail and extortion!' I shout. I have no real idea what those two words mean in the court of law, but they sound intimidating enough.

The man replies in his South London accent. 'Look,' he calls back. 'I don't know what you're talking about, OK? Everything we did was legit. Kind of. So, it is what it is, right? You know what I'm saying.' He starts to move slowly down the tree trunk.

I cringe at the passive aggressive, useless phrases that everyone uses nowadays. *It is what it is. You know what I'm saying.* No, I do not know what you're saying, meatball head. Except I don't say that.

'Excuse *me*,' I say instead, with the emphasis on the *me*, a bit too much like a hormonal teenager with attitude. 'But it is definitely *not* what it is.' Except that doesn't make any sense, really.

'You're not a bailiff. You're a fake. Or even worse, you're a fraud. And you'd better tell me where my mother's painting is, or I am calling the police. I'm warning you. Aren't there painting police as well? Police especially for paintings? Well, I'm sure I could call them, too.'

I'm finding it hard to hide my shaky breath. Confronting Gerald – a dying old man with cancer – was one thing, but this man looks like he could knock me out with a fingernail. He comes further down the tree towards me, and I take a few steps forward. I will not let him intimidate me like Clara did. Because look how that's turned out so far.

'Look,' the man says quietly now. 'I felt sorry for you the other day, alright.' His feet touch down on the ground and I notice he's speaking gently, much more so than he did when he was in Langswood. He places his tools down beside him, studying my face as if to pick out the lines where my boldness cracks. I force myself to meet his eyes. I don't blink.

'Well,' I say. 'I'm glad we cleared that up.'

'Cleared what up?'

My palms are sweating. Damn it. That doesn't make any sense either.

'I just need you to listen here,' I say.

Oh, for goodness' sake, Remi.

'I know Clara made you do it,' I say stiffly.

The man doesn't reply. But his eyebrow lifts, as if he's slightly amused. It's a risk, suggesting that I know anything about his or Clara's role in all of this. But I'm not stupid, even if Clara likes to think so. He works for her, like *really* works for her. He's not just a gardener.

'I was scared the other day. Fine. But I'm not scared now. And I won't hold it against you. It is what it is, like you say.' I try a different tactic now, pulling my very best *feel sorry for me* face and fluttering my eyelashes. Inside, bile threatens to erupt from my throat.

'Right,' he says, and I can tell he's softening to me by the way he puts his hand to his mouth, touching the pink part of his lip.

'Well,' he says eventually. 'And I'm only saying this because you're…'

'Because I'm what?' I cross my arms.

'A bit bizarre, I guess. I've got a niece a bit like you.' He pauses. 'But anyway, if you really want to know, the plan was to make it look like your mother had been stealing from you. That she'd been loaning against your name. We took other bits and pieces to make it look realistic. But it was the painting that we were there for. *Make sure you don't leave without that painting*, is what Clara had said. I don't know exactly how much it's worth, but she'd told us it was an original. Then me and Wayne looked up what an original Pieter Bruegel would be worth. Millions, apparently. Tens of millions, depending on what painting it is.'

I know he's telling the truth by the way he's shaking his head. He couldn't believe it, that we had an original Pieter Bruegel hanging in our house in Langswood. Something worth millions and millions of pounds.

It takes me a while to speak again. 'Right. Well, I knew that. That it was an original, I mean. So where is it now?'

'No offence, miss. But by the look on your face, I'd say that you had no idea.'

We stand there for a while in some strange standoff. 'Let's agree to disagree, shall we?' I say.

He laughs loudly now. He is actually laughing at me, and it is making me cross. My hands are now shaking out of anger as opposed to fear.

'So where is it?' I press.

'We were supposed to take it to the nursing home. The one where your nanna is. I don't know, it was Wayne that did that. It's not a huge painting, it's easy enough for one strong person to carry. Clara was going to pretend to find it and bring it back to you, to prove what a good auntie she is. So that you'd sign it over to her willingly. But by the way you're huffing and puffing and stomping about, I guess you've already done that.'

It's annoying me so much that this man can see right through me.

'But it isn't mine,' I say. 'The painting isn't even mine. So I couldn't have signed it over to Clara.'

'Look, as far as I know, the painting is Johanna's,' he says. 'Everything is Johanna's. This house. Your house. As long as Johanna is alive, then it's all hers. Who's it is after that, who knows? But I stopped short of becoming a murderer. That's not in my job description.'

He starts to gather up his things, like he's done giving up his secrets to me. 'I'll tell you one thing for free, though. Your auntie is one ambitious woman. Ambitious in the sense that she won't stop until she can get her hands on everything the Van Tams have ever earned. She's what you call *work shy*, you see. She says she's a vet, but she's barely there. Wants it all handed to her, she does. They all do, these rich kids. Clara says your mum's the same.'

He wipes the sweat from his brow and rubs it on his trousers. 'Clara wants it all, and she won't want you interfering. So I'd stay out of her way, if I were you.'

'Fine,' I say, retreating back to the house. 'But you want to know something? You didn't need to be so horrible at our house, did you? You were extremely rude and horrible. And I know you don't think so, but I bet your niece is awesome.'

And then just like Mum had done to Gerald, I add, 'And one more thing. Whatever Clara tells you to do. Don't you ever come near me or my mother again.'

Chapter Thirty-Three

'tegen de maan pissen'

To piss against the moon

Back in the house, the atmosphere is the exact opposite to what it was a few hours earlier, when we'd all excitedly met Fred. Luke is looking downright pissed off. He's gone and got our things from the bedroom, and he's pulling up his socks, about to walk the bags out to the car. I rub his shoulder reassuringly, but he goes to shrug me off.

'I'm leaving,' he says. 'Aye. I'm taking you to see your grandma, like I said I would.'

I turn to Fred.

'We need to find Johanna's will.'

Fred's face tells me he knows where it is. And that he's not sure about my intentions for wanting to see it.

'It's not for Mum, if that's what you're thinking. You might think that my mum is a money-grabbing so-and-so, but it turns out that she wasn't stealing from me, after all.' I'm pacing around the kitchen now, pulling my hair out of its messy bun and putting it back up again.

'Are you an anxious girl, Remi?' asks Fred.

'What makes you say that?'

Fred tells me that he suspected his mother had anxiety, except they didn't call it that in those days. That she used to blink excessively, and that she'd often bring her mouth up to her nose like she was kissing a baby. It's kind of strange, when someone diagnoses you by referencing their experience with somebody else entirely. As if women who act differently are all suffering from the same kind of disease.

'It would make me less anxious if we could find this will,' I say.

Luke sighs a long sigh again. I'm wondering if he's regretting coming on this trip with me, even after declaring his love for me a few hours ago in the car. Or, that now I've told him that I love him too, he doesn't have to pretend anymore.

But he looks at Fred and says, 'Can you help us, like?' and then I tell them what the man had said in the garden – that Clara was behind the bailiffs all along. That in fact, we didn't owe any money and that perhaps I didn't have a trust fund after all. And that Clara must have faked the handwritten note. Mum didn't know the bailiffs were coming. Mum likely had no idea about Clara's twisted plan.

I tell them that the painting might be worth millions. Tens of millions. Maybe even hundreds of millions? Fred listens to all of this in silence, and I wonder what he knows. Does *he* know the painting is an original? Now Johanna's mind has gone, is he Johanna's power of attorney? Will it all go to him, in the end? Why is *he* here and Johanna there? Does he even care?

'*Komen*,' he says eventually, and he pulls out of his pocket a set of keys attached to a wooden keyring in the shape of a clog. He unlocks the back door and we start to head out towards the outbuilding, the same outbuilding that housed the newspaper articles in the old mahogany desk. The articles that told me what a blundering paramedic my mum was.

The sky today is clear, and a black and white bird is hopping around the branches of some kind of small, pretty tree. I breathe in the fresh air, air that smells fresher after the threat of being stuck inside a building full of old. We're walking slowly, mimicking the way Fred moves. He's unlocking the door to the outbuilding and I get déjà vu from yesterday, and it's back again, that feeling of trepidation, that queasiness that puts you off your lunch.

Soon we're at the desk again. Johanna's will is in a different drawer, though, and Luke has to help Fred jiggle the drawer until it opens. I stand quietly until Fred hands me two pieces of paper, and then I go to read, except that they're in Dutch, and so Fred has to read them out loud for the both of us. He reads the words perfectly but awkwardly, his voice dipping in places.

Last Will and Testament of Johanna Van Tam

Declaration

I, Johanna Van Tam of *Bloemenhuisje*, Veenhoflaan 12, 6741 AB Oosterbeek, The Netherlands, being of sound mind and of legal age to make this will, do hereby declare that this is my last will and testament, revoking all previous wills and codicils.

Appointment of Executors

I appoint **Clara Van Tam** of *Bloemenhuisje*, Veenhoflaan 12, 6741 AB Oosterbeek, The Netherlands as the executor of my will. If they are unable or unwilling to act, I appoint **Fred Aaldenburg** as the substitute executor.

Distribution of Estate

I direct that my estate be distributed as follows:

I leave my house at address *Bloemenhuisje*, Veenhoflaan 12, 6741 AB Oosterbeek, The Netherlands, to my daughter, **Clara Van Tam**.

I leave 100% of my residuary estate to **Clara Van Tam**.

I leave my painting, Pieter Bruegel's Topsy Turvy world (the original) to my only granddaughter, **Remi Van Tam**.

If any of my beneficiaries predecease me, their share shall pass to the Hope for Tomorrow Foundation.

Signed by me, Johanna Van Tam, on this day in the presence of the undersigned witness.

General Power of Attorney

This power of attorney is made on 5th September 2017 by Johanna Van Tam hereinafter referred to as 'the Donor' to Clara hereinafter referred to as 'the Attorney'

Appointment of attorney

I, Johanna Van Tam, appoint **Clara Van Tam** to act on my behalf in relation to the following matters:
Managing my bank accounts, paying bills, and making financial transactions.
Buying, selling, or managing property on my behalf.
Signing documents necessary for my financial affairs.

Powers granted

The attorney shall have full authority to carry out necessary transactions in connection with my financial affairs, except for the following limitations:
The attorney may not sell my Pieter Bruegel painting until my death, when thereafter it will go to my granddaughter, **Remi Van**

Tam.

'So, the painting will be mine?' I say in astonishment. 'And everything else will be Clara's? Where is Mum in all of this? And where are you, Fred? You're just a substitute executor?'

The old Dutchman who is my grandfather is already putting the papers back. He closes the drawer and starts to walk out of the outbuilding without saying another word. I open the drawer, grab the papers and frantically roll them into a cylinder, passing them to Luke for safekeeping. I may have been naïve, but I'm not stupid enough to leave without a copy of what my mother had asked me for.

'Fred,' I call out after him. 'Fred! So, I need to get this straight. When Johanna dies, everything will go to Clara. Does that mean our house, too? Does that mean you'll have nothing? And Mum… what does that mean for her?'

We're out on the grass now, and Fred is looking at me like I'm the same old money-grabbing child that they all are. I wonder if I like him as much as I did a few hours ago, when we first laid eyes on each other. He looks as though his opinion might have very well changed on me.

'I told you to be careful,' he says with a sadness in his voice. He locks the door on the outbuilding, then carries on walking slowly over towards the house. I grab one of his arms as a way of containing him.

'And why have I been left the painting? Why not everyone? Why are we not all sharing everything?'

Fred carries on stumbling through the garden. 'It's a very long story,' he says.

'She's manipulated her, hasn't she,' says Luke, who is sort of jumping around beside us. It's like watching someone who after a whole grueling hour of guessing clues, has just found the key in an escape room. 'Johanna has slowly been losing her mind and Clara has used that to make herself the power of attorney. No wonder she's got houses in London and the like. She's got full access to Johanna's bank accounts, and she has free rein to sell her things and take the money for herself. Everything will be hers when Johanna dies. The only thing that Clara can't have is the painting. The painting that you were told is a cheap copy, but that really is an original. The painting that is probably worth more than all of Johanna's assets combined, like.' He delivers the last line with a satisfying Geordie *like*.

'So, you think now, that Clara is trying to manipulate me into giving it to her?' I say. 'You think she planned the bailiffs to make me turn against Mum? You think the bedroom was all a show to make out she cares about me?'

Luke nods with a genuine look of horror on his face. 'God, that's mental, like. But it makes sense, doesn't it?'

'And earlier, when we were talking about the painting, Clara asked me for my signature. Except I told her that the painting was Mum's. So I signed some document with Mum's signature instead.'

Luke shrugs and I look down at Fred, who is now reaching the paving stones by the conservatory. Through the house, I can see Jasper waiting patiently in the kitchen with his coat.

'The signatures mean nothing, Remi. It was a show, to throw you off course,' says an out of breath Fred. He puts his hand on mine, then, like Clara would do, except his hand feels cold and clammy, and his fingernails are fat and coloured pale yellow.

'If you're worried about the money… and everyone is always worried about the money,' he says. 'You can't sign anything over, Remi, not without witnesses and the usual formalities that come with signing important documents. And historical paintings are protected extremely well. There are many hoops that you have to jump through to prove a valuable painting is rightfully yours. Paintings are very hard to steal and then sell.'

'But everything else?'

'Well, yes. Clara will get it all.'

I think of Mum. Of the house. Of her having to leave Langswood. Of her in the middle of the cul-de-sac, being forked on the ground like an outsider by all the murderous neighbours. As a punishment for being an awful, bungling paramedic to her mother. Was *she* trying to steal the painting from me, too?

'So, as long as Johanna is alive,' I say. 'Clara can't get her hands on the painting, then?'

Fred looks at me. A strange, pained look. And I realise it then. *As long as Johanna is alive.*

She *can* get her hands on the topsy-turvy world that I loathe so much. Of course she can.

Clara is not going to England to reconcile with Mum.

She is going to England to kill Johanna.

And then she very well might try to kill me.

Chapter Thirty-Four

'de koe bij de horens vatten'

To take the cow by the horns

I hate travelling in the back of a car. For some reason, the front of a car and the back of a car are like two completely different vessels to me. If I sit in the back on a long journey, I will nearly always be sick, even when I do all the things that you're supposed to do – look out the window, avoid reading anything, focus on the horizon. My monster inside likes to misbehave, mostly in public, when I especially don't want it to. I puked into Mum's handbag in a taxi in Mykonos once, all over our travel money. It was either that or my lap, and in hindsight, the lap would have been the better idea. Or I could have just asked the taxi driver to stop, of course. Mum spent the rest of the journey rubbing my back like she used to do, when I was her *poorly-Remi-pukey-guts* daughter. That time though, she was really mad.

Could I not try a little harder to stop it from happening? Once, I overheard her suggesting to a neighbour that I did it for attention. She'd tell the *kleine bijeenkomsts* that I'd eat too much too close to a journey, which is why I'd always get sick, except that I never fancied eating before a road trip. She never let me live that Mykonos event down.

The sickness that I'm feeling now is different, though. I know that the lump that sits right in the top of my throat, like I've swallowed an extremely uncomfortable little sick bomb that's about to go off at any moment, is a lot to do with being in a car, but mainly all to do with the fact that we're on our way back to England, to Johanna's nursing home. And that I have no idea who – or what – we're going to find there.

I fold my arm under my elbow and pinch the bridge of my nose. In this situation, Clara's cardigan that I'd reluctantly thrown back on couldn't smell any worse, of a mixture of farmyard animals and of noodles, the result of the lunch that she'd made for us eight hours earlier. It had penetrated through the house and into the fibres of all of our clothes, even ones in wardrobes. My mouth starts to water, and I quickly try to swallow down the lump.

We're squashed into Jaz's Honda so that our limbs are almost touching in an uncomfortable way. I was hoping we could have brought the Rolls Royce, except that according to Jasper, the Rolls doesn't like to travel out of Holland. I wasn't quite sure what he meant by that, but it wasn't like there was much I could do to argue with him. And the fact that they're in here in the first place is all my fault, of course.

'You're coming with us,' is what I'd said to Fred back at the house. And then Jasper had insisted on coming, too. The problem is, that Jasper looks exactly what you'd imagine a Dutchman in his forties to look like – six foot five, size thirteen feet and long arms and legs. His foot keeps encroaching on the tiny bit of space I have in my footwell, and I wonder if Fred has put him in the back with me on purpose.

'Is Johanna really dying?' I say out loud. All I can think about is whether Clara has arrived in England yet, but that's not a question that Fred can answer.

'Unfortunately, yes,' replies Fred. 'But she's been dying for a long time. So we don't know when that day will finally come. It could be days, it could be months, it could be years.'

'Right,' I say. 'That's sad.'

There are so many things I want to ask him about Johanna. Do you love her? Why did you leave England without her? Does she love you? Why aren't *you* the one desperate to see her, like I am? But questions about Fred and Johanna's relationship are far too personal to ask my grandfather, especially in a Honda Civic full of people.

'Does everyone hate my mum?' is what I ask instead. It comes from deep down inside me.

Jasper coughs, as though he's shocked at such a direct question. As though it's impolite to ask your grandfather why he's allowed one of his children to take everything and the other, to be left with absolutely nothing. Because that is exactly what he's done, isn't it?

I can tell in Fred's voice, from his front seat next to Luke, that he's glad he doesn't have to look at me. 'Of course we don't hate Elise.' He says Elise like *Elishh*. 'But my question back to you is this – do *you* hate your mother, Remi?'

'I don't know,' is what I reply. Which is true, I really don't know. Do I care that she might be in danger? Of course I do. But can't you hate someone and want to save them anyway?

'Well, let me tell you something that might help you decide,' he says.

He takes off his seatbelt, as though he needs the room to expand his chest before he speaks. Perhaps he's feeling claustrophobic in this little car, too. Luke changes lanes and drives a little slower along the motorway.

'One night, in nineteen-ninety-eight,' he says. 'Elise was about fifteen. We were living in Holland then. Anyway, she'd been at a friend's house, a girl called Lara who played water polo, not very well actually, but a nice girl at that. Elise had dinner there and then made her way home, on her bike through Tulpenhof Park, when she was pushed off and robbed of her watch. It was a *verschrikkelijk* attack. She was beaten black and blue for her Christiaan Van Der Klaauw. So much so, that none of us recognised her when she got home. I wanted to kill the *kankerlijer*, the Dutchman who did it to her. Every night I went to that park, every night for a month, looking for him, waiting for him. But nothing. We never found out who did it to her.'

I suspect that the *k* word must be an awful, awful Dutch word by the way Fred crosses his heart as he says it. A word that fits the description of the man that did something terrible to my mother. Jasper squirms in his tiny backseat.

'Elise started drinking. Beer, wine – it wasn't crazy, but it was enough to make Johanna worry about her. Johanna believed she might need therapy, you know? So Clara found this place that she could go, some kind of rehab thing, is that how you would say it?'

'Yes,' says Luke. 'Rehab's the right word, like.'

I imagine Mum as a teenager, kept prisoner inside a place that's not home. I see her sitting on the edge of a stiff mattress, seeing the scary faces of the topsy-turvy world. Except those faces would be real, in a rehab facility. Those scary faces would be real.

'So, did she go?' I say.

'*Ja*, Remi, she did. And she was even more distraught, because it clashed with the world dance competition, the one that she had been training for her whole life. Elise was such a beautiful dancer, Remi. Clara was also a beautiful dancer, but Elise was better. Clara knew this. Elise was going to win that competition, but if Elise was in rehab, then Clara had a chance of winning. And she did. She won that trophy. And I was very proud of her.'

Luke opens his window as he says this, tossing his chewing gum out onto the roadside and closing the window back up again.

'But Elise wasn't happy, of course. They were always in competition about something. They always wanted something the other one didn't have. Or couldn't have. Like children. Like you, Remi.'

If I weren't already boiling, I'd blush. Could Clara not have children? Does this explain the creepy bedroom with the Minnie Mouse glasses?

'Her Oma and Opa were not happy about Elise going to rehab. They couldn't leave their money to someone who was *unstable*. That's what they called her. They called my daughter unstable. They told me I would never get a penny of their millions because they do not trust easily. That's what kind of people they were. While they were alive, Johanna was forbidden from giving anything to Elise directly. But she did what she could. She bought a big house for you both to live in, which is why it is in her name. Not Johanna Aaldenberg, but Johanna Van Tam. Her family were against us marrying. They were against her changing her name. The only time she went by Johanna Aaldenberg was in the newspapers, because they interviewed *me*, and I wanted her to have my name. That's what I've always wanted. Do you know what it's like to be controlled by your family, Remi? Johanna may very well have been cursed by those Van Tams.'

I stay silent in the back of the car.

'Samuel left you a little. But of course, Samuel – like me – wasn't rich like your great grandparents were.'

Is he jealous? Bitter, even? He sounds like one of the neighbours whose child wasn't clever enough to have passed their exams for one of the better private schools, when everyone else's had.

'I loved Johanna,' he says. 'But I should never have married her.'

We've barely had one drink, and yet the monkey is truly coming out of the sleeve now. I scratch at my wrists with the tips of my fingernails, letting the pain wash silently over me.

'She bought us a house. And she didn't try to take it back, even when she couldn't see me. So, she still cared about Mum, then? Even after everything?'

'Johanna never cut Elise out of her parents' will,' replies Fred. 'And she wanted Elise to be in *her* will. Except…'

'Except after the accident, Clara cut her out,' says Luke. 'Once Johanna went into the care home, Clara made herself power of attorney and changed what she could to suit her.'

'Oh, Remi,' says Fred, ignoring Luke entirely. 'You have the beautiful painting. The painting will be yours, and of course, you can do what you can to help Elise. You have nothing to worry about.'

I face the window, my mind going to Mum. I have a *lot* to worry about. Does he not care about his daughter? Or his devastatingly ill wife? Are the Van Tams all out to hurt each other? Does love not overcome greed? Are they just like our neighbours in Langswood, in constant competition with each other over who has the most *schimmelpennigs*?

Was I that stupid that I thought families were not like that?

We sit for a moment in silence, the hum of the motorway roaring beneath our feet. Then Jasper speaks.

'You know the painting wasn't a gift from your father to your mother, right?' He turns his head towards me, his green eyes covered in translucent eyelashes that fall over his pupils like a horse. Fred bows his head as if he doesn't want to be a part of the conversation anymore.

'Of course I know that, now,' I say.

Another person who thinks I'm stupid.

'The painting has been in the Van Tam family since the seventeenth century,' says Jasper. I'm looking back at him, marveling at the way he speaks in such perfect English, even though he's probably never lived in England.

'It was a family tradition, that one should be given it. Not to become rich, but to teach them a lesson. The naughtiest child was to have it, and they should look at it every day and every night, to witness the wickedness and foolishness of humans firsthand. You must know that it is not a beautiful painting. It is a terrible one. And I'm sorry that you will inherit it.'

He turns towards the window then, and again, I see them. The grotesque, exaggerated faces, warped and contorted, their expressions caught between idiocy and despair.

They're taunting me.

You can't trust Mum.

You can't trust Clara.

And, although he rescued us from that house today. Now? I don't trust Fred, either.

Johanna is alone in Cambridge and she could be in serious danger. And it might just be her *whole* family who has put her there.

And it's up to me to help her. Before my ghost grandmother becomes a ghost, after all.

Chapter Thirty-Five

'op hete kolen zitten'
Sitting on hot coals

The narrow suburban roads are squeezing us tightly, forcing us to weave in and out of parked cars. The light turns green and Luke accelerates round a particularly sharp corner, making things much, much worse. I start searching in my handbag for a plastic bag, one of those bags for life, except the bag for life is having a great life in a cupboard somewhere, and is never there when you bloody need it, is it? I decide an open handbag with its contents tactfully pushed to one side will have to do. I tilt my head back, close my eyes and start breathing in through my nose and out through my mouth, slowly counting to ten. Fred is turning in his seat to look at me in a concerned way, but he offers nothing to help, and neither does Jasper. I can smell heavy whiffs of Luke's aftershave and although it's a pleasant scent, it's making the nausea worse. My heart is feeling every turn of the wheel, every bump in the road. We've been driving for six long hours. How long is this journey going to take?

I open my eyes just as we pass a large sign for Ripley

Meadows, which must now be less than a few moments away. I feel tense, like a well-kneaded loaf of bread about to be shoved into a hot oven. *Brace yourself, Remi.* But what am I bracing myself for?

With one hand on the seat I sit up sharply and try to focus entirely on what's outside the window, my other hand grasping my leg which is jiggling uncontrollably, my thigh wobbling akin to a gigantic water balloon. I twirl my hair around my fingers and pass it through my lips, each strand turning red from my lipstick. Luke is humming quietly to himself, looking directly at the road ahead. Jasper and Fred are muttering inaudibly in Dutch about something which I can't understand.

The road to Ripley Meadows is unlit, and even with the satnav, we almost miss the turn. The tarmac is barely visible under the car's headlights. Beyond the beams, there's a slight fog in the air, like the ground is angry tonight and is breathing fire from its surface like a dragon. A cat darts across the road. Or maybe it's a fox. The cross on the GPS that tells us we have arrived is staring out from the screen on the dashboard like a final, unavoidable truth. We are here. We are finally here. Johanna is somewhere in that building. As long as Clara gave us the right address, of course. But that's what I brought Fred along for.

The building is big. Dark green ivy is creeping over one whole side of it, framing tall windows that look out over an exterior courtyard. Some curtains are drawn, some are open, and some windows glow with a low, blue artificial light. Wooden benches with street lights exposing names inscribed on silver plaques are dotted sporadically around the place. We are all peering silently through the windscreen as we drive up towards the guest parking area, while Luke maneuvers the car carefully between a blue Sedan and a small, silver hatchback. He turns off the engine and we sit, watching the leaves on the trees swaying from side to side. I wonder if I could be sick, now. But it doesn't come. The bile has turned into blood, blood that is pouring out of my pores, blood that is boiling up into my brain. I'm a woman scorned. Hell hath no fury.

I'm the first to swing open the car door. A clock somewhere starts striking for nine o'clock and I rush towards some double doors, but they fail to open. I turn and hurry towards another entrance, past Luke who is now standing motionless on the pavement. He's studying the scene, patiently trying to work out which way is the right way. This is why he's here, of course, to be the level-headed one among us, but it doesn't stop me from running around resembling the white rabbit in Alice in Wonderland, darting from left to right and right to left again, muttering things, negative things, *oh dear oh dear*, trying to work out where I need to go. I'm irritated that I'm not acting more composed, but I seem to have lost all control of my legs.

'Here, Remi.' Luke gestures towards a third entrance, the right one this time. It's incredibly obvious now I've seen it, and I clench my fists in frustration. A sign on the door says *Please ring for out of hours assistance*. Jasper is helping Fred out of the car as I go to press the button.

'Please let her be OK in there,' I mouth. 'But what am I going to say to her? I don't know what I'm going to say to Johanna.'

I start chewing at my nails aggressively. Only a few days ago, I'd thought my grandmother was dead. I never knew Clara existed. A grandad was a figment of my juvenile imagination. I'd thought that discovering them all would make me so happy. Except this story is not what I expected it to be. It's not what I expected it to be at all.

'Hello?' comes a voice on the intercom.

'Hi,' I say. 'We're here to visit Johanna Van Tam. She's my grandmother. Please.'

There's a long pause, long enough for me to start imagining what I would have to do if they tell me that visiting hours are over and try to turn us away.

'Please,' I say again. 'We really need to come in.'

A buzzer goes. 'I'm opening the door for you,' says the voice. *Thank God.*

Luke squeezes my arm, and as soon as the door is open, we are through it, looking for the reception desk. Inside is a little like walking into a high-end hotel, if not for the smell. It's not a terrible smell – better than bodily odours, of course – but it smells so strongly of ozone and antiseptic that I have to slyly pinch my nose. If I were to look around, I'd see that the lobby is spacious with comfy seating, and a long, polished desk where a couple of well-presented staff are sitting ready to greet us. Gentle, soothing colours and soft lighting help make the place feel peaceful. There's a home-like vibe, and it feels comfortable, not like a place that you would dread to end up in. In fact, if not for the clinical smell and subtle signs that it's a medical facility for the elderly – like sensor alarms and handrails on the staircase – you could think you're in some high-class serviced apartments.

I lunge at the man who is sitting behind a sleek electronic tablet perched on a stand. Fred is now in the building and is standing tentatively by the door.

'Hallo, Tomasz, *wie geht es dir heute*?' he says to the man politely. There seems to be no end to his linguistical talents. I turn around to see him show Tomasz a warm, sad smile, and Tomasz returns it in a genuine way. 'It's a pleasure to introduce you to my granddaughter, Remi, and her partner, Luke,' says Fred. He pushes me towards the desk like I'm a prized puppy of his, or perhaps so he can remain cowering behind us.

'Welcome to Ripley Meadows,' says Tomasz, extending his smile to the group. 'I didn't know Johanna had a granddaughter.' I recoil slightly, feeling self-conscious. Perhaps it's the way that he's looking at me, studying my face as though he's trying to decide if it's a *thumbs up* or a *thumbs down*. 'Beautiful, if I may say. Just like her grandmother.'

I shuffle uncomfortably. This is all going far too slowly for me.

'Which rooms is she in?' I ask, my eyes searching the building.

'If you could all sign in for me,' says Tomasz, 'And please, sanitise your hands.' Luke presses the tablet efficiently in front of him, then squeezes liquid from a container and rubs it into his palms.

'My hands are clean,' I protest, but there's no use, as Tomasz is already staring me down in a *do as you're told* kind of manner.

'Can you confirm that you're all well today?' he asks, as though it's a rhetorical question, and we all nod our heads in unison. 'Johanna was in good spirits this afternoon,' he says. 'We had a music session with Will today. They all enjoyed singing along to Rod Stewart and Lionel Richie! It's amazing how they can remember the words.'

Luke flashes me a look of confusion. Singing along to Rod Stewart doesn't sound like someone who is meant to be dying soon.

'Please,' I say to Tomasz. 'It's late and... if you could just tell me which room Johanna is in, please? I'm in a bit of a hurry.'

Tomasz nods at me, but his pace doesn't quicken. He hands us a set of visitor badges attached to lanyards that we are told to hang around our necks. Then, he walks out from behind the counter and leans towards Fred discreetly. 'Could I just have a quick word?' I hear him say, and he ushers him behind the counter, out of earshot of me and Luke. I watch as they exchange whispers and nods. Concerned looking ones – or at least, they're not smiling.

'Is everything OK?' I ask, as Fred wobbles back over to join us.

But Fred says nothing. Instead, he takes off his lanyard as quick as he'd put it on, hands it to Luke, waves at Tomasz, then starts walking slowly out of the building.

'What the...' says Luke, hot on his heels. 'Fred? What's wrong?'

But he doesn't reply. Jasper appears at the door and helps him to stagger down the concrete steps.

'Leave him,' I murmur, even though I'm as shocked as Luke is at what's just happened. Even Tomasz looks stunned.

'We're wasting time.'

I grab Luke's arm and pull him towards the staircase as Tomasz says, 'I'm sorry. I can only allow one of you to go up there this evening.'

Luke looks aghast. 'But…'

'That's fine,' I say, waving him away. 'I should do this on my own, anyway.'

Luke is hesitating on the stairs, like he has no idea if my *I should do this on my own, anyway* is what I really mean, or if it means *I should never be doing this on my own and you should be telling Tomasz to shut it.*

'It's OK,' I say, looking at him meaningfully.

'Fine. But please, Remi. Call me if you need me, OK? Promise me?' he says, and he kisses me hard on the forehead, right where my thoughts live, as though he's attempting to reach them and soothe them, pressing love directly into the place where I need it the most.

~

Upstairs feels even more like a high-end apartment block than the lobby.

I walk down a wide, well-lit hallway, treading on soft, salmon-pink carpeting that muffles my footsteps. Carers dressed in dark-blue uniforms and light-blue plastic aprons dart past, flashing me generous smiles if they happen to catch my eye. I pass by a few open doors, open enough for me to pick up small pieces of conversations about pills and cups of tea. Three similar-looking women sit watching TV in a common area, in more layers than they need for the heat in here. Thick, scratchy-looking jumpers lay over buttoned-up shirts, with vests underneath and tights, and I feel suddenly desperate to remove my own itchy cardigan. It's late, so I'm surprised to see their chairs arranged in a circle around an episode of *A Place in the Sun*, which is blaring out loud enough for the whole of Ripley Meadows to hear. A carer is sat on a stool in the corner, writing something down, and the scent of lemon and hot water – a much nicer scent than I found in the lobby – is silently drifting around the place.

I avoid any chance of eye contact, rushing on by past a small, empty kitchenette and a vending machine. And then, right at the end of the hallway, I see it. Her bedroom door is white, with simple, rectangular raised panels and *Johanna Van Tam* written on a plaque on the wall. The door is closed and for a moment I stand there, listening for noise.

And then I hear it. A faint sound of a lady's voice.

A voice that I know.

Chapter Thirty-Six

'hij laat zich de kaas niet van het brood eten'

He does not let the cheese be eaten off his bread

The chair that holds Johanna is a rich emerald green. She's dressed in a lavender-coloured cardigan draped over a buttoned-up white blouse, with just her small fingers showing. Like the other ladies in the TV room, she's wearing far too many layers for the heat in here. Or perhaps that's just my feeling. Two pearl earrings are clinging onto her ears like baby monkeys holding onto their mothers. I wonder if she should have been dressed down for bed already, but then I'm glad to see that I haven't walked in on her sleeping. I'm mostly glad to see that she's alive.

I've made it to my grandmother. I've finally made it.

'Johanna. It's me, Remi,' I say gently, tiptoeing over to her chair. I'm not quite sure where to put my hands, so I leave them hanging clumsily by my side. I can tell that her eyes have seen me, but they're wide and wild and bulging – feral even – as though she's feeling threatened. And even though it seems like she's trying to, she can't quite find me to look at me. I try to follow her eyes with mine, desperate for them to focus on me.

'It's OK,' I say, touching the top of her hand lightly. 'I'm not here to hurt you.' She recoils, still not able to look at me. I pick out her pupils, following her eyes to the corner of the room, where the painting – Mum's painting, or should I say, my painting – is positioned on a table, leaning against the wall. The villagers are there, like they always are, with their steely eyes and their crooked mouths, and *their* eyes can focus on mine. They can *always* focus on mine.

Johanna is looking at them, as though she's just as bothered by them. As though she's trying to tell me something.

Something bad is happening. I can feel it.

'Mmmph-mmff!'

There's that voice I heard from outside the room. It sounds like it's coming from behind the bathroom door – a desperate, stifled attempt at speech.

'Hnnnh-mmmph!'

'Mum?' I'm at the door now, kicking it open and forcing my way inside.

And then I gasp.

If it wasn't for Johanna, sat frail and hunched over in her chair, looking scared and confused, I would be tempted to scream. A sour smell of sweat lingers in the small square bathroom, bold against the antiseptic backdrop. Mum is there, sitting on the floor by the basin, her hands tied tightly to the towel rail by some sort of white cord and her mouth covered in tape. Mum is looking at me with a panic-stricken fear in her eyes, waiting for my reaction, like she knew that when I eventually found her, this would be the scene that I would walk into all along. She's almost naked, with only her bra and knickers on, but there's a dress folded neatly next to her on the floor, with a belt laid on top. I pick up the belt and the dress, studying the shape and the colours and the smell. The dress smells of farmyard and mildew and noodles. The belt has a CD at the buckle.

They're Clara's.

I pull the tape carefully from Mum's lips, leaving behind a bright red mark.

'Remi,' hisses Mum. 'Leave now, Remi. You need to leave now. She has tied me here and I do not know where she is, but she is coming back. And I am certain she is going to kill Johanna. And then I am worried she might hurt you.'

I look back towards my grandmother, who turns her tiny head to see me, her eyes clouded with confusion. Wisps of limp, silver hair frame her delicate face, and – for what feels like the hundredth time in the last few days – my body fills with liquid, like I'm very much about to burst, a big bulging water balloon that's being chucked violently to the ground.

'Do not move,' I spit. I realise how stupid that sounds as I say it. As if Mum could just untie herself from the radiator and start running off down the hallway.

'And I am not leaving! You and your crazy sister, messing up our lives! You're bloody crazy! I don't know who's crazier, you or her! And poor Johanna here is the victim of your stupid feuds, and I am fed up with it! I am so fed up of being lied to! So you better tell me what the hell is going on, or that is it! I am calling the police!'

I grab at the door, threatening to close it on her. I'm trembling with a mix of fear and anger. The way I'd felt only moments earlier was that the sight of Mum would bring me a feeling of such relief. Yet the sound of her voice now makes my skin crawl with rage. Even if she's on the floor tied to a radiator in only her bra and knickers.

'You told me she was dead,' I hiss at her. 'You told me Johanna was dead.' I rest my forehead against the cold white door, willing it to give me the strength to face my mother. Willing it to help me articulate what I want to say, without it coming out like self-centred, childish garbage.

I am an adult. I want so much to be an adult.

'It's been days, Mum. Almost a week, for goodness' sake! I've been going out of my mind with worry. You upped and left me, you ignored me. You tried to get me to do your dirty work with no mention of a psycho sister or a selfish grandfather, and now I've found you here, with your poor mother, your apparently *dead* mother! Are you *kidding* me?'

'I would not have known what to say,' she says, holding her tied-up hands together as if she were praying. 'Remi, darling. The whole thing. It is extremely complicated, and you need to leave. You need to leave now.'

'Complicated?' I scoff. 'But it all makes sense now, of course it does! Joyce told me that you were never at home on Sundays. I thought she was full of shit. But this is where you've been coming, isn't it?'

'She is in danger,' says Mum. 'Johanna has been in danger for a long time, Remi. I did not mean to disappear without telling you where I was. But when Gerald came to our door, and I told Pa that you knew, that you knew that Johanna was alive…'

'What do you mean, you told Fred? You were keeping in touch with him all this time?'

'I called him. I had to. He was supposed to be keeping watch, making sure that Clara never came back here to…'

'To hurt you, is that what you're going to say? To hurt me?'

'Yes, Remi. She is dangerous. I keep telling you. You need to leave.'

'So you thought you'd just leave me out of it all? And keep pretending like Johanna didn't exist?' The words tumble out like Tetris blocks as the selfishness of it all hits me all at once.

'I did not want you to come here,' says Mum. 'All these years, you have thought she was dead. How was I supposed to tell you, Remi? What would I have said?'

'Anything. You could have said *anything*. And I'd have probably believed you. Believed your damned lies, like I have done my whole life. Even though I've known something was off, ever since you told me that ridiculous *hit by a tram* story. Ever since you decided to make me another victim of your big mistake.'

My whole body is shaking violently now, enough to knock my glasses from my face. I'm not used to speaking to Mum like this, and I'm shocked at how easily the words are flowing from my lips.

I hate you, I want to say.

'Were you going to run away from me, too? Like you ran from the rest of our family?'

She sinks her top teeth into her knees.

'It was not me, Remi.'

I bite my tongue, feeling like I'm about to implode. 'Oh, it was *all* you,' I say. I widen my stance and press my feet into the floor to keep myself upright.

'I just don't think you understand what you've done, Mum. I know some awful things have happened to you. But your total inability to deal with things, or to have an open mind… it's forced you into hiding from everyone. And in the process, you've ripped away any chance of me knowing a family. The secret Van Tams. I don't care if they're dangerous or selfish or whatever. That is not the point. You have stolen my family away from me, and you have no right to have done that.'

The well breaks open and tears start to fall onto my face. 'By thinking about yourself. You've inflicted that on us, Mum.'

Mum watches as I cry in front of Johanna. I am so angry with myself that I'm crying in front of Johanna.

'But it was not *me*,' she says again. 'Darling, how many times do I have to tell you? You cannot trust Clara.'

'You don't think I know that it was you who was the blundering paramedic? The one who accused Johanna of being drunk? You don't think I know that Johanna was trying to see me for all these years?' I say.

'What are you talking about, Johanna was trying to see you?

Did Clara tell you that?'

'Clara didn't tell me that. She *showed* me that. I saw the letters. I have the letters.'

'You know, there is a saying in Holland,' says Mum. '*Een muur met scheuren zal binnenkort instorten.* That a wall with cracks will soon collapse. I think, right now, that is what is happening to us, Remi.' Her voice is clipped and it's her eyes that are watering now. 'But you are wrong about these letters. I don't *know* of any letters. You have to believe me.'

'Believe you? You expect me to believe you now?'

'Yes,' she says, a bit bolder now. 'I do. Or do you think I tied my hands here by myself? Please, help me untie them, Remi? Just do as you are told, please?'

I want to touch wood, but it won't make a difference. *Just do as you are told.* I feel like I could run up to Mum and pull at her hair, then untie her and grab her by her bra strap and attempt to wrestle her out of the high window, maybe. I could kick her. Slap her in the face, if that's what I felt brave enough to do.

But I don't know what to do.

Then, she says, 'Untie me, Remi. Or leave. Either way. Just do it. Now.'

And then I'm laughing. From somewhere inside, I let out a long, nervous laugh. And Mum is staring. Hard.

I hold my finger up to my mouth. 'Do not make a sound,' I say. 'If you want me to help you, you'll do as *you're* told, won't you?'

I take the tape that had been covering her mouth and I reapply it, pressing it firmly over her lips. My legs then start to move, pulling my torso out of the bathroom and away from the woman who made me. And towards the woman who made her. Mum tries to stand up, but I push my hand up just like a furious lieutenant would do. 'Do. Not. Move.'

I close the door of the bathroom shut.

'Johanna,' I say, moving back over to her emerald green chair.

'I'm so sorry, Johanna. I wish we didn't have to do that in front of you.'

Her mouth is moving like she's chewing on her thoughts, her lips pressing together and then releasing in small, unconscious motions.

And then she whispers, 'She's doing it again'.

'Who is doing it again?'

'The one in the uniform.'

'Elise?' I say. 'Mum?'

And then she shakes her head. 'No, no, no, no.' And her frail little arm goes up to point at the painting.

And now I know what to do.

I wait.

I wait for Clara to return.

Chapter Thirty-Seven

'de kip met gouden eieren slachten'

To kill the goose that lays the golden egg

Clara startles as she walks into the room and sees me. She knows I'm not supposed to be here. I'm supposed to be locked in her house two-hundred miles away in Holland. But I am here, sat beside Johanna, telling her about Copperfield and how he does this thing where he zooms full speed across the living room, skidding to a dramatic halt inches from the wall like a ninja warrior. I hadn't told her that I'm worried about him. He's been alone in the house for a really long time now and I'm sure it will be affecting him mentally. He's a smart cat, and he'll know that something is wrong. Except cats are brave. If Copperfield falls from the top of the stairs, he doesn't panic. He twists his body midair to break his fall. He trusts his own instincts. He knows that he will land on his snowshoe paws.

Copperfield walks into every room like he owns the place. He has no problem with staring down something that is much bigger than him, much bolder than him. And I need to do the same.

Clara does not scare me. I am going to be brave for someone who can't be. I am going to be brave for Johanna.

'Hello, Remi,' she says in that loud, twisted voice of hers. 'I have to say, I really didn't expect you. But you've come at just the right time.'

I take in Clara's uniform – an oversized midnight green shirt and shorts, black boots and a softshell jacket. She's wearing paramedic clothing, but she's not a paramedic. Clothing which she must have stolen from Mum.

When Johanna sees her daughter, she starts rocking back and forth quietly. *She's doing it again. The one in the uniform.* It all makes perfect sense now. Johanna wasn't talking about Elise, like I'd thought she was. She was talking about Clara.

'Hello, Clara,' I spit back.

Stay bold, Remi.

'I can only apologise for spoiling your plans. And I see you got the painting back? How very convenient.'

Clara laughs. 'Great, isn't it? Except you didn't really expect me to do all that hard work and then just return it to you, did you?' She pulls a stretcher in from the hallway. A stretcher on wheels, like you would see in an ambulance.

'What's the stretcher for, Clara? And the uniform?' I take a step closer to Johanna's bedside. 'So you can finally remove the one person who has been standing in your way of getting everything you ever wanted?'

Clara laughs again.

'It was you, wasn't it? It was you in the ambulance that night. Mum wasn't the blundering paramedic. It was you who mistreated Johanna, and then you let Mum take the blame.'

'Oh, Remi. You are so *clever*. I knew you'd be clever like your auntie. Except it wasn't me who suggested that Elise take the rap. I can't take the credit for that one.'

'So who was it, then?' I demand.

'Your grandfather, Fred, of course! He is a very clever man

too, you know. But he also likes money. Like me,' she smiles.

'Parents are funny, aren't they? So easy to wrap around your little finger, once you've found their weak spot. Fred was so scared that without me, he'd get nothing from the Van Tam's inheritance, and it made sense, right? No one wanted me going to prison, did they? Elise takes the blame, she gets a few months suspension and you get the painting. We take the rest. I'd say that was an extremely generous offer, wouldn't you?'

'You wanted her to die, didn't you?'

'Well, technically, no,' she says. 'She just needed to suffer a little. Enough for her to believe that she was losing her mind, so she'd sign her power of attorney over to me.'

'But how did you get in the ambulance in the first place?' I squeeze my necklace until my knuckles are white.

'We look alike – it wasn't hard to pretend I was Elise. And I'm a vet, remember? I put things to sleep in my sleep. So, I gave Johanna a little sedative, then waited for it to kick in. Gave her a little excuse to pop out of the house for five minutes and then positioned her in the road and hey presto – Gerald did all the hard work for me. Good old Gerald.'

Clara pulls out some black latex gloves and starts pushing them onto her fingers.

'You know what she wanted to do, don't you? She wanted to give it all away, Remi. Oh yes! All of it. To some ridiculous charity, to people who'd done nothing for it, absolutely nothing. I am *helping* you, Remi, can't you see that? We are the victims here. We've had riches dangled like carrots over us our whole lives and for what – to have them taken away by some charity? I told her to come to Holland with us, but no, she wanted to be here, near to you two, spending our inheritance on this fancy nursing home. Do you know how much they charge here, Remi? Well, it's not sustainable anymore. They'll take everything. And once Johanna is gone, then the fact is that without me, you will have nothing. Not now I've got my hands on this painting. Which means I guess you'd better be nice to your auntie Clara.'

I pull a face of disgust. 'So, if you were planning on stealing it, then why is the painting here? Why didn't you just have your gardeners – sorry, I mean *bailiffs* – take it straight back to Holland?'

'Oh, you know. I just thought I'd show it to Elise one last time, so she'd remember the cute little faces and so she could stop being such an arrogant little bitch.'

'Mmmph-mmff!' mumbles Mum from the bathroom. 'Hnnnh-mmmph!'

My fingers squeeze at the necklace. *Touch wood touch wood touch wood touch wood.*

Clara laughs again. This time, she reaches into her pocket and takes out a syringe.

'I've looked after Pa, haven't I? Gave him a place to stay while Johanna abandoned him? She chose this home before her mind went, you see. This was the one thing I couldn't control of hers. But enough with it now. It's Johanna's fault that I need your painting, Remi. And you *will* sign the painting over to me.'

'Or what?' I say, a little too antagonistically.

Suddenly, the cream room becomes a million shades of silver. Clara has lost it. She grabs my face as though she's a violent mother grabbing a teenager who's just sworn at her for the first time. 'I have worked so hard for this, Remi. I am in control now, and you will do as you're told.'

You will do as you're told. Another one who thinks I am an obedient fool.

I blink at her hard.

She comes closer towards me, squeezing my cheeks and looking me directly in the eye. Then, in a loud whisper, she mouths the words, 'It should have been me. Your mother didn't deserve you, you know. And if you stop being such a judgmental little cow, then it still can be.'

She lets go of my face, and I hold my cheek.

'Now come on, now,' she says. 'I know you are upset. It's a lot to take in, isn't it?'

'Those letters,' I pant. 'The letters from Johanna to Mum. You told me Mum sent them back to her. But she never got them, did she? You made sure Mum never got those letters.'

Clara is getting angry, now. She looks perturbed, like she doesn't have time for this.

'Mum never got them, did she, Clara?' I press.

'Oh, boo hoo,' she says. She turns the needle over in her fingers. And then her face turns bright purple, and she hits me, hard, a loud slap across the cheeks.

Johanna gasps. I hear Mum shriek from the bathroom.

'Well. Considering my mum didn't deserve me,' I say. 'You can't even hit me properly. My mum hits me better than that.'

Then, before she can say anything back, I'm grabbing the syringe out of her hand and plunging it into her, straight into her leg, pushing whatever liquid that's inside deep into her left thigh. It's Clara's turn to gasp now, and she recoils in shock, falling to the floor.

Without hesitating, I pull a black marker pen from out of my jean pocket.

'The thing is,' I say, walking over to the Pieter Bruegel painting that's still leaning against the wall. 'I didn't *actually* say that you couldn't have the painting, did I? And I'll tell you what. I'll put your name on it to prove it.'

The marker pen smells of alcohol and plastic, something almost sickly sweet. I take a deep breath in and then with the marker pen in my right hand, I scrawl C L A R A in huge capital letters, all over the ugly little faces of the topsy-turvy world.

'There,' I say. 'It's all yours.'

And then Clara jumps to her feet, puts her hands to my neck, and she squeezes, and she squeezes, until the room goes black and I fall.

Chapter Thirty-Eight

'komkommertijd'

Cucumber time

It's three days after yesterday. A bunch of wilted daffodils sit woefully on the bedside table. Three days before yesterday, all I'd seen in here is horror. The horror of a daughter scorned, someone who wanted all the *schimmelpennigs* she could get her hands on. No matter what she had to do to get them.

But it's beautiful in here now. Delicate lace curtains shimmer in the soft light of the room, framing a large arched window that makes it feel bigger than it is. I notice that the wall behind Johanna's bed is covered in hand-painted flowers, a mixture of pansies and poppies, and pale blue forget-me-nots. The TV is tuned into a classical station, with the gentle strains of piano creating a real sense of peace.

Johanna is sitting upright in her bed. Just like our surroundings, she's beautiful, too. The delicate lines that three days before yesterday looked deep and troubled, today seem softer and calm, and although her eyes are cloudy and distant, they are young eyes all the same. The twinkle in them is still very much there.

Johanna had pressed the panic button just in time for nurses to rescue me from Clara's grip. She had saved me. And I had saved her.

After all these years. We had saved each other.

I move towards her and she looks at me, searching for recognition, except it's clear that she's finding nothing from inside of her. I kneel down by her bedside and speak as softly as my voice will allow right now. The pain from Clara throttling me means it still hurts to swallow.

'Hello, Johanna. If you don't mind me joining you. It is so lovely to see you today. I didn't properly introduce myself before. But I'm Remi. I'm your granddaughter.'

I lay my hands on my lap and stay still for a moment, studying her face, hoping to spot a flicker of familiarity in her smile. Perhaps she'll remember the Remi who shut her tied-up mother in the bathroom. Or the Remi who stabbed her auntie with a syringe. Or the Remi who drew all over her Van Tam family painting.

I hope she's not scared of me. But thankfully, her face is soft. 'Do I know you, dear?' she replies kindly.

Mum takes a seat in the chair behind me, her hands folded neatly in her lap as she watches us both in anticipation. 'It's little Remi,' she confirms after a while.

'Yes, it's me, Remi,' I repeat, keeping my voice as steady as I can. The piano plays a few more jolly-sounding notes. 'I know it's been a while, but I'm here now.'

Johanna frowns a soft frown, and she tilts her head back and forth as if trying to knock a memory out of it. 'Remi. That's a pretty name.'

I smile at her gratefully and she blinks a few times, her expression unchanged. She's still trying to knock the memories around in her head. 'Do you work here, dear?' she says quietly, not quite as a question, but more as a fact.

I look to Mum, unsure what to say next. I realise that deep down, I knew Johanna wouldn't remember me. I knew she wouldn't suddenly say, *oh yes! Little Remi, the granddaughter I've been longing to see for all these years!* But my heart hurts from a quiet pang of disappointment. Mum eyes me encouragingly, willing me to go on.

'I don't work here,' I reply, my voice now trembling slightly. 'I'm here to visit you, Johanna. I'm part of your family. I'm your granddaughter, who has missed you terribly for all these years,' I say. I hear a sharp intake of breath from Mum on the bed, followed by a loud swallow.

Johanna lets me take her hand, and as I feel the frailty of her bones, her cold fingers go still. I'm not sure if she is hearing me, or if my words are simply here, floating hopelessly in the air. We stay still like that for a couple of minutes, until she closes her eyes, and then opens them again.

'Are you a princess?' she asks. 'Your eyes. You look just like a princess.'

I promise myself I won't cry. Not again, in front of my new grandmother.

'What's funny,' I say, 'Is that I was thinking just the same thing about you.' I smile at her lovingly. She is exactly the grandmother that I imagined she would be. Not because she said that I looked like a princess. But because of the way her eyes lit up as she said it.

'Your hair,' she says. 'That's a lovely wig you're wearing.'

This time I can't help but laugh, squeezing her hand lightly. Johanna doesn't react, except that she lowers her head, looking a bit like she might fall asleep. Then, after a while, she lifts it back up again.

'I'm a little teapot,' she starts singing, in her delicately beautiful Dutch accent. 'Short and stout.'

I'm so surprised by the sudden outburst of song that I pull my hand away gently and go to stand up. Johanna stops then and smiles up at me.

'Here's my handle,' she sings. Her voice has gone from soft and meek to now amazingly clear and jolly. I watch as Mum stands up from her corner of the bed.

'Here's my spout,' she joins in.

'When I get all steamed up,' sings Johanna. 'Hear me shout.'

'Tip me up. And pour me out.' I finish. The words come out of my mouth in the most unexpected but effortless way. I look at her in amazement. She used to sing that song to me, I'm sure of it. We lock eyes for a while, eyes that mirror each other's, eyes that are cut from the same cloth. And then, Johanna starts crying. A real, pained, sad cry.

'Oh, *moeder*,' says Mum, rushing over to her and giving her a comforting hug around her shoulders. It's almost too much for me to bear, seeing her cry like this.

'I'm sorry! I'm sorry!' Johanna cries in bewilderment.

'It's OK, Mama,' she comforts her. 'I think we'll give Johanna a rest now, don't you, Remi?' she mouths to me.

'Of course,' I reply, retreating towards the door. 'I love you, Nan,' I whisper, knowing that she won't hear it, but saying it all the same.

~

The sun is setting outside, casting a golden shadow over the lawn. On such a beautiful evening, it's angering me that I'm thinking of Clara, and of where she might be now. After the nurses came to rescue me, she'd grabbed the painting that I'd wrecked and wrestled her way out of the building. Am I scared she'll come back to finish us off?

Maybe.

I turn and tread silently to Mum's car, pulling the passenger door open without looking at her. I can hear her crying. Not a sob, like in the house after Gerald had turned up. This cry is more like a whimper. I can't make out whether it's a sorry, remorseful cry or a sorry, self-pitying one.

'Why did you want me to be a paramedic?' I ask. I feel bolder, now, to ask Mum questions like these.

She calms herself, breathing slowly in and out.

'Because I needed you to be ready,' she says.

'Ready for what?'

From the corner of my eye, I see Mum dab at her face with a tissue. We're still not looking at each other.

'Do you want to win?' she says.

'Win? Win what? What do you mean?'

'Do you want to win in life?'

'Yes,' I say. 'I think everyone wants to win, Mum. But I've got no idea what you're talking about.' I wonder whether now is a good time to tell her that, quite frankly, I've never really understood a word that's come out of her mouth in the whole twenty-one years that she's been my mother.

'The world is not fair,' she says. 'Which means, the truth does not always win. When your grandfather told me to lie about the accident, I was sure the truth would come out eventually. I stayed in the ambulance service. I was trying, Remi. Trying to be good and strong and right. I wanted you to carry that forward. I wanted you to be what is right in the world, just like your grandmother Johanna.'

She takes another shaky breath in. 'Except the truth never did come out. Not until a few days ago, anyway. The whole of Cambridge still thinks it was me who mistreated my mother.'

My eyes go to the ceiling, to the smooth and seamless fabric, with not a sag or a crease in sight. 'It doesn't matter what everyone else thinks, Mum. We know the truth, right? Isn't that what matters?'

'I wanted you to see people at their worst,' she says. 'Like my grandparents wanted me to see, in that God damn painting. And I wanted you to be prepared to deal with that, Remi. But now? I do not care that you are good. I do not care that you are honest. All I care about, is that you avoid being the victim. Look at what happened to me. You can be attacked, and then you can be punished for it. You do everything right? Then you are in a great position to be fucked over. People will tell lies about you. What is the use in being perfect, if that is all people believe, anyway?'

I go to rest my hand on hers, to do what I haven't done in a long, long time. But she pulls her hand away before I can touch her.

'Well, I've realised that I don't care what anyone thinks, now Mum. My classmates. The neighbours. I just don't care.'

'Hmmm,' she says, her tears dry by now. 'And you know what *I* have realised, Remi?' The darkness is spreading quietly around the car. 'Don't be like me. Be like Clara. Clara has won. I have not. So, like I said before...'

She tucks her wavy hair behind her ear so I can see it. For the first time, I notice a scar, not an obvious line or mark, but more of a patch. A tight, shiny stretch of skin like a burst or a splatter.

'Like I said before. You make a mistake,' she says. 'Then you admit nothing.'

~

After a while, Mum turns the engine on, and we drive home in silence. I try to focus on Luke, or on my beautiful meeting with Johanna. I think of the song that she had sung to me, the song that we'd sing in the bath together when I was three. And for a moment. Just a tiny moment. I feel a small break in the current of my anxiety.

I shall call it my cucumber time.

Some people can never find their *komkommertijd*, their calm pond in the midst of their bustling sea. They never feel that break in the tide, where the pace slows. Those people believe in evil. But I like to believe in love.

They just don't allow themselves that respite.

Chapter Thirty-Nine

*'men moet roeien met de riemen
de men heeft'*

One must row with the oars one has

Can you have a mother who is both always there, yet who is consistently absent? What would you call that? A bad mother? No, she's not a bad mother. I won't allow that.

Am I even a good daughter, anyway? I think so. It's been five weeks, and I'm still talking to her, aren't I?

My arms spread out across of the edge of the pool, and I feel satisfied with my twenty lengths of front crawl. I dip my head below the surface of the water, the coolness of the pool helping to soothe my raging thoughts. Mum's always told me not to use the pool alone – I could smash my head, or faint, and then drowning would be inevitable and no one would hear my screams – but although these are all plausible, I decide that they are very unlikely. This afternoon, I'd fancied my chances.

I wrap the towel around my torso, letting the water drain from my face. My hair is a tangled mess, something that takes me a good ten minutes to brush through, going from piece to piece, knot to knot. I slip on a black linen dress and a touch of make-up and I traipse back to the house to warm up.

Johanna died two nights ago. A carer went to her room to wake her, and she'd gone overnight in her sleep. Mum had said that it wouldn't have been painful. That it was probably the best way for her to go. Luke had said that he'd agreed. I didn't cry, when she'd told me. I haven't been able to grieve for her, yet.

I'm not sure that Mum can, either.

I know now, that Mum turned me against Johanna to protect me. To stop me from going to look for her, or for Clara, to save me from the topsy-turvy world that is her family. I know that she controlled my money so as not to allow me to get caught up in the trappings of wealth. Something toxic, that she was already trapped in. I'm learning to not hate her for it. We all have our reasons, after all.

Mum puts the apple pie down in front of us, and she cuts me a slice and spoons it onto my plate. I lift the jug of cream and pour it over her portion. Then we eat together quietly. This is what we do, now. We pretend like it never happened. It's quite simple, really. I don't ask, and she doesn't answer.

I scrape the last piece of apple into my mouth, and then move to the dishwasher with our dirty plates. Copperfield purrs around my feet. Mum sips her tea at the table.

'Johanna didn't know, did she? Johanna didn't know that the bungling paramedic was Clara. Not until she turned up in her bedroom, about to murder her own mother.'

Mum sips some more of her tea.

'She didn't know, because she likely couldn't remember anything about the night of the accident. She said it herself in one of her letters. She had no idea it was Clara who mistreated her. She thought it was you, didn't she? Those letters to you about me were real. Except you didn't know she'd forgiven you, did you? Which is why you only started seeing her when you knew her memory was gone.'

Mum takes a long gulp of her tea.

'Here,' she says. She pushes two tickets in front of me, which I can see are plane tickets to Berlin.

'What are these?' I ask. Mum and I have never been to Berlin, to the land of brutalist buildings and bratwurst.

'The Pieter Bruegel,' she says. 'The one that you drew over at the nursing home.'

'The one that I never want to see again?'

'Yes. The horrible painting that you hate, Remi. I understand. But it was a copy. I knew Clara would eventually come for it, and so I had a copy made.'

'What do you mean?' I say.

She takes another slow sip of her tea. 'I gave the original to a museum in Germany for safekeeping. It is yours, whenever you want to collect it. So, I thought we could go there. Would you like to go there together, Remi?'

I pick up the tickets, turning them in my hands as her words sink in. The painting is in Germany. I could collect it and sell it, and we could be set, for life.

I think for a moment.

I think of going to Berlin. I think of closure. Of putting the proverbs behind me.

'I would like to go,' I say. 'But just not with you. If that's OK.'

And then I take the tickets and I stand up, and I step outside, into the wind, that persuasive kind of wind that makes your back door bang back and forth. Luke stands with his short-shorts on, the ones that make his thighs look so deliciously sporty that I melt inside. And I don't care that I kiss him in front of her.

And I say see you later. Have a good afternoon.

And without smiling, Mum waves me goodbye.

Epilogue

I stand across the street, my hands clutching a tissue in my jacket pocket. I would rather not have to be mopping up my drool every so often, but it's been happening ever since she stabbed me with that sedative in Johanna's bedroom. My focus has been off, too. I've not been able to concentrate on anything, lately. Even that new Netflix phenomenon, *Deskman* or whatever it's called, has gone through one ear and back out again. It's boring, waiting for the muscle aches and the drowsiness and the fogginess to subside. But I'm here, now. And I need to be smart. I need to keep my distance. She can't see me. The CCTV can't detect me. I am to stay here among the crowds until it gets dark.

I watch as she moves up the steps, the same way Elise used to do when she was trying to sabotage my chances at the pageants when we were barely out of primary school. A ponytail falls to almost halfway down her back, swishing in a cat-like way as she walks. It's vile, the way she thinks so much of herself, now. I could grab that ponytail and pull her back down those steps like the disobedient little juvenile that she is. But I can't do that, because then my cover would be blown. I need to stay inconspicuous. I can't let her get to me. *Het vlees op de spit moet worden besmeerd.* The meat on the spit must be basted.

She needs my constant attention from now on.

The boy is there too, the one with the crooked nose and those ears slightly too big for his face. *Bless.* They're staring now, up at the banners draped over the entrance, looking as cold and as pale as the exterior of the Gemäldegalerie. I think for a moment that she might turn back. That she might see me. But she doesn't. I'm dabbing at my mouth with the tissue again as she steps up and into the building, disappearing amongst the Berlin crowds.

I know why they're here, it doesn't take a rocket scientist to work it out. It's just I haven't decided what to do with them yet.

But I've got options.

After all. I already told you, that I put things to sleep in my sleep.

I've got my eye on you, Remi Van Tam.

Acknowledgements

My first thank you goes to my husband, James, who always believes in me and who, over the course of a few years, read numerous drafts of this book without complaining!

To my sister Louise. Having a sister is a blessing and I couldn't have done this without your honest feedback and ideas. Thank you for always being there to read my latest creation.

Thank you as always to Mum and Dad, the finest and most hard-working parents I could ever wish for. I got lucky!

To my brother Matt. Thank you for allowing me to use what happened to you as inspiration for this novel. And, for being superhuman.

Thank you to Sarah and to Sue, for taking the time to listen to my crazy ideas. To my Dutch friends, old and new (who are very much like Johanna, and nothing like Clara or indeed Fred in this novel). Holland is a wonderful place, and I think of it as my second home. I encourage anyone who hasn't been to visit. To Monica at Cornerstones Literary. Thank you for your knowledge and for keeping me focused.

To my children, who have taught me the true meaning of love. And finally, to all the people who both amaze me and annoy me on a daily basis. Thanks for the inspiration!

About the Author

Firstly, thank you so much for reading my debut novel The Secret Van Tams. A small request from me – if you enjoyed this book, please could you leave a review on Amazon, or share via your social media channels. Even if it's just a sentence or two, it would make all the difference to me as an author and would mean I can keep writing books. Thank you.

If you would like to follow me on Instagram or TikTok, check me out here:

Instagram: carlybishopauthor
TikTok: carlybishopauthor

I don't post every day, but I'd love to connect. If I do post, it's mainly about books I've read and enjoyed, or about places I have eaten. I live near the famous Hampton Court Palace with my husband and my two boys. I love history, watching football, eating out and learning about (and tasting) wine. Lately, I have been attempting to play the piano.

Dutch Proverbs Directory

Although this novel is a work of fiction, Pieter Bruegel the Elder is a real artist and his sixteenth-century painting *The Netherlandish Proverbs* does indeed hang in the Gemäldegalerie in Berlin. Some of the chapter titles in The Secret Van Tams feature in his painting, and I would encourage you to view it, if you ever have the chance to travel to Germany. It really is a fascinating painting. Below is a list of how the sayings might be interpreted in English… take from them what you want, they are interpretations after all! Please also note – Dutch is not my first (or even second) language, so I do apologise if I have got anything wrong.

Promise is debt:
if you make a promise, you are expected to fulfil it.

To have the roof tiled with tarts:
to have lots of money.

Life is not always beautiful:
life is not a bed of roses.

He who has butter on his head, should stay out of the sun:
someone who is guilty should avoid drawing attention to themselves.

What can smoke do to iron?
You can't change the unchangeable.

To sit between two chairs in the ashes:
to be indecisive.

The sow pulls the bung:
negligence will be rewarded with disaster.

To play on the pillory:
to attract attention to one's shameful acts.

To put your armour on:
to prepare yourself for a challenge.

If I am not meant to be their keeper, I will let geese be geese:
if responsibility is not yours, you should not interfere.

To tie a scarf around someone's neck:
to ruin or betray someone.

He sits with the baked pears:
he's stuck in an unpleasant situation.

To nail someone to the pillory:
to publicly shame someone.

He carries water to the sea:
doing something useless or redundant.

One must strike while the iron is hot:
take action at the right moment.

To bell the cat:
taking on a difficult task that others avoid.

You catch more flies with honey than with vinegar:
kindness and persuasion are more effective that hostility.

One cannot serve two masters:
you cannot be loyal to two conflicting interests.

That is a bandage on a wooden leg:
a completely useless solution.

Looking for a stick to beat the dog:
searching for an excuse to punish someone.

To pull the chestnuts out of the fire for someone:
to take a risk for someone else's benefit.

One cannot carry fire in one hand and water in the other:
it's impossible to support two opposing causes.

To turn a wheel before someone's eyes:
to deceive or mislead someone.

He looks through his fingers:
to ignore something deliberately.

When the fox preaches passion, farmer, watch your chickens:
beware of hypocrites.

The fish starts to rot from the head:
problems in leadership affect the whole system.

He cannot leave the church in the middle:
someone who is stubborn and refuses to compromise.

To cover something with the cloak of love:
to overlook someone's mistakes out of love or kindness, or a desire to keep the peace.

He hangs his coat to the wind:
he changes opinions based on circumstances.

High trees catch a lot of wind:
leaders are exposed to criticism

The fish is dearly paid for:
a costly mistake.

His herring does not fry here:
that is not going to happen.

If the sky falls, we'll all have a blue hat:
we will all go down with the ship.

To piss against the moon:
a pointless or futile effort.

To take the cow by the horns:
to tackle a problem directly.

Sitting on hot coals:
impatiently waiting for something.

He does not let the cheese be eaten off his bread:
standing up for oneself.

To kill the goose that lays the golden eggs:
to destroy a source of wealth or fortune out of greed.

One must row with the oars one has:
make do with what you have.

Printed in Dunstable, United Kingdom